rebel elle

AN ELLE RILEY MYSTERY

STEPHANIE KINZ

also by stephanie kinz

Stubborn as Elle:

An Elle Riley Mystery

rebel elle

An Elle Riley Mystery

STEPHANIE KINZ

ISBN 979-8-9874789-2-9 (paperback)
ISBN 979-8-9874789-3-6 (e-book)

In Loving Memory of Sulee Adeline

1943— 2023

For James-
My own Best critic.

preface

Dear Reader,

Rebel Elle is the second book in the Elle Riley Mystery Series. Chapter One takes place approximately six months after the first book, Stubborn as Elle, concluded.

Although, Rebel Elle may be read as a stand-alone, for a greater reading experience, I recommend first reading Stubborn as Elle.

May you enjoy Elle's continuing story.

Happy Reading,
  Stephanie Kinz

prologue

THERE WERE three people in attendance at Clayton
Butcher's funeral. That is if you count the preacher performing
the service, who did not even know Clayton in life. The pitiful
gathering seemed to be fitting. After all, most people do not
wish to pay respects to a murderer. Least of all, me, almost his
last victim.

I can picture the scene in my mind as Sheriff Jack Lennox
describes it. The funeral home employees standing off to the
side, underneath the shade of a tree, smoking cigarettes while
they wait for his cold, dead body to be lowered into the
ground; anxious to throw dirt on the coffin so they can be on
with the rest of their day. The sun shone bright. There were no
tears from the angels for anyone who could be mourning his
death.

I feel relief at the thought of his demise. I suppose I should
feel some type of vindication or justice at his death, or even
guilt about the relieved feeling, but I don't. It is just simply
relief. Relief that I will never have to look over my shoulder in
fear he is there. Relief to know when I wake from the night-

1

mares of reliving the trauma he caused, I can remind myself it will never happen again.

His sister, Camilla "Cammie" Butcher Parker was, of course, at the funeral. She is perhaps the only person who could say if there was ever any good to be found within Clayton. That's if anyone cared to ask. They didn't. Whatever praiseworthy qualities Clayton could have possessed in this life had long since been eclipsed by a darkness. And if Cammie did describe any type of goodness, nobody would believe her. She is a manipulative liar who has spent her life being Clayton's puppet master for his nefarious deeds.

Sheriff Jack Lennox was the third person at the graveside service. He didn't mourn Clayton, nor will he miss him. He was there out of a false sense of guilt. Clayton was assassinated while in Jack's custody, killed by a single gunshot wound to the head as Jack was escorting him into the courthouse.

It did not take Jack long to discover the person behind the trigger was a skilled marksman. He made the kill without injuring Jack, who was close enough to Clayton to have his blood and bits of his brain matter scattered across him. Despite Clayton being a murderer and horrible human, Jack felt responsible for him since he was in his custody.

There is nothing Jack could have done to prevent Clayton's execution. Reiterating that fact to him is pointless. In his mind, he failed at protecting his prisoner. Much to his chagrin, there doesn't seem to be much he can do about catching Clayton's killer, either. The hitman is an enigma, who goes by the name Chromia— short for heterochromia— a condition which affects his eyes, making them two different colors. The name, eye condition and his various kills are the only known facts about him. A person must look deep into the dark web to hire someone with skills such as those Chromia possesses. The F.B.I. has been chasing him for years, so when his name came across their radar during Jack's investigation, they swooped in and quickly took over the case.

The F.B.I. taking over the case did not result in Jack ceasing his investigation. It only makes his job harder, as he must find ways to work around them. And they are missing out on a golden opportunity by not sharing all their information with him. In less than a week, Jack was able to learn as much about Chromia as the Feds discovered over several years.

"You know, if you need my assistance, all you have to do is say so," I say, to Jack who has been complaining about the F.B.I. He has no issues with the U.S. Marshals who were assisting him with the manhunt, and he works well with the State boys, but the F.B.I. is a different story.

He is sitting across the table from me at the pizza parlor. This is our first date. It isn't the fancy date he had planned, but with Clayton's murder, it is the first chance for him to escape his office long enough to have a sit-down meal. The opportunity for the occasion still would not have occurred if the F.B.I. had not stepped in, so I guess that is the one positive to their encroaching on his case. Talk of funerals, murderers and how he would figuratively like to strangle the Feebies isn't exactly romantic date talk, but it is what we know.

He dashes parmesan cheese on his greasy slice of pepperoni and sits the shaker back on the red and white vinyl tablecloth. "Thanks. No offense, but you are the last person who needs to be anywhere near this case," he says. "I do appreciate the offer, though."

"Sure," I say, shrugging as if it is no big deal. I am not certain he would accept an offer of help from me even if I wasn't close to this case, considering he both hired and fired me as a deputy in less than a week. Normally he would have a snarky or witty remark to my offer. But like everyone else, he seems to act as if he is walking on eggshells around me at the mention of anything related to Clay Butcher.

I'm not certain why I offered to help. Truthfully, I am glad he declined. He's right, I am too close to this investigation. If it were me who came face to face with Clayton's killer, I am not so certain that I would not shake Chromia's hand, rather than helping to make sure he is placed in handcuffs. Jack takes a bite of pizza and makes direct eye contact with me from his side of the booth. It's as if he can read my thoughts and his mouth quirks up at the corner ever so slightly. This may be our first date, but he knows me well enough to realize the handshake would win if I were faced with the choice.

"Besides, I am hoping this is the first of many dates. That probably wouldn't happen if you were working this case."

"You're right. Getting fired would make me as angry at you as the first time it happened," I say, giggling.

He chuckles and his dimple is on full display. "I was thinking more of how I don't date employees or coworkers. But, yeah, I would most definitely end up firing you again. I'd probably have to threaten to arrest you, too. That would really put a damper on our relationship."

Our relationship. Those two words sound so simple. It is much too early to think of us as being in a relationship. But the words are loaded with possibility. And for the first time in a long while, I feel hopeful for all the things I worried I would never have or want again.

one

FIVE MONTHS LATER

Nervous sweat trickles down my chest as it runs in rivulets to pool between my breasts. Thomas attempts to circle me yet again. I watch him, trying to anticipate his next move. He maneuvers right and then changes direction, quickly veering to the left. His eyes narrow as he realizes he hasn't distracted me as he had hoped. My eyes turn to slits in return.

We have been at this cat and mouse game for too long, both of us wondering what the other will do next. I am growing exhausted. I just want it to be over, but I know I cannot give in. That is what he is waiting for. I can see the fight is taking a toll on him too. He is starting to look fatigued. His stamina is growing weaker. But like me, he refuses to accept defeat. Sweat drips from the end of his nose. He reaches up to swipe it, never taking his eyes off me.

The seconds feel like hours dragging on. My muscles are taut, like a rubber band ready to snap. I can practically feel them humming from the determination coursing through them. My blood roars in my ears. More circling, more watching, and more calculating. Impatience takes over and I decide to attack.

I bring my right leg forward in a front kick, hoping to connect with his upper body and bring him down. Too late, I realize, he foresaw the upward trajectory of my foot. With a growl, he grabs me behind the knee, forcing me to the ground. I land hard on my back, surprise and the impact causing the air in my lungs to leave in a whoosh.

I have no time to recover my breathing before he is on top of me, straddling me, putting his left hand around my neck, and holding my left hip down with his right hand. I can smell coffee on his breath as it fogs me in the face, making my breathing even scarcer. His brown mullet is stuck to the sides of his neck from sweat. Another bead of perspiration threatens to drip from the end of his nose with a projected path of my mouth. I squeeze my eyes shut as panic sets in.

I must regain control and defend myself. My fight or flight instincts kick in. I remember the lessons from my kickboxing instructor Scotto regarding situations that mean life or death, like the one I found myself in several months ago. I resolved then that I would never again be a defenseless victim. I vowed to be more prepared to safeguard myself in the future.

With both of my hands I grab the one responsible for the death grip on my throat. I lock his left elbow into an arm bar. I sense his discomfort. He releases the hold on my hip. Bringing my right leg up under his left arm, I squeeze his back with my calve and foot using all my strength. This gives me just enough leverage to bring my left leg up and lock it around his neck, flipping him onto his side, with a loud thump. I can sense his body's duress even before he taps me on the hip indicating he has had enough.

"Say it!"

"Never!" he replies.

My grip tightens at his refusal. He slaps my hip again, harder this time. Although the strike stings, the pain is worth it. Finally, he says, "Fine! I'm a loser. Elle Riley is the best and kicked my ass."

"It didn't sound like you meant it. Say it with more heart."

With a grunt, he grudgingly repeats, "Elle Riley kicked my ass!"

"And?" I ask.

"I'm a loser," he mumbles breathlessly, grudgingly.

I release my grip. He rolls over on the mat to lie beside me, both of our chests rising and falling with our labored breathing. "I can't believe you made me say it. Bad enough I have to buy you lunch now."

"Well, Thomas, that's what happens when you're a *loser*. You get to buy lunch."

"Yeah, yeah," he says, as I slowly get to my feet. I offer him a helping hand up.

He looks at my outstretched limb with suspicion and refuses. "I'm not falling for that." He drags himself up off the mat and asks, "The Diner for lunch?"

"Sounds great," I say. We both down a bottle of water before I head for the lady's room and he to the men's room to freshen up.

* * *

People enroll in a kickboxing class for different reasons. Some take it up as a hobby, form of exercise, to learn basic self-defense moves, or because they think it will make them look cool. I treat every sparring session as if I am resisting a true predator, which I know from experience is much more likely to happen than I previously would have thought. Thomas, my usual partner, never goes easy on me, which is why I always choose him as my opponent. His height and weight give him a clear advantage, creating a challenge and making the victory that much sweeter when I win a match.

My name is Elizabeth Ann Riley. Everyone calls me Elle. I am a former investigative journalist. I still do some freelance journalism, but most of my days are now spent working as a Private Investigator for Art Bellamy, the proprietor of Art of Investigations. Art was formerly married to my mother. Although they are now divorced, he remains the father figure in my life.

The investigations gig is tame most of the time. But the element of danger persists in everyday life. When you spend your days prying into the lives of others, that element multiplies. You can never predict another person's behavior or actions. Some people can become erratic when their back is against the wall. And then there are others who enjoy chaos and are just looking for an opportunity to draw you into their madness.

This past spring, while investigating a case, I was abducted and almost murdered. Such an ordeal can leave scars, both physically and emotionally. I refuse to give into the emotional scars, because that would make me feel like more of a victim. Instead, I consider myself a survivor. Being a survivor indicates you were strong enough to come through the situation above ground. Even if the truth is a hero came to my rescue— I had to be smart enough to stay alive until the knight in shining armor appeared. If I should ever find myself in a similar situation again, I want to be as prepared as possible. I plan on always being a survivor. Afterall, the word victim is attached to those who don't live. I want to be equipped to be my own hero in the event no one comes to my rescue.

I lean over the narrow sink basin, splashing cold water

onto my face and then peer into the mirror. The fluorescent lighting in the otherwise dim room only enhances my haggard appearance. I take a long look at the puffy bags under my eyes and the little red lightning bolts shooting from my green irises. The evidence of many consecutive restless nights lately written all over my face. My cheeks are flushed from adrenaline, making the rest of my countenance appear pallid.

I straighten and take a step back from the mirror, deciding that examining myself too closely is causing my self-confidence to diminish. I use my fingers to fan my fringed bangs into a more attractive placement. The bangs are new, and I have yet to grow accustomed to them. My mother, Annie, who is a hairdresser, cut them to hide the recent scar on my forehead. It is one of two physical scars from my recent brush with death. The second scar is on my chin; hiding it with bangs isn't an option.

I sit down on a small wooden bench to take my shoes off, and frown at my reflection in the mirror, thinking once again about how tired I look. Then, my thoughts trail to the reason for the restless nights. The reason has a name. Well, two names to be exact. Jack Lennox, who is the county sheriff, and my current boyfriend. And Colton Ryan, my longtime friend and ex-boyfriend. Both names are currently tied for first place at the top of my bad list. I sigh as I shake the thoughts of them both from my mind. Thinking about them will only serve to put me in a bad mood. A foul attitude combined with my diminished self-confidence, fatigue, and emotions that have been too active lately, would be like a tornado heading for a trailer park.

I finish freshening up and change my clothes. I inhale a deep breath, the scent of bleach and Lysol mixed with sweat assaulting my senses. I take one last look at myself in the mirror, wipe the frown from my face, straighten my posture and square my shoulders before leaving the restroom. When I emerge from the short hallway, I find Thomas scrolling on his phone, guzzling another bottle of water as he waits for me.

"Why aren't you wearing the shirt I got you?" I ask, resisting the urge to smile as I anticipate his reply.

"This?" he asks, holding up a black tee shirt with 'Elle kicked my butt,' in red letters across the front. "This is trash. Although, I will admit it was clever of you." A shadow of appreciation crosses his face before he continues, "The deal is lunch. Not to wear this hideous shirt." He tosses the tee at me, and it lands at my feet.

"No worries," I say. I kick the shirt to the side and then unfold my arms from my chest, revealing the one I am wearing that says, 'Thomas got his butt kicked by me.' "I had an inkling you may feel that way, so I had myself one made also." I beam a sarcastic smile at him. His mouth ticks up at the corner ever so slightly; an indication that he finds it hilarious but doesn't want to admit it.

Ours was an unlikely friendship. We started out as enemies. He is a cashier at a local convenience store, with a deadpan persona that many do not like. I am a customer at the store and take great pleasure in antagonizing him in return for his pain in the ass nature. He seems to appreciate that I am a pain in the ass too.

He has one of those personalities that you must get to know before you can understand him. Understanding him means adjusting to his personality. Adjusting to his personality means recognizing his bluntness as authenticity, rather than rudeness. Sometimes I refuse to adjust, and it leads to us acting more like frenemies. He is brutally honest, and although I may win a sparring round occasionally, he usually wins when warring with words.

I bend down, picking up the shirt and hoisting my bag over

my shoulder as we make our way out of Scotto's Fighting Stance Studio, flipping lights off and locking the door. Scotto, along with the other spectators, including my mama, grew bored of our seemingly endless song and dance long ago and vacated the building.

I toss my bag into the back seat of my Ford Bronco and then lock the door. We walk past his older model Monte Carlo sitting in the side parking lot, opting to walk to the diner instead.

Autumn was late to arrive this year and is hanging on longer than normal. The weather could not be more perfect than it is today: sunny, with temps in the low seventies and a slight breeze that makes the leaves dance upon the street before being blown onto the sidewalk by passing motorists. The flowerpots lined up along the street are exploding in an array of fall flowers. The various colors of pansies and mums showing off, competing for most vibrant and beautiful. Sweet alyssum emits a honey-like fragrance as they pool in a snowy white blanket surrounding crotons that stand tall and buoyant in their beds. I am reminded of why fall is my favorite season.

The door of the coffee shop swings open as we pass, and the scents of fall drinks waft out into our path. The pumpkin spice and mulled cider fragrances mix with the nutty aroma of coffee beans. My stomach growls, reminding me I haven't been eating well the last few days. The sparring session seems to have stirred my appetite. Perhaps after I eat lunch, I will catch my second wind. I'm optimistic that maybe an afternoon nap will put me on the road to feeling more like myself. For the first time in over a week, I feel as if restful sleep will be possible when I close my eyes.

two

JENNIFER, the waitress glances up when she hears us enter the diner. Her smile quickly turns to a frown when she sees my lunch partner. The restaurant is bustling today as it normally is during the weekend.

The phone rings. She rushes toward it, no doubt in hopes that if she busies herself, she can avoid taking our order. Her coworker snatches the receiver and Jennifer's face falls. I consider dining with Thomas a social experiment. I am waiting to see how long it takes before Jennifer rings his bell with one of the ceramic mugs or stabs him with a fork. Judging by the look on her face, today may be the day that happens.

We slide into our favorite booth in front of the big window with a street view. Regular diners try to avoid this stall because the red vinyl seats are ripped and patched with duct tape, often catching on your clothes as you slide across the bench. It is also situated beneath an air conditioning vent, often causing diners to chill, leading to them being uncomfortable as they try to enjoy their meal.

With shoulders slumped in defeat, Jennifer grabs her order pad, slowly walking toward our table, cutting her way through the greasy haze, din of clanging dishes and conversations. I can hear her mumbling "Dear Lord, grant me patience," as she nears the booth.

She turns to me first, choosing to save the worst, Thomas, for last. "Hey Elle. The usual?" she asks me, smiling.

"Yep," I say. Today is Saturday and my Saturdays are always predictable. Farmer's Market with my Mama at nine a.m., kick-boxing class with her at ten o'clock, then lunch at the diner—where I will always order a cheeseburger, fries, water and a vanilla shake. I usually feel that I have earned the meal after class. Lastly, a stop by the investigations office before heading home to relax with Buddy, my Bernese Mountain Dog.

Jennifer cuts her eyes toward Thomas, lowering her brows. "And what for you today?" she asks, as she taps her foot, crossing her arms over each other. Thomas is not a creature of habit like me. He never orders the same thing twice. Which isn't a problem, but the ridiculous instructions about his meal and the excessive amount of time it takes for him to place his order are. I focus on her as she waits for his response, wondering if today will be the day that she loses her cool with him.

"I'll have the same as Elle." Her foot stops tapping. A slow, suspicious smile appears on her face until he continues with an evil grin, "no tomato, onion, lettuce or pickles."

"So, a plain cheeseburger?" she asks.

"No, not plain. I want *mayo* on it." Jennifer clenches her teeth and glances heavenward. "And I only want a half order of fries. *NO* salt. Do onion rings for the other half. And... I want peanut butter in the vanilla shake."

"Okay. Cheeseburger—mayo only, fries, onion rings and peanut butter shake?" she asks.

"If you want to call it a peanut butter shake," he shrugs.

"Well, that's literally what the menu calls it, so," she lifts a shoulder in return as he looks at her deadpan. "And extra salt on the fries?" Now she is just messing with him. I can't help but to giggle.

"No. I said no salt!"

"So, extra salt. Oh, I mean no salt," she corrects herself, smiling mischievously. "We'll get that right out," she says, turning on her heel.

"Can you believe her?" Thomas scoffs. "She is definitely not a people person."

"And you are?" I laugh, looking at him unblinkingly.

"No. But I never claimed to be. The customers I deal with at the convenient store aren't nearly as nice as people who dine in restaurants. May have something to do with not wanting spit in their food if they are being jerks," he says, tilting his head, considering the possibility.

"I really need a career change," he continues. "I've been thinking your line of work seems intriguing. How often do you get to use your kickboxing skills in the field? Because that's something I would *definitely* enjoy."

His incessant chatter regarding his disappointment with the general public drones on, sounding like a smoke alarm chirping from a dying battery. I glance out the window as my mind wanders uninvitedly, once again, to Jack and Colt. The thoughts drift a little further, pulling me into their murkiness, until Thomas's voice is no longer penetrating my ears. I'm uncertain how much of the one-sided conversation I have missed when he snaps his fingers at me, bringing me back to the moment. "Yoo whoo, Elle. Where'd you go?"

"Sorry," I mumble, swinging my attention back to him. I clear my throat, trying to find the right tone of voice before joining the conversation. It's a balancing act, speaking honestly without being callous or rude. Being gentle, yet harsh, as if scolding a child. "You are too offensive to hack it as a private investigator. People would never cooperate with you. In my opinion, you would be suited to a job where you would have the least amount of interaction with other humans or where it doesn't matter if you're rude. And yes, you're right about people not wanting spit in their food. You should be nicer to our waitress, so it doesn't happen to you," I say, while pointing a finger at him.

He scoffs in response. He isn't offended, but rather thinks my opinions are ridiculous. "What's up with you today? You seem to be a little off and extra snarky. Don't think I haven't noticed those awful looking bags under your eyes. Boyfriend dump you?" he asks, as he uses the saltshaker to run circles around the pepper.

"I'm just peachy and I'm not snar....Wait. Why would you think *he* dumped *me*?" I ask, jerking my head up sharply, staring at him, waiting for an answer. Gossip spreads faster than wildfire in this town and his question makes me wonder if he has heard a rumor. Jack did not break up with me, nor did I end our relationship. Right now, our relationship could best be described as complicated. I am still unsure of the long-term effects of the complication.

He laughs. "Oh, you're serious?" he asks, sobering, as I think surely, he must have heard a rumor that Jack has ended our relationship. Perhaps a bit of gossip about me pushing his limits too far this time and him tiring of the situation. Maybe I am the only person who is unaware, considering that I have refused to speak to him in over a week.

He moves the salt and pepper shakers back to their original spots, then interlaces his fingers on the table, preparing to give me a lecture. "Surely, you know that you're a *lot*," he says, sliding his hands apart, as he waves one of them in the air indicating my whole person. So, he hasn't heard a rumor, this is just going to be his brutally honest opinion. I inwardly sigh with relief, but the feeling quickly changes to a grunt of irritation as he continues. "You're moody." He holds up a finger. "Not the best at communicating your feelings." He raises a second finger. "I'm sure you run him ragged keeping up with you. Always putting yourself in dangerous situations because of your rebellious nature," he says, while pointing to the scar on my chin. "And then there are your anger issues," he continues while adding more fingers to his count, holding the five digits splayed in the air.

The truth of his opinion strikes a nerve. His tone sounds callous and rude. I bristle and defensively lash out in return. "I don't have anger issues!" I say, swatting his hand away. "You do realize people don't call you TNT because your initials are T and T or due to a dynamite personality? They call you that because *your* personality is explosive, Thomas. So, who has anger issues?"

"Ah, I see I've hurt your feelings. Remember that the next time we spar," he says, reaching for the salt and pepper shakers again.

"Oh, trust me, I will!" I narrow my eyes at him.

"See? Anger issues. And you're like an elephant. You never let things go," he says, tapping the side of his head with a straw as Jennifer sets our plates on the table.

"I'll admit maybe I do have anger issues, but mainly just with you," I say, tilting my chin up indignantly.

"Same here, Elle," Jennifer says, giggling. She pauses to read my tee-shirt. She claps her hands. "Best shirt ever! Is that a club I can join?"

Thomas rolls his eyes upward in response as he dumps salt on the French fries that he ordered unsalted.

three

I LEAVE the diner with a full belly, my victory high over defeating Thomas at sparring now deflated. My disposition has turned broody, leaving the meal sitting like a lump in my stomach, rather than giving me the second wind I had hoped for. Today clearly turned into a frenemy day with Thomas and I'm okay with that. Right now, I'm okay with not adjusting to his personality or having to tailor my own to accommodate his.

I take a slurp of my milkshake. The sweet creaminess instantly curdles on my stomach, causing me to lose my appetite for it.

I look down at my feet, regretting leaving my vehicle at the Dojo, before heading down the sidewalk in the direction of Art of Investigations. I pass a two-story brick building, which houses the old theatre, where a man is on a ladder. He is removing skeletons that have been hanging along the front of the building and appearing as if they are climbing the wall. In their place, he is hanging a Happy Thanksgiving Banner. A woman stands on the sidewalk supervising. "To your left," she yells over the sound of a truck engine passing by. No, no, your other left." She rolls her eyes, causing me to suppress a giggle.

I step around a mountain of pumpkins stacked along the sidewalk. The Fall Festival took place last weekend. Halloween décor is coming down but Fall decorations will remain until after Thanksgiving. The fall fest is one of two held yearly in Justice County, my small Appalachian hometown, which is nestled in the mountains of Kentucky. The second festival is the Christmas fest. The town and residents go all out for both. The result is usually a scene that looks like it could have been taken directly from a Hallmark Movie.

The rest of the year, the town is your typical middle of nowhere destination. Beautiful, yet struggling. Bountiful, yet weighed down with the problems joblessness and drugs bring.

It is a place where the ladies buy their mayo by the gallon during the summertime, to allow for all the potato salad they make, and where if you don't own a cast iron skillet, chances are you're not considered a good cook. A place where bacon grease is regarded as an essential oil. Most people say Grace over their dinners, and "Bless your heart," can be taken literally or it can be meant as an insult. Drivers still pull their cars to the side of the road when a funeral procession is passing. It is a region where quality is considered greater than quantity when it comes to most everything and hard-working people believe that if you are going to do a job, you should do it well.

It is a poor community and for the most part always has been. The only exception being when the coal mines were open. They have been gone for many years now, along with the well-paying jobs they provided. Now the only remnants of those days are the lands that have been raped, causing problems such as flooding, and the elderly men with black lung from inhaling coal dust. Still, most of us sport license plates on our vehicles proclaiming, *Coal keeps the lights on.*

Because despite the problems that came from the mines, it was the only time our region was prosperous with well-paying jobs.

When the jobs went away, our community was re-allotted its rightful place in the world as poster child for poor America. After all, who would represent the indigent, destitute and uneducated, if not for the pitiful Appalachians? Most of the people with this opinion are well-intentioned. They have no idea that many people here still believe there is a difference in needing a helping hand up and a permanent hand-out.

The stereotypical opinion of poor Appalachians always has been and always will be. Certainly, it can be offensive to our population. But it is small potatoes compared to the drug epidemic our region has been facing for years— a crisis that makes me furious and should also enrage everyone else.

It used to be that when someone did something wrong, others would say, "They sure weren't raised that way. It must've been the devil that made them do it." Now, most of the time, it really is the devil who tempts them. He doesn't come to people with horns, wearing a red cape, or even as a seductive temptress. He comes in the form of a pill that sometimes shape-shifts into a needle. He goes by the name opioid, promising to rid people of their ailments or boredom. He had plenty of disciples in the form of pill mill doctors with prescription pads. No one could have fathomed years ago that those light slips of paper prescriptions could carry the weight of our population, let alone bury so much of it.

I always thought of drug addicts as being like the junkies you see in movies. When I was young, you did not see people like that on our street corners. I had never even seen a homeless person until I moved away to attend college. They can be seen now, roaming the streets long after most people have gone to bed. Kids that were bright enough to pass math and science in school, but never cared enough to try, are now doing chemistry in the form of cooking meth.

On the heels of opioids and meth came fentanyl, which is far more dangerous than the devil we had gotten used to. Addicts are playing roulette each time they meet with their dealer to score. Small town America is slowly being drowned by an ocean of big vices.

I couldn't wait to escape from here as soon as I graduated high school. I had big dreams and wanted to give those dreams wings. As a teenager, when most girls were reading the Twilight books, I would be found reading classic novels or listening to old broadcasts of Walter Cronkite with my Granny. An old soul, she would call me. Book smart, polite people would say. But the truth was, I was a nerd. My idea of a fun time was helping Art with investigative cases. I was curious and often determined to solve a mystery, which some would define as nosy and stubborn. Naturally, I keep a running tab of those descriptive words of myself in my head; nerdy, nosy, stubborn and naïve. I certainly didn't need Thomas piling onto the list today, pointing out more flaws.

With my desire to meet challenges and solve mysteries, it was no surprise when I decided I wanted to be an investigative journalist. Between my excellent grades earning me scholar-ships, my mother working extremely long hours, and my working through college, I was able to pursue that goal.

So, the end of the summer after I graduated from high school, off I went into the world, wide-eyed and naïve. I met my now ex-husband, Liam while I was still attending college in Boston. We married shortly after I graduated. I got my feet wet working for a prominent paper— my dream job.

If I were to define the word naïve, it would be to think those two things would last forever. The end of both is two of a handful of the hardest life lessons I have learned in my thirty-two years. Hearts are broken when your wedding vows and trust are, and sometimes when your dreams come true, they aren't nearly as ideal as they were in your mind. Tough lessons that were taught to me by a philandering husband and a news media that seems to have developed a different idea of how journalists are supposed to report. With heroes like Walter Cronkite, I felt the sting of disappointment when I found out there really did not seem to be a place for me in this ever-changing era of news, unless I was willing to compromise my journalistic integrity. I wasn't.

A couple of years ago, after my failed marriage and giving up my career at the paper, I couldn't wait to flee Boston and return to Justice. Some could view it as tucking tail and running home to my mama. I choose to think of it as coming full circle. An ironic full circle. But that is the way of life in Justice: an unexplainable, often unhealthy love for something that is incapable of reciprocating it, leaving you yearning, yet satisfied at the same time. Like I said, it's an unexplainable love.

Returning to Justice to live wasn't an immediate decision. The upsetting life changes came with a desire for the comfort of home; more so, the comfort of my Mama and my Gran. So, I came to visit for a couple of weeks. Those two weeks turned into two more, then a couple more. The next thing I knew, I was living in the apartment above Art's office, working cases for him with no desire to return to Boston. I had my belongings shipped here, sold my expensive car, and the rest, as they say, is history.

I was stuck in limbo for a while after I returned. I fell into a routine— freelance journalism and part-time P.I. My high school sweetheart Colton and I re-sparked our relationship— a no strings attached affair. I told myself that I was content. I was content with the safety of not being in a serious relationship after getting my heart broken by Liam's infidelity. Content to do freelance journalism after giving up my job at the newspaper because I was burned out. Content to say I was just helping Art out with investigations, because that meant I could stop if I wanted. Content to be living in a small apartment above the office because that meant I could pack up and leave if I felt the desire to escape again.

Then one rainy night, when I was abducted by Clayton Butcher, that contentment I felt was stripped away. One night of being faced with death is all it took to make me realize that being content and being happy are two different things.

Contentment is often a word people use to describe an illusion of satisfaction. It is a cousin to complacency. It is a fear of what may happen if you try to change things. It is being perfectly fine with a hollowness. So perfectly fine, that you convince yourself you do not want more.

After that night, I decided I no longer wanted to be content. I wanted to be happy. I chose to be happy. I would like to be able to say that the epiphany is all it took for my life to be perfect afterward. However, my life is kind of like trying to fold a fitted sheet. I always start out with great intentions, high expectations and confidence, that I will be able to do it right. Halfway through, frustrated, sometimes sweating, I roll it into a ball and realize that I did the best I could. That is what my life is like when I am lucky. Other times, I feel more like I am the sheet and life the one rolling me into a ball.

My happiness is something I am the steward of; however, luck can contribute to that state of mind. Sometimes we can make our own luck, and sometimes it just happens out of nowhere. For instance, Clayton Butcher's death. Unlucky for him— but lucky for me. I did not feel that I had been robbed of getting to see his face when he was sentenced in court. I have faith in our judicial system, but when it rests in the hands of twelve peers, you never know how things will end. The peace I felt at another person's death used to alarm me, but now I have become perfectly *content* with it.

Jack, aka the current boyfriend and Sheriff, stays involved with the case in hopes that his suspicion will be confirmed that Clayton's sister, Camilla, is the person who contracted his murder. Clayton was an evil puppet, but Camilla was the person pulling the strings of their nefarious activities. With Clayton dead and buried, Camilla will most likely receive a slap on the wrist for her part in their crimes. Crimes that include kidnapping and wanting to murder me, murdering Kurtis Abbott, and attempting to murder two more people. This makes it personal for Jack. His wanting Camilla locked behind bars goes beyond him just performing his honorable duty as Sheriff. It speaks to his desire to be a protector beyond his duties as a sworn officer of the law.

The events that transpired with Clayton Butcher took place six months ago. Life has been a whirlwind since then, leaving me without much time to ruminate on the past. Occasionally, I still wake in the middle of the night, from a nightmare. One in which I am tied to a chair, gun pointed at me, ready to go off. I always awake before the trigger is pulled, drenched in sweat, heart racing from fear. Reliving that horrible night in my dreams leaves me tormented for days afterward.

Three months ago, I moved out of the small apartment above Art's office after I purchased an old farmhouse. The home is a work in progress. The list of tasks that need to be done in order to restore it to its former glory is endless. I am up for the job. The exhaustion that comes from staying busy and working hard helps keep the nightmares at bay when I close my eyes at night. And I have the rest of my life to work on the house, considering I no longer foresee the desire to flee my hometown.

Not only did I become a homeowner, but also a pet owner. I took on the responsibility of Buddy, my dog, when his previous owner, Gertie Rose, went to live in an assisted living community, Croaking Creek Adult Living. The facility/community is named after the creek that runs in the area. I cannot decide if the person who came up with the name is hilarious or morbid, but either way they should not have been given responsibility for naming accommodations for the elderly.

Buddy is a mammoth ball of fur. He is well-loved and provides endless entertainment. A couple of months ago, I released my first children's book, titled *Buddy the Dog*. The book was well-received. Turns out other people love Buddy's antics, too. The royalties from the book contributed to the remodeling fund for the house. It's a good thing I have the rest of my life to work on the home because my fund quickly diminished, with many projects still left to do.

I haven't been committing myself to very many freelance journalism jobs lately. Between the house, being a dog mom, working investigative cases, and life in general, I don't seem to have much time to devote to journalism.

Writing is something I always poured my heart into, trying to give an unbiased voice to my stories. It seems lately my voice has become jaded and cynical, making me feel as if I am unworthy of representing an impartial opinion. I have always striven to see the good in people and situations, but that is an aspect that I struggle with now. I am making a conscious effort to still try to see the good without being naïve. It doesn't always come easily. The ability to do so is one more thing Clayton Butcher took from me that I wish I could get back.

Journalism is a part of my life I thought I would miss, but I don't. Turns out, it has always been the investigative aspect of the career that I relished. The P.I. cases I take on seem to satisfy my curious mind and offer enough of a challenge to keep me occupied.

Before buying the house and adopting Buddy, Colton Ryan and I broke off our romantic relationship. He was ready to get serious. Although I do not have an aversion to finding true love and settling down, I just didn't feel like Colt is my happily ever after. We make much better friends than we would life partners. We were best pals before becoming high school sweethearts and remained close through the years. It was natural and familiar for us to fall back into the routine of friendship after ending our latest romance.

After our breakup, I started seeing Jack. I've known him since I was a teenager. He is an older cousin to one of my best friends, Daphne. She and I took great joy in irritating him when we were younger, and even sometimes now. I suppose I always had a secret crush on him. He is a couple of years older than me. When you are in high school, that may as well be an age difference of one hundred years.

As soon as Jack graduated, he joined the Marines. When his enlistment was up, he returned to Justice and eventually became Sheriff. I would run into him from time to time when I was home visiting, but I was married, and he was grown up Jack with a badge and a pen at the ready to write me speeding tickets. He had not forgotten what a pain in the ass I was when we were younger.

We were forced to spend time together while working the case to catch Clayton. There was an attraction between us that we both denied. When Jack learned I was no longer involved with Colt, he worked up the courage to ask me out. Things between us seemed to go well from that point: so well that he has a key to my house. It just made sense because he spends more time at the farm than he does his own home. Everything about our relationship made sense until a little over a week ago, when a misunderstanding led to a chasm between us.

He was in New Orleans consulting with the FBI, who had a lead on Chromia. Sally, the bartender at the Troubadour, called me late on the last night Jack was out of town, saying that Colt was drunk and in no condition to drive, asking if I could come get him. I picked him up from the bar. I did my due diligence as a friend and acted as his designated driver. When I pulled into his driveway, we realized he had lost his keys, so he came home with me, where I put him to bed on the couch.

Jack came home earlier than expected to find Colt standing in front of the fridge in his underwear drinking milk out of the carton. He assumed the worst. Colton did nothing to dissuade his line of thinking and instead antagonized him. The two ended up in a punching match that shifted from the kitchen into the back yard.

Between the ruckus they were creating and Buddy going wild, I woke up to find the screen door to the back porch torn off and the two of them rolling around on the lawn. They were full of piss and vinegar, each man determined to kill the other. I turned the garden hose on them to break up their battle.

After finding out what was going on, I became angry and made them leave. By that point Jack had realized he was mistaken, profusely apologized to me and even gave Colt a ride back to his house. The apology was useless, the damage was already done, and I was too angry to see beyond the hurt inflicted by what Jack thought had transpired.

I have refused to speak to either of them since. Colt's apology text and call went unanswered along with Jack's numerous calls and texts. I even had the locks on my doors changed so Jack's key wouldn't work. Hurt has continued to fuel my anger. Hurt that Jack thought I had slept with Colt. He knows my history with my ex-husband, Liam, and knows how much his extramarital affair destroyed me. Jack and I never had the "we are exclusive" talk. I never considered it necessary. Now I am left to wonder if it would have even made a difference. In those early morning hours, I learned Jack thought he could not trust me, and it wounded me deeply.

My anger at Colt is exactly that— anger. I'm mad as hell that he would encourage Jack to think such a thing, even if he did so with the thought it would be funny.

I love both men in different ways. Jack is the pleasure of my life. I love him whole heartedly and up until that point, he was the person I could see as my happily ever after.

If Jack is my pleasure, then Colt is surely my vice. Not a vice in the sense that my relationship with him is forbidden, but a vice in the sense that I will always forgive him, no matter what. He is like a lovable puppy who soils your new rug but is so adorable you immediately forgive it. He has always had that effect on me. I can't help it; I have a soft spot for him. I just don't love him in the same way I love Jack. Colt is funny, charming and handsome. Most women would think I was insane not to have wanted to become serious with him, but the heart is a tricky beast and mine just wasn't in the same place as his. I also cannot help but to think that he was more in love with the idea of settling down and I was his option at the time. I do not want to be someone's one and only out of convenience.

Both men are an important part of my life and the one thing I don't need is the two of them in a pissing contest.

As if on cue with my thoughts, I hear someone calling my name. I recognize Jack's voice without turning as he jogs across the street trying to catch up to me. I keep walking purposefully, ignoring him, as he keeps pace, stalking behind me up the sidewalk.

"You can't stay mad at me forever, Elle. At some point you're going to have to talk to me," he says.

"Wanna bet?" I say, over my shoulder, knowing that he is right that I can't stay mad at him forever. I have no inclination of talking to him right now though because if I do, I will forgive him and I am not ready to not be angry anymore.

"It was all just a misunderstanding. Why are you so mad anyways? I told you I would fix the screen door," he says.

I turn abruptly to face him, almost tripping over my own feet. He reaches out a hand to steady me. I slap it away, stomping my foot hard in frustration. It feels as if a jolt of electricity shoots up my shin from stamping my foot too forcefully. I have never been graceful when I am upset, much to my chagrin. "The fact that you don't know why I am angry is one reason why I am angry!"

"That doesn't even make sense. I can't read your mind so how can I know?"

"Of course, it wouldn't make sense to you... you obtuse," I struggle to find the right word, finally settling on "Jack*ass*!" I say, crossing my arms over my chest in a stubborn stance.

He balks as if I have slapped him and then narrows his eyes, never happy when I use Jack*ass* as a spin-off of his name. I avoid looking directly at those narrowed blue eyes because I will get lost in them if I do. I try not to take in his blonde hair, perfectly mussed up from running his fingers through it one too many times when he gets irritated, because I know I will forget my own reasoning. "Now you're just being mean spirited," he says, hands on his hips.

He should know me well enough to realize he needs to wait until my anger subsides before we can have a reasonable interaction. "Well, go away and I won't be mean to you," I say, lifting a shoulder nonchalantly, acting as if the mere sight of him doesn't still make my stomach flip.

"Fine. You know what? You drive me crazy! Stay mad forever. See if I care!" he says, as he turns and tramples the sidewalk under his feet in displeasure.

But I know he does care, the same as I know I won't stay mad forever. At least, I hope he still cares. Thomas's words come back to me; I am a lot to deal with, I'm moody, I am not the best at communicating my feelings, and I have anger issues. I wince internally as I realize all these things about myself are true and seem to be out of my control these days.

Most of my problems at communicating my feelings stem from another one of life's hard lessons that has nothing to do with the failed dreams of marriage or my career. It has to do with growing up without a father and his family refusing to be a part of my life. Promises were made on their part and broken repeatedly, until I did not even bother hoping for a relationship with them. That teaches a child to have trust issues from an early age and experience much more disappointment than a kid should have to live with.

My mother and grandmother ensured that I had the best life, despite being shunned by my father's family. Still, it hurt. I learned not to show how it crushed my heart, because if my Mama saw it, it wounded her. The situation created some unhealthy coping mechanisms. Hiding my feelings and emotions. Tamping down anger until I eventually imploded over a minor incident that had nothing to do with why I was irritated to begin with. Now, even hurt feelings or wounded pride seem to manifest into anger. I am still undamaged enough to realize this is a problem, but I'm flawed enough to not be able to control it.

The one valuable thing that came from having negligent paternal relatives is it taught me not to break promises. When you tell a child you will do something and don't, it shatters

their little heart, so keeping promises has always been important to me.

Jack is little better at communicating than I am. That's one
reason I think our relationship works. We don't have to talk
things to death. We understand each other most of the time
and neither one of us is an easy person sometimes.

I watch his retreating back going in the opposite direction.
I hope he will still care by the time I am finished being angry.
Damn it if he doesn't look good walking away, I think as I
admire the view.

* * *

Having lost my appetite for the milkshake, I toss it into a
trashcan before rounding the corner to the office. I take a deep
breath and try to plaster on a face that doesn't betray my bad
mood. As I open the door, Art reaches for a bottle of whiskey
sitting on his desk, prepared to shove it into a drawer, until he
sees it's me entering.

Lawrence "Teeny" Tulane is sitting on the other side of the
room with his massive tree trunk legs propped up on the desk
and a newspaper spread open in front of his face. He folds the
paper and lays it on the desk when he sees me. Teeny is a
former member of a biker gang, an ex-con, and the largest
man I have ever seen. He is the perfect example of why casting
stereotypes aren't accurate. The time he pulled in prison was
due to tax evasion. Someone else in his gang funneled their
dirty money through his identity, which was, I suspect, the
reason he was able to walk away from the gang so easily. He
now works for Art. I consider him a close friend in addition to
being a coworker. He also acts as my self-appointed bodyguard sometimes, which he is excellent at. Even though he
really is a gentle giant, he can instill fear in men just by

looking at them. Occasionally, the stereotype works to our advantage.

"What's up, Sunshine?" Art asks.

"Not much. What's up, Buttercups?" I ask, trying to sound cheerful.

"I take it your kickass session went well this morning?" Art asks, nodding toward my tee shirt.

I giggle in response.

I've got a job for ya'," he continues, as I take a seat at the desk I normally occupy. "A lady called. Requested you. Said you were recommended by someone she knows. She didn't go into a lot of detail on the phone other than to say she thinks someone is entering her home and messing with her things when she's out. Nothing the cops can do because nothing is ever missing and there isn't real clear evidence of an intruder."

"Hmm. That sounds interesting. Stalker? Crazy ex? Or crazy stalker?" I ask as I drum the tips of my fingers together considering all the possibilities that intrigue me. More of Thomas's words come to mind— 'Always putting yourself in dangerous situations.' *Dang it, Thomas, get out of my head*! It isn't that I want the world to be full of psychotic people. I try my best to avoid them, but it sounds much more interesting than workers comp fraud or cheating spouses.

"Hopefully none of the above," Art says. "She has some trouble with her schedule and can't come to the office. She asked if you could meet her at the Queen Bean Coffee Shop tomorrow."

"Tomorrow? Tomorrow is Sunday. And the Queen Bean is a twenty-minute drive. Thirty, if you get behind a slowpoke." I stare at him, unblinking.

"Yeah, I know. It's the only day she can meet though. And I'll entice you to do it by paying for you a manicure from that fancy nail salon down the street from the coffee house," he says in his laidback tone. He knows that my Sundays are usually reserved for spending family time at my Granny's house. He smiles hopefully. I will not refuse his request. I never do, but I decide to up the ante.

I run my thumb across my nails, trying to look like I am considering my answer. I haven't had a decent mani/pedi since Mei Ho opened her shop in Justice, Ho's Nails. Not that Ho's Hand Jobs (as someone thought it would be funny to nickname the shop), doesn't give great manicures. But I refuse to go there after my mom's nail tech, Gina, quit to work there, leaving my mother unable to offer nail services. My mama paid for Gina to go to school to do nails and then she quit her salon to work for Mei. My mother doesn't begrudge Mei or Gina and would encourage me to offer them my business, but I would rather have ragged nails. "Deal, if you throw in a pedicure too," I say.

"Deal. Pedicure too," Art says, without hesitation. "Now, tell me why you had Teeny change out the locks on your doors."

I give Teeny a sharp look. "What? You didn't say it was a secret," Teeny shrugs.

I asked Teeny to change my locks because I knew he would not ask any questions. I should have known that he would blab to Art. Art knowing my business is not a big deal, but he usually tells my mother my business and she turns everything into a much bigger deal. "It's a long story. I won't bore you," I say, waking the computer screen in front of me, pretending to busy myself.

"Please do bore me," Art says. "I'm guessing it has something to do with Jack since he has keys to your place and could have changed your locks himself. So, I want to know if I need to dig a hole."

I tell Art and Teeny what transpired between Jack and Colt. "I am not speaking to Jack, so I couldn't very well ask him to return his key. Rather than do that, I had the locks changed." When I finish, they both look like they are still waiting for a plot twist or punch line to emerge.

"You're mad because Jack is jealous?" Art asks. "The man carries a gun on his hip. You should just be happy he didn't shoot Colt."

"I would've shot him," Teeny says.

I roll my eyes at Teeny. He has never cared for Colt. He often refers to him as pretty boy— not as a compliment— and has threatened to crack Colt's skull on numerous occasions. "No, I'm not mad because he was jealous. I'm mad because Jack thought I was a two-timer," I say, lifting my chin indignantly, feeling fresh insult again at the thought.

"It seems to me like it was Colt's fault. I'm sure he done something to antagonize Jack. I like the Ryan boy, but he can be a turd sometimes," Art says.

I open my mouth to respond but Teeny interrupts me by clearing his throat and says, "I think what Art is trying to say is that Jack might not think you are a cheater so much as he was mad because he knows Colt would like for you to be a cheater. Put yourself in his shoes. If he still hung out with an ex-girlfriend, how would you feel about that? He just hasn't ever said anything about it because he doesn't want you to perceive him as jealous or controlling. It's obvious to everyone but you that Colt is still in love with you. If you want me to crack Colt's skull, just say the word," he says as he pounds a fist into his other palm.

"Yeah, what Teeny said," Art says, as he splashes whiskey from the bottle into his coffee mug.

Teeny sometimes offers pearls of wisdom like a scholarly intellect instead of a burly ex-con. He has a way of putting things into perspective. I never considered that my friendship with Colt is a problem for Jack because he has never said anything about it. Colt has always been my best friend. I don't think of him as my ex-lover, Colt. I think of him as my funny, always there for me no matter what, Colt.

What if Colton is holding onto me not out of friendship, but because what Teeny says about him being in love with me is true. I scrub the thought from my mind as quickly as it appeared. Colt is not lacking in the romance department. Even if I had broken his heart, which I do not think is the case, he moved on quickly. But I hang onto the possibility of Jack being jealous.

"Thanks, but skull cracking won't be necessary," I say, noticing Teeny looks slightly disappointed. Colt seems to have that effect on other males. Women love him and men hate him because they are afraid their women love him. "I'm sure I can think of ways to punish him and Jack all on my own." Neither Art nor Teeny disagree with me.

four

SOME COUPLES TRAVEL TOGETHER, take dance instruction, cooking classes, or find some other common interest to spend quality time together. Teeny and Sally have decided they want to be a P.I. couple: a dynamic duo, as Sally just told me. She wishes to become a licensed private investigator.

"What do you think? Would you be willing to sponsor me and help me prepare for the exam?" she asks, as I strain to hear her over the cover of a Waylon Jennings song the band is performing.

Sally is a big personality packed into a petite body. Teeny is muscle and brawn. The two are opposites, and the law of opposites attracting works in their favor. "Of course," I smile. "But what about the bar?" I do a circle with my finger indicating the space. "You're here most of the time. Especially now that you own the place."

First Thomas and now Sally. I am not sure what it is about my line of work that seems enticing to them. It entails a lot of grunt work and frequently making numerous people angry with you. Both of which they seem to have at their current jobs.

"I'll still be here most of the time, but I think Stevie can hold down the fort when I'm not."

I glance down the bar to Stevie whose previously hot pink hair is styled in bright green pigtails today. I wondered about her work ethic after interviewing her for a receptionist position at Art of Investigations. She doesn't like normal work hours and is also usually high on marijuana. Bartending seems to suit her, though. The customers love her, and I must admit she does a great job. The more I get to know her, the more I like her. It almost makes me wish the interview with her had gone better.

Sally continues, "Ya know, I spend a lot of time with Teeny when he is doing surveillance for Art, so I figured what the hell, I may as well become official."

"Sure, sure," I say as I bite into a hot wing. "I am meeting with a new client tomorrow. Maybe you can help me with the case if I need assistance. I can teach you how to do background checks next week, too."

"That would be great." Then she continues, a nostalgic look on her face as she uses a dishtowel to dry the inside of a glass. "Remember the day I got a shot off at Clayton Butcher when he had his gun to your head? The day he was holding you hostage right over there!" she exclaims with a sparkle in her eye.

I don't need to follow the direction of her pointed finger to be reminded of that day or the exact location it transpired. It isn't necessary to look at the hole in the wall made by Sally's shotgun—the hole that she decided to put a frame around rather than patch. "How could I forget?" I ask. It's etched in my memory as if it happened yesterday.

"That's the day I realized how exciting these cases could become," she continues. "A lot more interesting than listening to a bunch of drunks cry into their beers." Fred Jones looks up at her from across his frosty mug of Blue Moon. "No offense, Fred," she says, winking at him. He nods his head toward her, raises his glass and takes another swig.

I cough as I choke on a bite of cheese stick. "By exciting, you mean terrifying and by interesting, you mean dangerous?"

"Terrifying for you," she says. "Exciting for me. You had a Desert Eagle pointed at your temple. I was the one holding the shotgun," she chuckles.

And there it is. Both her and Thomas's reasoning for thinking that the P.I. life sounds alluring. He wants to use his kickboxing skills, and she wants to shoot people. Neither of which I have ever done as an investigator. There have been times when I have wanted to beat someone up or shoot them, but I have refrained. Jack is a stickler for rules, and I know I would get no special treatment from him if I were arrested for either offense.

"Don't remind me," I say. "I was more worried that I was going to be shot by you than Clayton Butcher!" I laugh. "But in all seriousness, thanks for being my hero that day."

"My pleasure," she says.

Stevie breezes by, sliding an order of bacon and ranch fries in front of me. The band's song comes to an end. There is a pause in music as they take a break. Stevie cranks up the sound system and the thumping of the music once again drowns out the din of voices.

"You and Jack still on the outs?" Sally asks. My raised brow tells her I do not want to discuss it. "It's a logical conclusion. You're carb loading and drinking Diet Mountain Dew. *At a bar.* That may be one of the saddest things I've ever seen."

She isn't wrong, I think as I toss a French fry at her. What led me here this evening is that I grew tired of lying on my couch like a sad sap of a human being. Even Buddy abandoned his usual post at my side, instead opting to camp out in front of the door in hopes Jack would be walking through it soon. *Traitor dog.*

She leans across the bar, lowering her voice. "Don't look now, but the reason I asked is because he just walked through the door. A.J. Parker has him hemmed up in a conversation. Want me to distract him while you slip out the back?"

Ignoring her warning not to look, I slide my eyes in the direction of the entrance. Jack has disengaged himself from A.J. and is making his way across the crowded barroom. He is out of uniform, wearing jeans, a black long-sleeved Henley, and a ball cap. The shirt is just tight enough to cling to his muscular arms and hug his mid-section: muscular arms that often embrace me and a mid-section that I know looks even better without the shirt. And damn it, he knows I love it when he wears a ballcap.

He only takes a couple of steps in my direction before being stopped by someone else. I debate whether to stay or go, deciding on the later. When we do talk, I don't want it to happen in a crowded bar or in the parking lot with prying eyes watching. It's bad enough that our interaction on the sidewalk earlier today is probably already the talk of the town. I've had two missed calls from Mama asking about it and a text from Daphne, who works at the Sheriff's office.

I turn my head back toward Sally. "Look at you Sal, being my hero again today," I say.

"I'll always have your back." She smiles mischievously, pulling a bullhorn from underneath the bar and yelling, "Ladies and gents, looks like our nice Sheriff has graced us with his presence tonight. Who wants to be the first to buy him a drink? Be a complete turn-about if one of y'all had to be his designated driver!"

Amid all the laughter and boisterous shouting, I slide off the barstool and amble to the kitchen for the back door exit.

five

THE QUEEN BEAN is in a community known as Little
Justice, a twenty-minute drive from Justice proper. It is a nice
drive that starts out with the mountains in the distance. Then,
suddenly you are driving along a curvy stretch of road through
the shaded side of the mountains, where the air feels ten
degrees cooler. When you emerge on the other side of the
kudzu covered basin, you enter the lovely town of Little Justice.

At the time the community was named Little Justice, it was
small enough the name suited it. When the interstate came
through, that all changed. The convenience of being close to
the interstate, coupled with its proximity to a man-made lake,
resulted in the town flourishing. It became a desirable location
for people who need to travel for work, but still wish to live in a
small-town setting.

It may as well be on an entirely different planet. The rat
race runs quicker here. The traffic is much worse. The homes
are nicer, the shops more highbrow. It's a beautiful area that
maintains its quaintness amid its bustling environment,
making it nice to visit but better to leave.

I parallel park in front of the coffee shop after leaving the nail salon. I admire my fresh pedicure peeping out from my open toed Freebird sandals as I walk into the cafe. Colder weather will be here soon, and I am taking advantage of the unseasonably warm day by wearing the shoes before boot season arrives.

I am a few minutes early, so I order an iced coffee and have a seat at one of the outdoor tables while I wait for Tara Daniels to arrive. Japanese maples are planted along the front of the wrought iron fence that runs the length of the alfresco dining area, giving it a private feel. Raised garden beds line the patio, with a few stray tomatoes and peppers hanging from vines. A slight breeze is blowing, rustling leaves along the sidewalk and street.

Many people dislike autumn because it is a prelude to winter, but I love it. It's as if God has opened a giant jewelry box and is allowing us a glimpse of the gems inside. Rubies and topaz richly decorate the landscape. The sun is a crowning diamond on a perfect day.

Two squirrels flit from limb to limb of a tree, wrestling for an acorn. It makes me think how similar animals are to humans. Acorns dot the ground, yet they both have their sights set on the same one, much like humans who are jealous of what each other have.

I look over when I hear, "Excuse me. Elle?" A lady is standing nervously beside the table.

"Yes. And you must be Tara," I say, standing and extending my hand.

"Thank you so much for meeting with me," she says, smiling at me shyly.

"Of course. My pleasure." We chit chat about the weather and our favorite coffee drinks to break the ice before discussing the reason I am here. The wind tosses her blonde hair, the strands intertwining with the diamond studs in her earlobes.

She reaches up, tucking the strands behind her ear, as I notice a faint scar peeping out along the band of her watch. I wonder about the white, ropy lines of the scar, obviously old. I advert my eyes as she quickly lowers her hand onto her lap to hide it.

She removes her sunglasses, revealing brown, doe like eyes. There seems to be a sadness hidden in those brown orbs. She appears to be in her thirties, perhaps just a couple of years older than my thirty-two. She looks like the typical girl next door.

"You said on the phone that you think someone is breaking into your house? Breaking, as in more than one time?" I ask.

"Yes. I know someone is. I just can't prove it. That's why I need you," she says. I nod my head, indicating that she should continue. "At first it was just a feeling as if someone had been there. Then I started noticing things moved out of place, such as pictures, clothes in my closet would be hanging in a different spot, I could tell my drawers were rifled through. I could smell my perfume when I would enter the bedroom. It's a Tom Ford scent. I volunteer at the Assisted Living Facility and some of the residents are sensitive to smells, so I am not in the habit of wearing it. Normally, just on special occasions, so I haven't worn the perfume in months. The odd thing is that nothing of monetary value is missing. My jewelry is all still accounted for. To be honest, I'm just baffled by the whole thing."

"And you contacted the police?" I ask.

"Yes. I'm sure they think I am a raving lunatic. I have a security system and the alarm has never been triggered, so no proof," she says, raising her hands palms up. "The security company here is a joke. With nothing taken and no concrete proof, there isn't much law enforcement can do."

"There isn't anyone who could have the code to your security system?" I ask.

"No. Nobody," she says, shaking her head emphatically.

"I have a six-year-old daughter. Her name is Emily." She makes a couple of swipes with her finger to her phone and pulls a picture of the child to show me. She is adorable, with two missing front teeth and a smile spreading from ear to ear. It is the first time I have seen a spark in Tara's dark eyes since she sat down. "After I gave birth to Emily, I wasn't in the best place mentally. I suppose the shift in hormones and sleepless nights really affected me. I started having panic attacks and paranoia to the point that I gave up my nursing career. I had these terrible, irrational fears of horrible things happening. What if I administered the wrong medication to a patient? What if something happened to my child? What if my baby choked while she was sleeping? The list of things that crippled me with worry were endless."

I think about the scar again and wonder if it could be six-years old too.

She continues. "I was adopted. My mother told me on her deathbed. I suppose she wanted to clear her conscience before she passed. She told me that my birth mother suffered from mental illness, perhaps schizophrenia. I think back to things that have happened in my past. Things I seemed to have had an explanation for before, but now I cannot help but to worry about genetics. I guess what I'm saying is, I need you to prove that I'm not going crazy."

Her eyes are sad again, almost woeful. I am filled with empathy. I know all too well the paralyzing feeling of having a panic attack. The hyperventilating, the racing heart that seems like it is going to explode out of your chest, the sickness in the pit of your stomach. The rational part of your brain telling you to get it under control, your body and mind refusing to cooperate. I can understand how frequent attacks could have effects on a person's career or other aspects of their life.

46

"Emily's father and I divorced three years ago so I am a single mother. I would never want to be put in a position to lose my daughter or worse to not be able to be the best mother to her."

"Is it possible Emily's father could be gaslighting you making you question yourself mentally, so he can get custody of Emily?" I ask gently. He could know about Tara's biological mother having a mental illness. And if so, he may be aware this is something Tara worries about.

"I hope not." The corner of her mouth lifts slightly as she elaborates. "He's deceased. Died in an accident a year ago. So, if it's him, then I really do have a major issue," she says trying to make light of the heavy subject. "I guess I should have led with that when I mentioned being divorced. I'm never quite sure how to say it. I'm not a widow since we were divorced and saying Emily's father is dead always feels cold to me. It's almost as if people expect me not to have been affected by his death because we were divorced, but that isn't the case. We were great friends and coparents even after our marriage dissolved. We just weren't good at being husband and wife anymore."

"I understand," I say. "I don't have children, but I do have an ex-husband. A part of me will always love him regardless of our divorce."

"Exactly," she says.

I feel a connection to this lady. Her being a single mother reminds me of my own mama. Her daughter growing up without a father reminds me of myself. She even likes the same flavor of iced coffee as me. If we were meeting under normal circumstances, rather than P.I./client, I could see myself becoming fast friends with her. I don't have many girlfriends. There's Gertie, who is in her eighties and has occasional dementia. Sally, who is hilarious and seems to get funnier when I'm drinking. Then there are my mother and grand-mother. If you take all of them out of the equation, then I suppose that technically I only have one gal pal, Daphne, who has been my friend since we were children. She's so far in now that she couldn't get rid of me if she wanted.

"I'm assuming your security is Justice Security?" I ask, already knowing the answer. It is the only security company in Justice. She nods in response. "Okay, I'll need a list of everyone involved in your life. Maybe if I solve this case quickly, we can meet for coffee under normal circumstances." I smile.

"That would be wonderful. It will be a short list. It would be nice to have a coffee date with someone else that doesn't double as a mystery," she says, smiling too. "My circle is small. I would hate to think that anyone I know could be responsible. So not only do I want to know who is invading my privacy, I'd also like to know why."

"Let's get started. Tell me everything, including any strange coincidences you may not have thought anything of at the time they occurred."

* * *

Tara wasn't exaggerating when she said the list of people that she associates with is short. She and Jacob Daniels moved here five years ago from Silicon Valley, after his brother Mark had settled here. Mark and his wife, Janie, relocated here due to her family being local. Jacob was a software engineer, and the couple was anxious to leave San Francisco and settle some-where like Justice to raise Emily. After their first visit with Mark's family, they decided to make this place their home. Tara is an introvert who was busy raising her daughter and never took time to make friends once she settled here.

Jacob left Tara a substantial amount of money when he

passed away to ensure their daughter will always be taken care of. Tara isn't employed, but she volunteers at the local assisted living facility. She isn't social with anyone employed at the facility outside of their work environment. She doesn't date. There is an orderly at the home who is overly flirtatious with her. She strongly discourages his behavior, but he is very persistent.

Her mother and father are both deceased. She has some interaction with her ex-husband's widow, Celeste Daniels, because Celeste is still involved in Emily's life. According to Tara, Celeste never liked her. But she adores Emily and Emily adores her. So, she allows their kinship to continue out of respect for Jacob and the wellbeing of her daughter.

Then there is her ex-husband's brother and his wife who are a big part of Emily's life. They have a son around the same age as Emily and the two children are the best of friends. Tara has grown more uncomfortable in her ex-brother-in-law Mark's presence since Jacob's death. She often finds him looking at her intensely or a little too long, making her wish to limit her time around him. She is closer with his wife, Janie, and even considers her a friend.

Her social life and friends are mostly acquaintances who are parents of Emily's friends. She seems devoted to filling the role of mother, father and everything in between for her child. Tara is completely happy to have lost all aspects of her own identity to motherhood. I wonder if the devotion to her child became heightened after Jacob Daniels's death, by trying to fill the void, leaving no time for herself. But I get the sense that Tara hasn't had many interests of her own other than doing volunteer work since Emily was born. She told me that volunteering was important to her because it gives her a purpose outside of her home and makes her feel as if she is making a difference in someone else's life.

So, who would want to cause chaos in Tara's life? The girl next door, caregiver, mother of the year, puts others before herself, Tara. Could there be a creep stalking her? Someone with a deviant mind, waiting for an opportunity to misuse a vulnerable woman? Could someone be trying to make her think she's crazy to try and gain custody of Emily, in the process gaining control of the massive trust that Jacob Daniels left for her? Or could Tara be imagining the events? The last option doesn't seem likely to me. Tara appears to be very grounded. She also doesn't seem like the type of person to make enemies.

Experience has taught me to try and be a better judge of people. Tara seems to be a genuinely good person. A devoted mother, a caregiver to the elderly and invalid, and the type of person unselfish enough to let Celeste Daniels have a relationship with her daughter because she knows her daughter loves Celeste.

Whether a person is decent doesn't affect my decision to accept a job. I am, however, more mindful of the people I associate with now. I have learned that naivety about a person's character can possibly put your life in danger. I even had Jack teach me how to read people, showing me techniques he uses during questioning suspects. Tricks to help deduce if someone is lying by paying attention to their speech, body movements and eyes. But you can employ all the tips and techniques in the book and still be fooled by a master manipulator. These are the types of people I wish to avoid.

Which would be better? Someone invading Tara's life creating havoc or her mind creating the havoc for herself? Neither one is a prime option. I am hopeful that it is something much simpler, but I don't see how anything else would make sense.

Tomorrow, I will stop by the security company's office

before surveying Tara's house while she is doing her volunteer work. Then I will delve deeper into her associates, particularly the orderly from the assisted living facility. But tonight, I need to go see Jack. I have decided it's time to let go of my anger. Regardless of how much hurt, disappointment or ire I felt toward him, he is worth the effort of forgiveness. I cannot let another day go by while being at odds with him. If he truly thought that I slept with Colt, that speaks of a trust issue and I'm not sure where our relationship will go from there. But I plan on figuring it out before I lose sleep again tonight wondering.

six

THE MOON SITS HIGH and bright in the sky, leading me like a beacon as I drive to Jack's house. Although not quite full yet, it holds the promise of the brilliant harvest moon slated later in the week. A moon so beautiful that we are only graced with it once every several years. Along with it will come the exceptionally crazy behavior that its pull seems to spark in people.

I pull into Jack's driveway and park beside his truck. I did not call ahead. I prefer the element of surprise. I waited late enough to give him plenty of time to be home from the office. The light of the lamps in the living room filter through the curtains, telling me he has had time to get settled in for the evening but hasn't gone to bed yet.

I look at the house, admiring how cozy it looks with the warm light spilling from inside. Or maybe it is the thought of the man sitting inside the house that makes it seem like a comfortable dwelling. When he bought the charming blue craftsman style house several years ago, his mother and sisters made it their mission to turn it into a cozy home, rather than the characterless bachelor pad they knew he would inhabit. The result is a welcoming space that seems atypical for a single man such as him. His pleather sofa and blank walls were replaced with timeless pieces of furniture, art and fake plants that he wouldn't have to worry about watering. Jack could care less about tasteful décor. But he knows when to pick his battles and it was easier for him to let the females in his family have their way with his house.

I have been playing out various scenarios in my mind all afternoon about how I should initiate the settlement of our spat. An apology on my part is a ridiculous idea since I did nothing wrong. An apology on his part doesn't seem to be forthcoming since by his own admission he doesn't even know why I was angry. After my conversation with Teeny yesterday, I realize that perhaps Jack has deeper reasons for reacting the way he did. I should be more open considering those reasons.

I miss him and have been miserable. My anger about the situation has dissipated, unclouding my judgement, as is usually the case when I decide to let something go. I may have a temper and a short fuse, but I am equally as passionate in forgiveness as in anger.

Short of offering an apology that I do not feel I owe; I decide that the next best thing is to just seduce him. I'm sure he will be agreeable to that. After all, isn't the best part about fighting the making up?

Buddy is whining and dancing across the front seat. He stretches across my lap, pressing his nose to my window, pawing at the door handle, excited because he knows we are at Jack's house. I am not the only one who missed Jack.

I do a final check to make sure my boobs look perky. I peer over the top of Buddy into the visor mirror to make certain my hair looks nice, then I swipe some glossy lipstick across my lips. The lipstick probably isn't necessary since I chose to wear Jack's favorite dress tonight, but I put forth the effort anyway. "Okay, Buddy, let's go," I say.

As soon as I open the door, Buddy catapults across me, digging his back paws into my leg as he makes his exit and charges up the walkway. "Ouch, that is going to leave a mark," I mumble to myself, stepping down out of the Bronco. I run my hands down the front of my dress, hoping I do not have dog hair on me and follow Buddy up the sidewalk.

Buddy scratches at the front door before I have a chance to knock. Jack opens the door wearing gray sweatpants and a white tee shirt. Buddy stands on his back paws. He leans into Jack's chest, anxious for his hug. "Hey Buddy! I've missed you," he says, scratching the dog behind the ears and petting him. "At least someone is happy to see me." He looks to me searchingly and asks, "Are we at war or peace, Elle?"

Ignoring his question, I step around him into the living room. A glass of bourbon and what's left of the bottle sit on the coffee table. Chris Cornell's voice comes oozing out of his Bluetooth sound-bar, crooning about how he "nearly forgot his broken heart." Between the bourbon and the song, I'm guessing Jack has been as miserable as I have been. The thought leaves me feeling more certain that he does still care, despite Thomas so ungraciously pointing out my various flaws that Jack must contend with.

Buddy races toward the kitchen in search of his water bowl, making himself at home as Jack closes the door. I remain quiet. He draws his brows together in confusion at my silence. I smile wickedly and walk over to him, running my finger down his chest. He looks both surprised and suspicious, then is taken off guard as I grab his shirt and pull him in for a heated kiss.

The sweetness of the bourbon on his lips mingles with my

tongue. The masculine scent of him is mixed with the bleached cotton of his shirt. The effect leaves me breathless, making me wonder why I ever wasted time being hurt and angry at him. He returns the kiss momentarily before drawing back. He pushes me to arm's length and steps away.

He wags a finger and says, "Oh no, no, no! This," he says using the same finger to swing back and forth between us, "ain't happening until we talk."

"Huh?" I ask, confused about his refusal of physical contact and his insistence of wanting to talk. "*Talk*?"

Perhaps I was wrong, and this isn't his favorite dress after all. Maybe I chose the wrong shade of lipstick. I have never known Jack to refuse my advances. In fact, he is usually the one making the advances. Maybe he wants to talk about ending things with me. My heart sinks a little at the thought.

"That's right. Talk. You can't avoid me for over a week, change the locks on your doors and then just waltz in here looking like a million bucks, thinking everything is A-Okay," he says, while making the symbol of an "O" with his hand. "You need to tell me why you were so angry. Talk to me." He scrapes a hand through his hair. His hands go on his hips, then he crosses his arms over his chest before placing his hands back to his hips again, nervously. He intakes a deep breath and releases it as he waits for me to reply.

Okay, so this apparently isn't an 'it isn't you, it's me,' talk. Of course, in this situation he would probably say it's definitely me and not him. Now that I have had a chance to calm down and think about things logically, I would probably be inclined to agree with him. Just not aloud.

"You think I look like a million bucks?" I smile, thinking the dress and shade of lipstick were the right choice.

"What? Were you even listening to me? That is not the point I was trying to make."

"Yes, I was listening to you. Alright, okay. It's like you said, it was a misunderstanding," I say, looking down as I pick at an imaginary fuzz ball on my dress.

He scratches his jaw and says, "Yeah, a misunderstanding on my part. I'm not sure what the hell was going on with you on your part. You're going to have to tell me why you have been acting so crazy."

"I'm not crazy!" My head swings up and my eyes turn to slits as my temper flares. I take a calming breath and remind myself not to get upset. I am here to work things out, not make them worse.

"I did not say you are crazy," he says with a measured tone, hands palm out in front of him. "I said you were acting crazy. There's a big difference."

Buddy has been rabidly trying to destroy a stuffed toy. He stops in the middle of a ferocious head shake to take stock of our conversation. Seeing our conversation isn't going to become heated, he resumes the murder of the stuffed rabbit.

There really isn't a big difference in my opinion of being crazy and acting crazy, but PotAYto, potAHto. That's an argument I decide to reserve for a different time. I scoff and say, "fine." I plop down on the couch, petulantly. I pick up his glass of bourbon from the coffee table and drain it. "I was hurt and insulted because you thought I had slept with Colt." I refill the glass, draining it a second time, preparing for the remainder of our *talk*.

He rubs one of his eyes, then picks the bourbon up from the table, taking a swig directly from the bottle. He sits next to me on the couch, making direct eye contact. "I did not think you had slept with Colt. Elle, you are the most loyal person I know. Loyal to a fault even, that's why Colt was at your house to start with. I came in exhausted, in a bad mood from dealing with the Feebies over this hitman case. Colt pissed me off and I took my anger out on him. I know it was his earlier inebriated state that made him mouth off, but I didn't care at the time. I suppose I lied when I said it was a misunderstanding. It wasn't at all. I understood that Colt thought he was being funny, but I didn't care. I just wanted to kick his ass," he says, raising his hands palms up, smiling sheepishly.

"So, you weren't jealous at all?" I ask suspiciously.

"Please don't tell me you were mad because you thought I was jealous and now you are going to be pissed because you think I wasn't jealous," he says, leaning against the back of the couch, exasperated.

"No," I say, rolling my eyes. "It's just I was talking with Teeny yesterday and he mentioned that perhaps it may bother you that I am still friends with Colt."

"You have to stop getting your relationship advice from Teeny and Art," he says. "It doesn't bother me that you are friends with Colt, despite your romantic history with him. I know that the two of you have been friends since you were kids. If I'm being totally honest, what bothers me is that I feel like Colt is your backup plan."

"Backup plan?" I ask, drawing my brows together in confusion.

"Backup plan. Meaning if your relationships go south, you will still have Colt. Which also means that maybe you expect our relationship to fail." Taking my hands in his, he continues, "I don't know if you've noticed or not, but I am crazy for you. You can be mean as a snake and you scare the shit out of me sometimes. And often you drive me insane, but I am crazy for you." He smiles, showcasing the dimple in his cheek.

I clear my throat trying to discourage my tear-filled eyes from spilling over. "Colt is not my backup plan. Colt is the person I would call if the plan were to get rid of a body with no questions asked."

He raises a brow. "See that's the 'you scare the shit out of me' part I was speaking of."

"Not literally." I tilt my head, "Well, I mean, if it was a literal body, I would definitely call Colt. But that's beside the point." I wave a hand. "What I'm trying to say is *you* are my plan, Jack. If our relationship doesn't work out, then I'm not so sure that there would be hope for me with anyone."

I never expected our talk to go like this. I am a *I thought you knew* person, and Jack is more of a *show* me how he feels, rather than have to say it person. I assumed tonight there would be some yelling, a few snide remarks and a passionate make up. But this is much better. Apparently, he really does love me, despite all my faults.

I want to tell him he has ruined other men for me, but I don't. I leave a lot unsaid, because the truth is I disclosed such things in the past to my ex-husband. He tried to use my feelings as a path to obtain forgiveness for his indiscretions. I tried to forgive him; I really tried, but his infidelity continued, and he played me for a fool. So, there are some things I will not say aloud to Jack until I am sure he wants forever too.

"Yeah?" he asks, smiling timidly.

"Yeah," I say, meeting his smile with my own. I am fairly certain he can tell I am crazy for him too.

He leans in close to my face in anticipation of a kiss as he twirls a lock of my hair between his fingers, "I really do love you in this dress. What do you say we pick up where we left off when you first got here?"

I suppress a fake yawn. "Gee, I don't know. I'm exhausted after all this talking." He gently shoves me back against the couch cushions. His hands go to my sides in what I assume will be an embrace until he starts wiggling his fingers, tickling me until I erupt into giggles.

Buddy abandons his stuffed rabbit and jumps up onto the

couch with a happy yowl, needing to be involved in the action. I am still giggling, Jack laughs, and Buddy starts howling.

Turns out talking wasn't as horrible as I thought, and the best part about fighting really is the making up. Still, I hope it is a long time before our next quarrel.

seven

BUDDY and I spent last night at Jack's house. After dropping Buddy off at the farm this morning, I met Jack at the diner for breakfast, where he decided to accompany me to Justice Security.

When he pulls into the parking lot of the building that houses the security office, there are no parking spots available, so he parallel parks behind the other cars, presumably employees' vehicles, in front of the office. "This shouldn't take long," he says. "I'll keep an eye out in case I need to move the truck."

I wonder if this will be a fool's errand. Many businesses aren't forthcoming to Private Investigators due to privacy issues. Occasionally you'll encounter a lax employee that doesn't know or care about such rules, but not often. There is the option of calling Tara if I run into any problems, while I am here so that she may speak to someone and give her permission. Perhaps when they see the Sheriff, they will assume it's okay to disclose information.

Dating the Sheriff has its perks sometimes. Unfortunately, speeding tickets don't fall into the perk category. He still issues citations to me if he catches me over the limit. No warnings for

me. I have overstretched my bounds when it comes to warnings. He acts as if it pains him to write me a speeding ticket, as
he states it is a matter of safety; not just mine, also everyone
else's. I know him well enough to know that he thoroughly
enjoys every swirl and line of the ink as he pens the citation.

"You ready to go in?" he asks.

"Yep," I say, as I open the door and jump down out of his
truck.

He holds the heavy, glass door to the office for me, like the
gentleman he is, and we enter. A man with the name William
stitched over the pocket of his blue button-down shirt is
manning the front desk. He has a phone pressed to his ear,
saying, "Uh huh, uh huh, I see." He cups a hand over the
mouthpiece and says, "I'll be with y'all in just a minute. I was
on hold for forty-five minutes before I got to speak to an actual
person," he says, explaining why he doesn't rush to end the
call.

Five minutes and several "uh huh's" later, we are still
patiently waiting. William cups his hand over the phone
receiver again and yells toward an office down the paneled
hallway. "Billy, can you come up here and help these fine
people?"

Billy, who looks like a younger, slightly heavier William,
emerges through the office door with his eyes trailing his
shoes. He finally glances up halfway down the hall, and his
eyes land on us. His gaze scans Jack from top to bottom, taking
in the Sheriff's uniform, and his face pales. He halts in his
tracks. Hesitating momentarily, he then does a turnabout,
running for the back door.

"What the hell?" Jack mutters.

I shrug. William is glancing around, oblivious to Billy's
evasion, as we walk back out to the truck. Neither one of us is
concerned with chasing Billy. A green Kia Soul is parked in

front of the office with a decal on the windshield that says Billy Boy. Chances are he is going to run around the back of the very long plaza and make his way to the front for the car, which is blocked in by Jack's truck. This is one of those work smarter, not harder situations, so we both lean against the car, chit chatting about the weather, while we wait for Billy to appear.

Finally, he emerges from the side of the building. With the fear of being chased over, he is walking now, instead of running, which is probably a good thing judging from the way he is holding his side. He looks down the sidewalk and sees us. He stops and bends over at the waist. Still panting from his long sprint, it is a moment before he raises up and turns to run in the other direction. We can tell his heart isn't in it. Clearly, Billy is not in fit shape.

"They just get dumber by the day," Jack says, as he pushes away from the car and takes off jogging in Billy's direction. It doesn't take long for him to catch up. He grabs him by the nape of the shirt, directing him back to the front of the office. Billy holds up a finger indicating Jack should give him a moment and bends at the waist again trying to catch his breath. I can see Jack give an exaggerated eye roll. I can tell by his expression that he is stifling laughter.

He deposits Billy in front of the building, where he slides down the brick wall, crumbling into a squatting position, holding his side and panting to catch his breath. "Mind telling me why you ran when you saw me?" Jack asks.

Billy's pale face has red, mottled splotches from exertion. His ginger-colored hairline glistens in the early morning sun with sweat. He is still struggling to breathe as he holds up a finger again indicating he needs a moment. When he is finally able to speak, he says, in a high-pitched tone, "I don't know. Seemed like a good idea at the time." He starts coughing and

Jack steps back so that if he vomits, the trajectory won't be his shoes.

"That is the dumbest thing I have heard in a while. Although, it is just Monday, so someone may still top it this week," Jack says, as Billy looks at him wide eyed. "Listen Billy, never, ever run from law enforcement. Now, once again, why the great escape?"

It has started to dawn on William that something is amiss. He stands and walks toward the big, plate glass window, as far as the phone cord will allow him to go. I can see his lips move in a final "uh huh, bye," as he hangs up the phone and rushes outside.

"I'm no dummy," Billy says. "You know I know exactly why you're here." He tilts his chin up defiantly.

"Why don't you remind me?" Jack asks, scowling, his patience starting to ebb.

"Come on Sheriff, I know Richie snitched on me."

I can see the wheels of Jack's mind turning quickly as he says, "Richie? Richard Carter who was arrested a few days ago for a string of burglaries. What did you have to do with that?" I can see the enlightenment dawn on Jack's face. "I'm guessing you were a big help to Richie by being employed here."

Billy's face turns an unnatural shade of gray and his eyes grow even wider. His Adam's apple bobs as he gulps while looking toward William, before asking Jack, "You mean Richie didn't rat me out?"

William looks like a grenade someone has pulled the pin halfway out of, ready to explode anytime.

"Nope. You did that all on your own. I appreciate it though," Jack says.

William finally speaks. "You're fired Billy! You better hope this doesn't affect my business!"

"Sorry, dad," Billy mutters. "All I did was tell Richie when I thought houses were vacant. I didn't know he was going to steal anything. I swear! I just thought he needed a place to stay since his old lady kicked him out."

"Well, look at you, aren't you a true friend thinking you were helping him become a squatter," Jack says, sarcasm dripping.

"The way I saw it he had three choices: Homeless. Squatter. Or sleep on my couch. No way I was letting him stay with me. I'd never get rid of him," Billy says.

"Well, now he has a nice warm cell to sleep in, Billy. And looks like you may get to be his roommate after all."

"Ah man," Billy says, nearing tears, "I'll never make it on the inside. If someone tries to make me their bitch, well, I'm sure you could tell I can't outrun 'em'."

"Calm down Billy, I'm sure your dad will post bail for you," I say.

"I wouldn't count on it!" William yells. "Just wait until your mom hears about this. It'll break her heart."

Billy looks manic. "He'll calm down," I whisper to Billy. "And your mom won't want you to be in jail." I have no inkling if William and Billy's mother will calm down enough to bond Billy out of jail, but it seems to pacify him. He gives an uncertain nod before standing.

I look at my watch. What I thought was going to be a quick trip has turned into a lengthy ordeal. "Let's go," I say, anxious to leave before William can reiterate his refusal to post bail and Billy have a possible meltdown. "I'll talk to Billy on the way. If he's no help, I'll come back and talk to his dad after you drop him off."

Any concern I had about questions for Tara's security company were unwarranted. Turns out, Billy is a nervous talker. He talked during the entire drive to the Sheriff's Office. He spilled the beans on everything he ever knew about anyone, including his pal, Richie. I wondered if he had ever heard the term 'snitches get stitches.'

He was insistent that Tara's home wasn't targeted by Richie's burglaries, even though he still maintained he knew nothing about Richie being a thief. He had spoken to Tara himself about her supposed intruder. Her home alarm has never been triggered, meaning that whoever entered had her security code. Which, according to Tara, no one else has.

After Jack parks in front of the Sheriff's office, he and I exit the vehicle. He meets me at the rear of the truck. Billy is craning his neck, peering out the window anxiously looking at us. The hue of his face has returned to an almost normal color. Jack asks, "What do you think?"

"I believe him. Her home hasn't been burglarized and I'm sure Billy would have told if he knew of anything suspicious to do with her residence. You?"

"I believe him, too. I'll have a crack at Richie today to see what he has to say about it." He glances off into the distance before saying, "Elle, I don't have a good feeling about this case. I almost feel like it's a premonition of something bad about to happen. Maybe I should just check into it for your client."

"Seriously? You have a bad feeling about *every* case I have worked since Clay Butcher."

"Yep. And you know how that ended. I don't know why you don't take on more journalism gigs and fewer P.I. cases."

This conversation isn't new, but it is growing tiresome. We have it every time I take on a case that requires the least bit of investigating. So, pretty much every case I work. He grew up the only male sibling in a houseful of girls with a Marine father. It was ingrained into him to be a protector. That's exactly how he has tried to live his life. First by being a Force Recon Marine, then by becoming Sheriff after his baby sister died from a drug overdose. In his mind, he didn't save his sister, Hannah, but he will do his best to save everyone else—particularly me. I would like to think his desire to be my protector stems from his overwhelming love for me, but the truth is he wishes he could save the world.

I narrow my eyes at him. "You know what? You are right. Perhaps you could knock me up, so I can just stay home barefoot and pregnant while you carry your caveman club into the office every day."

He holds up a finger. "That is not what I mean, and you know it," he says, checking his tone.

I cup my hand around his finger, lowering it. "And... One of your deputies couldn't help to start with because it couldn't be proven a crime had been committed. Now, you want to personally take over because I'm on the case and you have a bad *feeling*?", I ask, putting air quotes around the word feeling. "That's rather biased, don't you think?"

"Call it whatever you want but it is what it is," he shrugs. He can tell by my stubborn stance that I am not going to agree. "At least pass it off to Art or Teeny."

"She requested me personally. I'm not passing it off to you or anyone else," I say. I remind myself he is well meaning, so I add in a gentler tone, "If I need help, I promise, you'll be the first person I ask."

"Fine," he says, scowling. "I know you are no damsel in distress, Elle, but I still worry. I'm at least going to have someone driving past her house on a regular basis, though. I have a vested interest in your safety."

"Oh, yeah? And what would this vested interest be?" I ask,

smiling seductively as I inch closer, placing my hands on the front of his shirt.

"I've gotten used to your cooking," he smiles sheepishly.

"So... barefoot, pregnant, and *cooking*." I lightly slap at his chest.

He displays an amused grin, then he glances back at his truck and says, "Let me go book blabber-mouth Billy and I'll drive you to the diner for your Bronco."

"No need. I can walk," I say, as I tiptoe to give him a kiss bye. I wave at Billy, who is probably in danger of getting a crick in his neck from peering at us. He smiles and raises his cuffed hands, wiggling two fingers to wave goodbye.

Jack wallows his eyes. "You're the only person I know who can spend ten minutes in a vehicle with a criminal and come out as friends with him."

I laugh and say, "Some criminals are nice," as I head off down the sidewalk toward the diner.

"Elle," he calls after me. I stop and turn back toward him. "Please be careful."

"Always," I say, walking backward as I blow him a kiss.

eight

I INSTALLED cameras in Tara Daniels's spacious home that has a backyard view of the lake. I also placed clear tape along the top of the door jams, a little trick she can use to see if someone has opened her door. Now I am settled into my car parked along the street in front of the house. The inside comfort of her home is alluring, but the chance of coming face to face with her intruder is not something I wish to do. My focus is discovering who her intruder is and their reasoning for doing so, not serving as security or running personal interference.

She volunteers her time Monday through Thursday from Nine a.m. to Two p.m. All the incidences have occurred during those times, so I decide to conduct surveillance today to see if anything out of the ordinary happens.

I was surprised when I learned that she did not already have cameras installed inside the home after what she has been experiencing. Considering her ex-husband was a tech guru and the neighborhood is posh, I would have thought cameras would be a standard feature for their home. But then again, it seems as if this would be a safe neighborhood so perhaps, they felt there was no need for them before now.

When Tara called Justice Security to ask questions after her home intrusions, she spoke to Billy, who became indignant, feeling that she was being accusatory. He was probably searching his memory to recall if her home was one of the addresses that he had given his pal Robber Richie. Their conversation did not end on nice terms, and she decided to switch to a new security provider before she had a chance to inquire about having cameras installed. But considering her current situation, and with Justice Security being the only security company in the county, she did not want a lapse in security. She also feels that cameras inside the home are something of an invasion of privacy. She put her trust in me, allowing me to put them in place, with the promise that she is the only one who can view the footage unless she chooses to show me.

With the equipment in place, there isn't much of a reason for me to surveil her home. If I am being honest, it is my way of avoiding the other case I need to pursue, which involves possible worker's comp insurance fraud. Those are the worst cases. If someone finds out you were the one who discovered they were defrauding insurance, not only do they decide *they* hate you, but so does their family, friends, and anyone they consider close enough to invite to their house for dinner.

I have been settled in for about forty-five minutes observing the home, routinely raising my binoculars to get a closer look at the house sitting beyond the sprawling front lawn. I yawn from boredom and lift the binoculars again. A face appears in front of my vision, distorted, resembling a fun house mirror. My breath catches with alarm.

"Hello there," a lady says, rapping on my window as I lower the binoculars. "Car trouble?" Her voice raises a few octaves on the word trouble. She appears to be middle-aged and is holding a brown chihuahua on her ample hip like an infant.

I push the lever lowering the window. "Nope, no car trouble. Everything is fine."

"You sure? You've been parked her an awfully long time. You aren't a burglar, are you?" A forced laugh lets me know she really thinks I could be. "Elaine Smith, Community Watch," she says, patting her chest with her hand, as if community watch is an endearing term that she holds close to her heart. The dog points its bug eyes at me suspiciously. "This little doll is Princess," she says, indicating the pet. Princess pulls her lips back revealing her teeth, letting out a snarl that would put Buddy to shame.

I conjure a bright smile and say, "Do I look like a burglar?"

"Well now, maybe you don't look like the typical thief. But it takes all kinds, you know." Her mouth sets into a hard line as she flips her over-bleached blond hair over her shoulder. Her forced pleasantry is over and now she is intent on the important business of minding the neighborhood.

"That is true, it does take all kinds," I smile. "I promise I'm not a burglar. I am working."

"Oh, a working girl, are we? And what are we working on?" She sounds like she has her doubts about what type of working girl I am. Her brows are much darker than her hair and look like two caterpillars perched above the bridge of her nose as she lowers them at me.

I bite my tongue, holding back the many replies that come to mind, instead I smile again as I drop the binoculars onto the seat. I don't think I look like a burglar or a hooker, but like she said, it takes all kinds. I reach for my wallet to show her my credentials. Her intent gaze follows my hand as I stretch across the console for my pocketbook to retrieve the wallet. She spies the gun lying on the passenger seat. The caterpillars crawl up her forehead as her eyes grow huge like a set of saucers.

"Gun!" she shrieks. "Please don't shoot me!" Princess the chihuahua starts yapping and snarling, ready to lunge at me. Elaine tucks the dog under her arm like a football as she turns in preparation to run.

"What? No, no. I'm a private investigator," I say, trying to calm her down. "See?" I cautiously hold the license out the window. Curiosity causes her to swivel her head and look at the license.

She laughs nervously as she comes out of her panic mode. "For a second I thought I was a goner," she says, clutching her chest. The dog's barking quiets as she senses Elaine's demeanor calming. She readjusts Princess to sit on her hip again.

I fake a laugh, hoping her time at my window is up and she will return to her base of operations, aka her house. She squints in the direction of Tara's house. "P.I.? I always knew that Daniels woman was up to no good. Anyone who is that reclusive must have a lot of secrets. Probably kinky, sordid ones."

I detect a sense of bitterness. Tara must have done something in the past to make Elaine feel slighted. "Tara Daniels is the person I am working for, and I think she just likes her privacy like most normal people." Elaine doesn't seem offended by the possibility I could be insinuating that she doesn't fall into the normal category. Perhaps she is just well-meaning, but she seems like the type who takes their role as a community watch member seriously due to nosiness, rather than safety.

"As a member of the community watch, you probably notice a lot of things other people don't. Have you seen anyone else out of place in the neighborhood? Maybe someone at

Tara's house?"

"No. Why? What happened? Do I need to call a meeting with the neighborhood?"

"That won't be necessary. I'm just here making sure Tara's security system is up to snuff after installing some equipment." That isn't entirely true, but I don't think Tara would appreciate Elaine spreading her business about.

She narrows her eyes slightly— an indication she knows I am keeping something from her. Princess yips at the shift in her energy. "The only people I've seen at that house are Tara and her daughter. And of course, the dead husband's new missus. Other than them, Jacob's brother and his wife."

"*Ex*-husband," I mutter.

"Right. Ex, dead husband. The brother kind of gives me the creeps," she continues. "Looks just like Jacob, but sleezy if you know what I mean. I always feel like I need to rinse my eyes out after looking at him. Oh, and of course it's just weird the dead husband's new wife spending time with the girl." She places her hand on my door like we are having a heart to heart. "That whole family is weird."

I can add judgmental to Elaine's list along with nosy. It seems unnecessary to probe her with further questions. If she had seen anything out of the ordinary, she would remember, and probably be more than happy to share with me. "Something told me you were an integral part of the community watch, and I was right. Thank you for the information and thanks for checking on me." I plaster on the best fake smile I can muster, hoping she will take the hint and excuse herself.

"No problem. If you need me to gather any information for you, just let me know. I'd be more than happy to help."

*Never in a million year*s. "I'll keep that in mind. Thanks, again," I say, raising my window.

"Really, I wouldn't mind a bit," she says, speaking above

the glass closing. Princess gives one final ferocious bark. I give her a wave and pick up my phone pretending to answer a call.

I breathe a sigh of relief as I see her in the mirror walking away. I lift the binoculars, focusing on Tara's house once more. I know the chances of seeing anything amiss are slim, but I decide to wait it out, if for nothing more than to irritate Elaine by being parked on the street for an excessive amount of time. But if I see her walking toward my vehicle again, I am out of here.

I toss the field glasses onto the console and adjust my seat to settle in more comfortably. I am in the middle of a yawn when someone pulls on my passenger side door. Although the door is locked, the suddenness startles me. I reach for my gun until I notice that it is Jack, who is now rapping on the window. I hit the unlock button. He slides into the passenger seat.

"I'm glad to see you had your doors locked," he says, in place of hello.

"Yeah, well, seems you are the only person who ever tries to enter the vehicle with me when I am parked somewhere."

"Fair point. But still, safety first."

"What are you doing here? Did you talk to Richie?" I ask.

"Yeah, I talked to him. Dead end. I'm here because it's a slow day at the office and I figured you could use some company," he says, extending a bag of strawberry Twizzlers in my direction.

"Sure," I say, skeptically, taking the candy. I tear open the bag. "So, this has nothing to do with you wanting to babysit me because of your 'bad feeling'? Don't think I haven't noticed both Eli and Brittany patrolling this street today." I take a bite off a licorice.

"Nope. I told you I was going to have someone patrolling.

And also, a lady called into the office saying a pervert that fit your description was lurking on the street," he laughs.

I bite back a few choice words, as I pick up the binoculars and point them toward Elaine's house. I see a curtain move and raise my focus to it. She is looking back at me with her own binoculars. She quickly drops them and steps back from the window.

Jack has his head tilted and eyes squinted looking out the window too. His laugh deepens.

"You are really enjoying this, aren't you?" I ask.

"So much," he says, wiping tears of laughter from his face.

"I'm surprised she did not call back saying I tried to shoot her."

He momentarily sobers. "You didn't try to shoot her, did you?"

"No. Of course not. I may have thought about it, though." His merriment returns. "Okay, you've had your fun. You can leave now."

"I am in no hurry. Like I said, slow day at the office. Besides, if you grow bored, we can make out." He waggles his eyebrows at me.

"Sheriff Lennox, I'm not sure what kind of training you've had, but that is not how I was taught to conduct surveillance," I say primly. "Maybe I should sign up for your class, though. It sounds much more interesting." I giggle.

"Oh, it is," he says. "I'd be willing to give you your first lesson now." He moves across the seat toward me.

I place a palm on his chest, halting him in his path. "As tempting as it sounds, I really am working, so, you are going to have to skedaddle." I say, making a walking motion with my fingers.

"Fine," he says, pulling me in for a kiss goodbye. His radio squawks to life, indicating his presence is needed elsewhere.

"Duty calls, anyhow." He leans back into the car before shutting the door. "Make sure you lock your doors again."

Jack doesn't always verbalize his *I love you* as such. There are times it comes out as 'It pains me to write you this speeding ticket, but I want you to be a safer driver' or 'I have a bad feeling, please, be safe', or 'lock your doors'.

"I love you, too," I reply, causing him to flash a dimpled smile before he jogs away.

After he leaves, I scroll through my phone, looking for a podcast to listen to while I am keeping an eye on Tara's house. Finding a story that sounds interesting, I let the voice of the host play across the car's Bluetooth system. The voice is meant to sound ominous but instead comes across as cheesy.

Today we bring you the tragic story of how Christmas never came one year for several young women of a small town. That's because Santa Klaus visited them early. That's right. Santa Klaus. Klaus with a K for killer, because he only chose victims with a chimney in their home to stuff their dead bodies into, after he decapitated them.

The murders sent shock waves through the otherwise safe community.

Seriously? What type of demented personality chose to dub the killer Santa Klaus, even if it is Klaus with a 'K'? How about Chimney Sweep or Smokestack? Or anything other than Santa Klaus.

The first victim, Beth Woods, a twenty-eight-year-old grocery store clerk, was on her way home from work one beautiful afternoon. When her phone pinged with the sound of an incoming text message, Beth did the responsible thing as a driver, and pulled onto a sleepy side street in her lakeside community to check the message.

A shiver skids down my spine as I look out at the sleepy side street next to the lake where I am parked. Perhaps this isn't the ideal listening material, after all. But I am intrigued now and want to know what happened to Beth.

She never had time to respond to the message, which was from her mother,
asking her if she was coming for dinner that evening.
Beth's mother never received a response because....
Santa Klaus busted Beth's driver side window from her Nissan Altima,
and drug her from the car. He then took her to her house....

Maybe I will just save this podcast for another time, I think as I reach to turn it off. A rap on the driver's side window causes a jolt of fear to course through me. I shriek as I reach for my gun, expecting Santa Klaus with a K to be there.

When I look to the window, Colt is standing there laughing. He thinks startling me is hilarious, until he notices the gun pointed in his direction. He quickly sobers. I was so enthralled by the serial killer story and focusing on Tara's house that I did not hear his diesel truck pull up or see him walking up to my vehicle.

"Gee, Elle. I know you're still mad about the other night, but do you think you can put the gun away?"

I lower the weapon that my delayed faculties still have me pointing at him, as I roll down the window. "What are you doing here, besides giving me a heart attack? Are you following me?" Jack is the person who normally follows me to my stake-outs, giving me a meltdown by startling me.

"Following you? Why would I follow you?" he asks, with a confused look on his face.

"I don't know. Maybe to apologize."

"I've already apologized to you. Besides, I'm the one who should be upset. I had to ride into town with Jack, in my underwear, soaking wet. And I've been having to walk around with this," he says, pointing up at the black eye he is sporting, courtesy of Jack.

"Serves you right," I huff.

He rolls his eyes. "Since when did you and Jack become too sensitive to take a joke?"

His question is met with a harsh look that is meant to whither him. "Whatever," he says. "No, I wasn't following you, or even looking for you, for that matter. I was coming to that house." He points at Tara Daniels's home.

"Do you know Tara?" I ask.

"Tara? Who's Tara? I was looking for Samantha."

"Who's Samantha?"

"Do you really want to know?" he asks, with a wicked grin on his face. "I met her a couple of weeks ago and—

Now it is I who rolls my eyes. "Nope," I say, holding up a hand, interrupting him. "But you've got the wrong house, pal."

He rubs his jaw and says, "Hmm. I guess it's possible I got some bad directions."

"I suppose the black eye didn't deter you from attracting the ladies?"

"Makes me look like a bad boy," he winks.

Colt doesn't need any help looking like a bad boy. He could

be dressed as if he was ready to sing with the church choir and still put off a bad boy vibe. I take a long look at him. The deep eyes with long dark lashes. It should be against the natural order of things for a man to have such luxurious eyelashes. Yet he and Jack both have eyes that make me envious as a female. Where Colt's eyes are dark like obsidian, Jack's are like the bluest ocean.

A tendril of Colt's dark hair falls just right to lay across his forehead perfectly, probably by design. Jack often runs his hands through his blonde hair when he is distracted, giving it a perfectly unkempt look. Colt's grin is often mischievous, whereas Jack's is more polite, the mischief part of Jack reserved for those who know him well.

Colt may have a bad boy persona and a proclivity to raise hell at times, but Jack is much more formidable when riled, as evidenced by the beating he gave Colt, which is no small feat. Jack's restlessness and anger brews just below the surface, tucked away from others. When he is provoked, there is only one word to describe him. That word is dangerous.

The difference in the two men is like night and day. The one thing they have in common is the effect they have on the female population. Colt owns the fact that the ladies swoon over him, whereas Jack tries to pretend he is oblivious to how women react to him.

When Colt and I broke off our romantic relationship, I had to flip off the switch in my brain that acknowledges how attractive he is. Even before I became involved with Jack, I cut ties with those thoughts. Otherwise, it would have just been a matter of time before we fell back into the same habits, and he fell back into my bed. I may refuse to allow myself to think of him in that way, but I still have eyes and understand that his eyes could be swollen shut and he would still have luck with the females. He may be a bad boy, but he has a heart of gold, which is why I keep him in my life.

"What are you doing here?" I ask.

"I already told you, looking for Samantha."

"No, I mean why aren't you out of town working?"

"Deer season." Apparently today he is looking for a *dear* instead of a deer.

"Well, I guess if there's no Samantha, I'm out of here. You really should tell me you accept my apology, though. You know you and I go together like peas and carrots. I can't stand the thought of you being put out with me," he says.

"Fine. I accept, under the condition that you learn how to read a room," I say, holding up a finger. "Despite what you may think, you aren't hilarious all the time." I get a fist bump and a mischievous grin from him in return as acceptance to my term. "Good luck finding Samantha," I add.

"Thanks. She had the most amazing..." I hit the lever to raise my window as he brings his palms up to cup his chest.

I look up the street to Elaine's house and see her curtain flutter again. I grimace and start the engine as I watch Colt's retreating back in the side view mirror. I may as well give up on the task of surveilling Tara's house. If her intruder were to have shown up this morning, they would have gotten scared off by all the visitors I've had.

Out of all the homes in Justice, it's an odd coincidence that Colt ended up at the same house as me. Sometimes coincidences are just that— coincidences. Tara is not Samantha, and she doesn't seem the type to go for a bad boy like Colt.

nine

WHEN I LEFT Tara's neighborhood, I decided to pay a visit to Croaking Creek Assisted Living to see what I could find out about the orderly, Devin Harlow. Tara did not seem to think he is her intruder, but I would like to find out what I can about him. I could ask the office manager at the complex about his schedule to see if any of his off-time correlates with Tara's intruder. But chances are, the manager will not disclose information and I do not want Devin to know Tara hired me. If there is a chance he is stalking her, it would tip him off. And if he isn't her stalker then it could make an awkward work situation between him and Tara. Gertie Rose lives at the complex and I decide to ask her about Devin. I know she will spill the tea about him.

I pull into the empty parking spot in front of Gertie's apartment. I can see her peeping out the living room window. I wave and she immediately rushes to open the door.

I take in her Hawaiian shirt covered in pineapples and the bright yellow lei around her neck. "Oh, Elle. I wasn't expecting you today. What a nice surprise."

"Sorry that I didn't call ahead. Did I catch you at a bad time?"

"Oh no, not at all," she waves a hand. "I was just getting ready for our luau, but it isn't until later." She ushers me through the door, and I have a seat on the sofa. "You didn't bring Buddy with you?"

"No. Not this time. I'm working today."

"Anything interesting?"

"Not really. I just wanted to visit with you and ask you about a couple of people who work here while I am visiting."

"Gotcha," she winks, indicating she knows the people I am going to ask about are probably the subjects of an investigation. Sometimes her faulty memory can be a blessing and I hope she forgets that detail before she sees Devin again.

"I have a new friend who volunteers here. Her name is Tara Daniels. Do you know her?"

"Oh yes. Tarrie. She doesn't like it when I call her Tarrie, though. She's a real hard ass about rules, but other than that a sweet girl. A little quiet. She's like a clam and stays in her shell most of the time. But I like her. I even make her laugh sometimes."

"I'm sure you do," I giggle. "What about an orderly named Devin? Do you know him?"

"Hubba bubba, do I ever. Hunk of a man. Why? Are you thinking about dating him?"

"Um, no. You know I am in a relationship with Jack."

"I don't see a ring on that skinny finger of yours," she says, holding up her gnarled, bony ring finger for reference.

"We haven't been involved long enough for that."

"Hogwash. My Joe and I only dated for three weeks before he proposed. We were married for fifty-two years before he passed. He liked it, so he put a ring on it."

"You were blessed with a wonderful marriage," I say,

refusing to think about what the 'it' was that Joe liked well enough to put a ring on it.

She nods her head and looks mournful for a moment. "So, what do you want to know about Devin?"

I let out a breath. "Oh, you know, Tara mentioned him, and I have never met him. So, I was just wondering about him is all."

"What do you want to know?"

"I'm just curious as to who he is." She whirls her eyes, indicating she isn't buying it and I should just get to the point, so I do. "Well... is he creepy? Does he seem like he is a pervert?"

She smiles impishly. "Hah. So, you do want to date him."

"Again, no."

"Oh, okay," she says, winking conspiratorially. I suppress the urge to wallow my eyes around in my head. "No, he doesn't seem to be a pervert. But he is good looking enough he could get away with being one. And my goodness, he is such a flirt." She blushes slightly, patting her gray hair.

"Does he flirt with Tara?"

"Yes. He flirts with all the ladies, old and young. I think I can see where you are going with this," she says. If she insists that I want to date him again, I may scream. "Does he have a lady who thinks he is cheating?"

"Not exactly." I continue before she can insist my curiosity is because I am romantically interested. "Tara said he usually works when she is here, but there are times he calls off when they are on the schedule at the same time."

"He does miss a lot of days. But it's because he usually takes his mom for kidney dialysis on the days his sister can't. He's a great son. I can see why you would want to date him."

I press the heel of my hand to my left eye, trying to ease the stabbing pain that threatens to turn into a headache caused by this conversation.

"Do you want to give me a lift to the rec center? You can stick around for a few minutes and see him in action for yourself."

"Sure. That sounds great."

"Okay. Just let me grab my stuff and I will be ready." She walks over to the small kitchen bar and picks up a grass skirt. She shimmies it up and over her bright pink, polyester pants. She then grabs a plastic cup that looks like a coconut. "All set. How do I look?"

"You look great Gertie. Luau ready for sure."

"Thanks, Elle. Now remember when we get there, if you decide he looks perverted enough for your liking, just say the word, and I'll put in a good word for you."

"That's not what..." I trail off, pressing my fingers to my temple to ease the tension as I realize there is no point in correcting her. "Sure, thanks," I say.

She giggles. "I hope we get to do the limbo."

Oh boy, I think. I hope they have a stretcher on hand in case someone throws their back out or breaks a hip.

ten

AFTER OBSERVING Devin yesterday and interacting with him, I feel that Tara is right to think he isn't her intruder. Most definitely flirtatious, but not in a creepy sort of way. So, I decided to move down the list of people Tara knows. I called Sally this morning and she agreed to accompany me to Celeste Daniels's art gallery.

When we arrive at the old Victorian house turned art gallery, we are the only people in the exhibition room. She and I have been staring intently at a painting for around five minutes. The dark, hollow eyes of the blurry man's framed face seem to be staring back at us. A shiver works its way up my spine and I move along the wall to the next canvas.

"Gee. Someone seems to be channeling their inner demons through their art," Sally says, as we glide three steps to the right and peer at the next painting. This one is of a child, dead flowers sprouting out of her head and weeds protruding from her ears.

Every painting in the gallery shares the same disturbing quality, along with a hefty price— meaning that people pay big money for what I consider disrupted art. Even the still life works look somewhat sinister. The normally aesthetically pleasing bowls of fruit are instead fruit that is pitted and rotting.

"I think it's eyes are following us," Sally says, as she glances back at the first painting.

"Hello ladies." We both jump and gasp at the jolt of an unexpected voice. I look back at the art to make sure the sound wasn't coming from it, then I turn a quick circle to see where the voice materialized from. Celeste stands before us, having emerged from somewhere near the back of the room. "What brings you into the gallery today?" she asks.

I resist the urge to grab my chest, so as not to betray that my heart feels as if it is knocking on Heaven's door. Sally has her hand pressed to her bosom, unconcerned with betraying that she was almost scared into a heart attack.

"I did not mean to startle you," Celeste smiles, seemingly amused. "My work has that effect on people sometimes," she points to Sally's hand placed across her chest.

"It was just so quiet in here and we were so engrossed in the paintings that we forgot anyone else could be here," I say, taking in her appearance. A short sleek black dress, with a long, flowing, black kimono that almost trails the ground behind her. Crimson high heels that match the shade of her lipstick perfectly. Her dark hair is a mass of flawlessly coiled curls. Her caramel skin is flawless. Her hazel eyes are vibrant. Celeste Daniels is a stunning woman.

"An acquaintance of mine said I should check out your work," I smile. "Tara Daniels," I say.

"How odd. I've never known of Tara to recommend anything about me," Celeste says as she fixes her gaze on me intently. "Nevertheless, did you find anything that interests you?" she asks, curiously.

Sally has been unusually quiet. I glance at her, hoping she

will chime into the conversation. Hand still over her heart, she seems to be lost in a trance, mesmerized by Celeste.

"Well, um," I stutter, "Your work is extraordinary. I suppose I would be interested to know what influences your art?"

Celeste's smile grows amused. "Life. I would say that is the biggest influencer of all, wouldn't you....? I'm sorry what was your name?

"Elle. This is Sally," I say, indicating the still dumb struck lady standing beside me.

"Well, Elle, would you ever consider letting me paint you? That exquisite bone structure of yours, those beautiful green eyes, ah, the perfect muse!" She looks at me with an intensity that feels like it is searing into my soul.

"Oh, I don't know. Although flattered, I am too impatient to sit still that long."

"Nonsense. I could take photos and paint your likeness from them."

"Again, very flattered, but I don't think—".

"—What Elle means is she would love that," says Sally, suddenly finding her voice. I give her a sharp look that says, seriously, you finally speak, and this is what you say. She shrugs, nudging me forward. "It's not every day that someone tells you you're beautiful enough to be a model."

"Excellent!" Celeste says. "Follow me, Elle. Sally, make yourself at home. This shouldn't take long."

* * *

I emerge from the back room that serves as Celeste's studio to find Sally lounging on a red velvet bench, phone in hand, taking a selfie in front of a painting of a woman wearing a snake as a hat.

Seeing me, Sally springs to her feet, following me out the door.

"How was it," she asks as we get into the car. "Did you have to get naked? Did her studio smell like Sulphur?"

"I am starting to rethink this whole sponsor you and help you prepare for your P.I. exam thing," I say.

"You wanted to figure out if Celeste is the one messing with Tara. What better way to do that than by getting to know her. So, what did you find out?"

"I'm not ruling her out. She certainly has the personality for it. However, according to her, Tara is supposed to be having an affair with her ex-brother-in-law, Mark."

"Do you think she is?"

After some consideration, I say, "No. I don't think so. But the important thing is maybe Mark's wife Janie thinks they are having an affair."

"So, she could be dicking around with Tara as revenge because she knows Mark is literally dicking around with Tara?" Sally asks.

"Possibly. There is also the chance that someone could be trying to make Tara think she is losing her mind— rendering her unfit as a mother. Which would make it possible to gain custody of Emily, which would lead to gaining control of an insane amount of money. That basically comes down to three people— Celeste, Mark or Janie. Celeste is already rich. Mark and Janie have money but not the substantial amount that comes with Emily's trust. Then there is the chance that it could be a creep or that Tara may actually be imagining it."

"I'm so confused," Sally says. "How do you keep all these people straight?"

"I suppose the same way you remember everyone's usual at the bar." I shrug.

"Hmm. Maybe I should assign drink names to these people to help me remember them. Or better yet, maybe I should invent a drink at the bar and call it the 'Celeste'. Wait, no, I've got it!" She claps her hands together. "I'll invent a drink called 'The Muse'. It will be green like your eyes, and I'll serve it in an exquisite glass," she says, laughing. Tears spill down her cheeks from mirth.

I shoot her the side eye, unamused. "I'm so happy you are enjoying this. Lucky for you, you saved my life that one time. Since you are already having fun at my expense, maybe you can help me decide how to explain to Jack that Devin Harlow may or may not think I am romantically interested in him. Also, he may or may not think I am into kinky stuff."

She sobers and wipes the wet streams from her cheeks, as I pull my vehicle onto the street. "Why would Devin Harlow think either of those things?"

"Two words: Gertie Rose."

"Enough said," she says. "Are you though? Into kinky stuff? You just don't seem like the type. I have been wrong about people before, though."

"No!" I reach over and lightly pinch her arm as her laughter starts to bubble up again.

* * *

After dropping Sally off, I make the drive to Tara Daniels's house. As I pull into the driveway, her garage door is open. She and her daughter are unloading groceries from the back of Tara's minivan.

"Hey, Elle," she says, when she sees me. "Emily, this is my new friend, Elle," she tells her daughter.

"Hello, Elle," Emily says, with a slight lisp from her missing front teeth.

"Hello, Emily. It's very nice to meet you. Your mother has told me so much about you."

"Did you come for dinner? Mommy is making spaghetti!" The child is obviously a fan of her mother's spaghetti.

"No. I just stopped by to talk to your mommy for a minute," I say as I grab the remaining grocery bags.

"Well, if not dinner, then at least a cup of coffee?" Tara asks, pressing a lever with her foot to close the back gate of the van.

"Coffee sounds great," I smile.

I keep Emily occupied while Tara puts away her groceries by presenting her with one of my '*Buddy the Dog*' books and reading it to her twice. Tara brews two cups of coffee and then says, "Emily, why don't you go pick out the perfect spot on your bookshelf for your new book while Elle and I talk."

"Okay," Emily says, as she skips off through the house toward her room.

"She really is a lovely child," I say.

"Thank you. I think so but I suppose I could be biased," she laughs lightly. "How about we have our coffee on the back deck?"

I follow her through the open concept kitchen into a great room with a stone fireplace that runs the length of one wall. I stop to glance at the various photos gracing the mantle.

"That's Jacob," Tara says, indicating a picture of a man with a younger Emily.

The man with dark hair and eyes is caught in a candid photo lying on the grass with the little girl. They both have their elbows out; their hands tucked behind their head and look like they have just shared the world's funniest joke. He is handsome and full of life. My heart aches for his loved ones at the loss of this man that I never knew. "Very handsome. He had kind eyes," I say. She nods her agreement. "You said he died in an accident? If you don't mind my asking?"

"I don't mind at all. He had bought a big spread of property out in the middle of nowhere. He had a cabin built and then he and Mark decided they were going to be preppers," she smiles at the memory. "Celeste hated it. Drove her nuts. So, naturally, I encouraged him," she giggles.

"Next, came an off-the-grid bunker. He and Mark started spending a lot of time there. They were supposed to be getting everything situated but I suspect they were just using it as a man cave."

"He was driving home from the property one evening and a deer ran out in front of him on the mountain road. He swerved and the car flipped, went over an embankment and caught fire. It was a while before anyone realized the wreck had happened. The coroner said that he most likely died on impact. Whether he said that thinking it would be a comfort or not, who knows. Just like that, gone forever. We didn't even get to see him one last time. His funeral was closed casket, of course."

"I'm so sorry. That's terrible," I say, as she wipes at her moist eyes.

"This is Mark, Janie and their son Maverick." She picks up a photo further down the mantle, trying to put distance between herself and the sadness of Jacob's death. "Mav is a year younger than Emily. They have always been thick as thieves."

Mark and Jacob were not only brothers, but twins. Alike, yet different. They have the same dark hair, eyes, facial features and builds; yet the genetic factors that make them individuals left Jacob strikingly handsome and Mark average.

If Mark is average, the only word I can think of to describe Janie, is plain. Quite literally, a plain Jane, with mouse brown hair, and nondescript features. The type of face that nobody would probably remember seeing in a crowd, unless she was smiling. The smile, to me, would be unforgettable. It's one of the kindest smiles I have ever seen and would leave an impression on me if I saw her in a sea of other faces. According to Tara, Janie has the kind personality to go along with the smile showcased in the photograph.

I glance further down the mantle, taking in a photo of Tara with what must be her parents. If she had not told me she was adopted, I would have sworn she looks just like her adoptive dad. The man's gray hair is the white gray that often comes to a blonde person. The eyes have the doe-like resemblance that I first noticed about Tara's. I can imagine a younger version of him and the resemblance to Tara would seem uncanny.

I wonder if there is more to the story of her adoption than what her mother told her. Surely, Tara knows that she bears a striking resemblance to her father. Perhaps there is more to the story and Tara knows but chose not to divulge the information. She did not mention seeking out her birth mother and it wasn't any of my business to inquire. I keep my thoughts to myself as we step through the wall of windows that serves as a door to the outside deck. Beyond is the lake with landscape of fall colors mirrored on the water. The sight is breathtakingly beautiful. I love the view from my little farmhouse that is nestled in a valley amid mountains, with a small stream running on the property, but if I had this view, I don't know if I would ever leave home.

"What did you want to talk about? Did you discover anything?" She twirls the diamond stud in her ear; a nervous tick that I have noticed she has. She settles in to one of the Adirondack chairs and takes a sip of her coffee.

"Unfortunately, no. I visited Celeste's gallery today," I say, after taking a sip of the bold coffee. I told her I was a friend of yours and you had mentioned her gallery."

A wry smile forms at the corners of her mouth. "I'm sure that went over well."

"Surprisingly, she seemed to take a liking to me. She insisted on painting my likeness."

"Well, that's something. At least she did not hold it against you for introducing yourself as a friend of mine," she giggles.

I chuckle in return.

"So, tell me Elle, what did you think of her gallery?"

"It was," I pause to search for the right word. "Different," is the only word I can think of.

Now Tara laughs mirthfully. "Different. Sure. That's a nice way of putting it. Creepy is how I would describe it."

I laugh in return, agreeing with her, before changing the subject. "I have watched the house while you were away for the last two days. I haven't noticed anyone snooping or anything amiss. I hope this does not sound insensitive, but I really feel as if I am just robbing you of money. With the cameras in place and your security system, perhaps it would be best if you just called if you need me. The Sheriff has someone patrolling your street now, so maybe whoever has moved on. I know that is of little comfort, but like I said, I hate to bill you for unnecessary hours.

"Of course, you're right. The money isn't important but I'm sure you have other cases you need to be working. Nothing has shown up on the camera footage either. I do feel more secure with those in place. How about I keep you on retainer and anything we can think of you can check into?

"That sounds perfect," I smile, glad that she wasn't offended that I essentially just told her I was wasting my time surveilling her home. "You still cannot think of anyone you may have forgotten you shared your security code with?"

"No. There have been workers here at the house in the past who have had the code, but I have always changed it as soon as their job was finished." She chews her lip, contemplating. "You agree with me that Devin seems harmless?" I nod my head in agreement.

After a moment of pondering, she continues, "Celeste is the only one I know personally that seems to have a problem with me, and I can't fathom that it would be her."

"I'm sorry to bring this up, but Celeste seems to think you are having an affair with Mark. I did not want to mention it because I didn't want to cause any type of drama between you and Celeste. I am not prying. It is your business if you are, but could it be possible Janie may think so too?"

Her face pales. She appears as if she may be physically ill. "There has never been anything between Mark and I other than being in-laws. He has always made me uncomfortable, even before Jacob's death. He seems to have grown more pointed and bolder in his behavior toward me since Jacob passed. Janie knows deep down that I detest Mark and she would never assume otherwise. I do not know why Celeste would say such a thing. It's an ugly and malicious accusation."

"Again, I'm sorry to have brought it up. You understand why I did?"

"Yes, of course. I am glad you did." She lets a calming exhale slip past her lips. "I can assure you Janie is not the person responsible for the break-ins. Despite Celeste being devious, I do not think it is her either. I have been paying more attention to my surroundings and haven't noticed anything out of the ordinary. I'm sorry, Elle. I know this is as perplexing to you as it is to me."

"It's fine, Tara," I say, with a smile that I hope appears comforting. "Although, I am glad that it hasn't happened again. Hopefully we can get to the bottom of it, for your peace of mind."

And for my peace of mind also, I think after leaving her. I feel a sense of unease about the situation.

eleven

THE FOG BILLOWS out in front of me like a veil of smoke as my feet pound the ground during my early morning run. The mystery of Tara's intruder seems impenetrable like the thick mist floating before me. I wind my way up the gravel road toward home.

I awoke this morning with Tara's case nagging at my mind. Anyone else would probably be happy to collect a small paycheck for a situation that seems to have resolved itself. I'm not happy about it, though. Something teases at the edge of my brain, causing my thoughts to fray. I have never worked a case before that has been unsolvable. Complicated cases, yes. I've had plenty of time-consuming investigations but never one that has simply ceased to exist.

I do not think someone being inside Tara's home was a figment of her imagination. I also do not believe the person decided they did not want to invade her privacy anymore. Either he or she was looking for something and found it. Or they know about the security cameras and the fact Tara hired me. Which leads me to think once again it could be someone involved with her life. Could it be Celeste?

Despite Tara's refusal to think Celeste capable of such a thing, I would not rule her out. Celeste seems like a pleasant enough person if you can get past the part of her persona which creates such visually disturbing art. The darkness I saw portrayed on those canvases wasn't just channeling creativity. That darkness was born from somewhere.

Celeste is financially secure. She was well-off in her own right before collecting any life insurance from Jacob's death. Money would not seem to be a motivating factor for her. Maybe she wants custody of Emily and is attempting to gaslight Tara to make her appear unstable. Or perhaps she simply wants to mess with Tara's mind because she gets some sick thrill from it. Tara said herself that Celeste is no fan of hers.

Or could Tara be wrong about Janie Daniels? Perhaps she does believe Tara was having an affair with Mark and is culpable. Catching Janie in the act would be the only way to convince Tara of Janie's guilt. The possibility of that happening is zero considering that she knows Tara hired me. If Janie is responsible, she is smart enough to play it safe now.

And then there is Mark, whom Tara loathes. Could it run deeper than just overt stares and off-handed remarks toward Tara? Perhaps he is obsessed with her. Tara doesn't seem to think so. Investigating her former in-laws is not something Tara is supportive or comfortable with me doing.

Either way the case is stalled unless the perpetrator makes another move. I hope he or she does. Not to have the satisfaction of solving a case but because if I were Tara, I would feel insecure knowing someone was inside my home uninvited. Not discovering who or why would leave me feeling uneasy forever. My being able to solve the mystery would be a bonus.

A bonus I would look forward to reaping much more than the case I will be working today. Trailing Leonard Shipley to prove he is committing worker's comp insurance fraud isn't exactly a mystery. He has been doing so for years. Fortunately for me, it shouldn't take long to collect physical evidence proving Leonard's injury is a sham.

Leonard has spent his adult life making a living by suing people. If his coffee scorches his tongue— lawsuit. If he is involved in a fender bender— lawsuit. If someone looks at him the wrong way, he sues them for discrimination. Not all his suits pan out, but enough have that he hasn't been forced to work much. A couple thousand dollars here or ten thousand there. Then the money runs out and he must resort to getting a job until he can come into another windfall.

When a stack of boxes fell on him in the warehouse of his latest job, he started complaining with his back. The cartons were empty, but Leonard claimed that he was injured while trying to move from the path of the tumbling boxes. His boss said that he had planned on firing Leonard that day but then the accident happened. Little did Leonard know if he had bided his time until the end of his shift, he probably could have screamed discrimination for some made up slight. Then he would not have to go through with the ruse of a probable fake injury.

Unlucky for me, Leonard has eleven siblings and a whole slew of family. Which means that a large portion of Justice will be angry if they discover I caught him committing fraud. I don't necessarily care what people think of me but some of his relatives work at the restaurants and shops I frequent. Like Thomas, I do not want spit in my food.

I was hoping Art would get caught up with his own cases and volunteer to take this one. He knows how much I dislike insurance jobs. Teeny isn't exactly inconspicuous when it comes to sneakily taking photos. People tend to notice him when he is spending time in a parked car, so he is not the ideal person for these cases. Which means they get passed to me when Art is busy.

I may as well set my mind to getting it over with. I round a bend in the road and see my house in the distance. "Come on Buddy, race you to the porch," I say. Buddy has been patiently waiting for me to announce our usual relay game. He takes off at full speed and then stops at the bottom of the porch steps. He is happy to remind me that he still has plenty of time to bound to victory before I near.

When I am five paces away from the bottom step, he rushes up the planks. His feet slide out from under him, and he plops down on his belly with his tongue lolling from exertion.

I stride up the steps and walk past the broken screen door. I sink down onto a rocking chair next to the one Jack is occupying while having his morning coffee. He spent the night here last night. Things have gone back to normal after our talk and make-up session.

"Uh oh, I know that look," he says. "The only time you run this early is when you have something on your mind." He passes me a bottle of water and points to a steaming cup of coffee that he has waiting on the side table for me. "Are you upset about the screen door? I am going to try to fix it this evening."

"No, not the screen door," I say, before guzzling a drink of water. "Leonard Shipley," I exhale with a tired breath.

The upward tilt at the corner of Jack's lip and his scrunched-up nose tells me that no explanation is necessary. "Well, I think it's a terrific thing someone decided to nail Leonard for the scoundrel he is. I know you're worried about his family getting angry at you, but they all know he is a scoundrel too," he smiles.

"Hmm," I say, distractedly.

"Is it really Leonard that has you in a mood this morning or is it the Daniels' case?"

"Both, I suppose."

"Well, I for one, am glad the case seems to have resolved itself." He shrugs.

"You aren't a woman who had a stranger in her house. You haven't had an unknown person going through your personal belongings," I say, pointedly.

"True. I am all about thwarting crime, though. Maybe you amping up Tara's security accomplished that. That may not be solving a mystery but an ounce of prevention..."

I roll my eyes at him, and he chuckles. He stands then stoops down giving me a kiss. Next, he pats Buddy on the head. "I'm off. I'll try to get in early this evening. Maybe we can take advantage of the remaining pleasant weather and throw a couple of steaks on the grill." Buddy's ears perk up— steak being one of the words he understands. "Make those three steaks instead of a couple," Jack laughs.

"Sounds nice," I say, standing and wrapping my arms around his neck. I give him one last kiss before he walks off. Buddy follows him to the truck with his tail wagging. I blow him a kiss as he backs his pickup out of the driveway. I have already forgotten about Leonard as I look forward to a simple evening with Jack.

* * *

Leonard Shipley is a crook. Although not exactly dumb, he has never worried about being caught while committing fraud. Nobody in the past has ever bothered to try to catch him, until now. Everyone has usually flung money at him so that they wouldn't have to deal with him. His latest employer probably doesn't care either, but the employer's insurance company does. I'm counting on him being lax with his daily activities, making my job quick and easy.

After stopping by the office to swap out my Bronco for the black Toyota Camry, I park across the street from the diner where Leonard spends his mornings. Everyone that knows me knows what my Bronco looks like. I would prefer to be inconspicuous at this task.

He is a social butterfly. When he leaves the diner, he will make his rounds. I just need to follow him and wait for the perfect photo op of him doing something his bad back is supposed to make impossible.

After he leaves the diner, he makes his way to the barber shop, where he spends what seems like an eternity sitting on a bench outside gossiping with the other men. Finally, he gets in his truck and leaves. I follow him to the Post Office then to the Dollar Store, where I park a few rows behind his truck. He enters the store. I remove the lens cap from my camera and make sure it is ready to snap pictures.

A commuter van with the name Croaking Creek A.L.C. pulls in a couple of spots over from me. I spy Gertie Rose through one of the windows. The assisted living community where she resides often takes the residents on outings and shopping. I raise my hand to wave toward Gertie and quickly lower it when I remember why I am here. I slouch down in my seat, hoping she did not notice me. At a time when I need to be inconspicuous, Gertie is the last person I need around. I peek out of the corner of my eye, noting that she seems unaware of my presence. I exhale a small sigh of relief.

Leonard emerges through the automatic doors of the store with a fifty-pound bag of dogfood slung over his shoulder. He effortlessly strides toward his truck. I raise my Nikon and start clicking the button to capture photos. I take a continuous stream of pictures showing him carrying the fifty-pound sack and easily tossing it into the bed of his truck.

"Yoo whoo, Elle. I thought that was you," Gertie says, almost plastering her face to the car window. I tap the lever to lower the window, while keeping one eye on Leonard.

"Hello, Gertie. How are you?" I ask distractedly.

"I'm good. How are you? Are you working?" she asks when she notices the camera. She follows my line of sight. She squints and says much too loudly, "Oh! Are you taking pictures of Lawsuit Leonard Shipley?"

I place my finger over my lips indicating she should be quiet. She repeats the question in an exaggerated whisper that isn't much lower than her normal voice. Leonard has his truck door open ready to get onto the driver's seat. He hears Gertie as his head snaps up and swivels in our direction.

Well, *shit*, I think as he walks toward us, scowling.

"Uh oh," Gertie says, in her loud whisper.

Uh oh is right. Leonard stalks across the parking lot and tosses a cigarette to the ground. His face looks furious and as red as the glowing tip of the embers scattering from the butt. He approaches the driver's side door. His scowl deepens. "What are you doing?" he demands suspiciously. "Are you taking pictures of me?" he asks, incredulous when he spots the camera.

I do not have time to reply before he is reaching through the open window, trying to grab the camera. I slap his hand and toss the Nikon onto the passenger seat. For a split second it looks like he is going to reach for my throat. Maybe I can put some of my self-defense skills to use, I think, until I see Gertie's bony fist lash out and bop him on the ear.

He jumps back, exclaiming, "Ouch!" Gertie whacks him with her handbag. "Stop that!" he yelps as she gets several more hits in. I attempt to open my door in case Gertie needs help, but the pair are blocking me in. I don't think he would hurt Gertie, but then again, he did just seem as if he was going for my neck. I grab my taser and hang out my window in case I need to zap him. But Leonard looks like he may be the person who needs rescued. Gertie is surprisingly strong and agile for her age and size. He tries in vain to anticipate where her purse will land next, so he can block it. "Tell her to stop that!" he shrieks toward me. I shrug in return.

"You like picking on little girls?" Gertie sneers at him in a disgusted tone then she kicks him on the shin. "Why don't you try taking me on?" She tosses her purse to the ground and raises her fists. She begins moving from side to side, resembling a boxing kangaroo. "Bring it on, big boy!"

"You're crazy! You're both crazy," he says. He looks manic as he darts for his truck and almost trips over his own feet.

"That's right, run away," Gertie yells. "And don't you even think about suing me or there's more where that came from!"

I should be upset about Leonard discovering me taking photos of him for the insurance company. Instead, I start laughing causing tears to glide down my cheeks. So much for being inconspicuous. It was worth being caught because it led to witnessing Gertie's boxing skills on display.

"Wow, Gertie. Thanks for the backup." I wipe at my eyes to dry the moisture, and I notice a small twitch in my left eye.

"You're welcome. Anything for my Elle," she says, patting my shoulder. "Did you decide if you want me to put in a good word with Devin for you?"

"Thanks for the offer, Gertie, but I don't think so," I say, as my eye spasms again. I hope Gertie did not notice the downward tick of my eyelid. She has a habit of being indelicate when it comes to commenting on physical flaws.

"If you change your mind, just let me know. And if you call ahead before coming to visit again, I will make sure Jared and

Stevie bring some brownies for us to eat," she says, winking at me. I bat a wink toward her in return and my left eye twitches once again. Her grandson Jared and his girlfriend Stevie are known to add an *extra* ingredient to their brownies—pot. I have only eaten them one time. Gertie eats them regularly. I cannot help but ponder if that is one reason why she is so lively for her age.

twelve

WHEN I ENTER THE OFFICE, Art is hard at work behind his desk. There's no sign of Teeny today.

"Afternoon," he says, as I walk into the room.

"Good afternoon."

Never one for leading with small talk, Art says, "Great news. You don't have to worry about the insurance case with Leonard Shipley. Fella from the company called. Apparently, Leonard is one hundred percent better and ready to rejoin the work force. Rather than try to prove fraud and make him pay the money back, they are willing to let it go... so long as he isn't trying to milk them for more."

"Hmph. Too little, too late. I spent my whole morning dealing with Leonard." My left eye spasms. What started as a small twitch has become more persistent. I think it may somehow be Leonard's fault. Or Gertie's. It's probably a toss-up between the two since it started while I was in both of their presence. "I even got pictures, which is the reason for his miraculous recovery. Gertie beat the snuff out of him in the Dollar Store parking lot with her handbag. She thought he was getting aggressive toward me about taking the pictures."

"I know I should be surprised, but nothing about Gertie surprises me." He shakes his head in amusement. "Did you get pictures of that? Maybe a video?"

"Sadly, no," I say, wishing in retrospect that I had.

I move the mouse bringing my sleeping computer to life. I begin googling mini cows. I have been thinking of getting some animals for the farm. Miniature cows may not seem like practical farm animals, but they are adorable.

"What are you working on?" I ask after a few moments, looking toward Art.

"Oh, nothing important," he says, removing his reading glasses and rubbing his eyes. He then locks his hands behind his head and asks, "How did it go with the lady from Little Justice? The one with the intruder breaking into her house?" This is a tactic on his part to change the subject.

Art is normally forthcoming with information about investigations. I suspect he is working with Jack, investigating the Chromia case, and neither one of them want me to know. They are worried that I will attempt to get involved. Their secrecy is fine with me. I have no desire to get tangled with trying to catch Clayton's killer. Jack suspects Cammie hired the hitman to prevent any possibility of Clayton testifying against her. Proving her guilt *is* tempting, but it is not worth the risk. That they think I am too dim-witted to figure out what is going on, is somewhat insulting. But for the time being, I will give them the satisfaction of thinking they are keeping me in the dark.

"Fine. Fruitless. I installed cameras inside her home. There really isn't much more I can do with absolutely no clues to go on."

"Maybe it was just her imagination."

"Hmm. Maybe," I say, as my eye jumps again. Although, I really do not think she is imagining the incidences. I hope that I can figure out for certain what happened.

"Something wrong with your eye?"

"It's just a twitch." I wave my hand to dissuade him from worrying about it. "Where is Teeny? I messaged Sally last night to ask if she wanted to tag along with me today. I never got a reply. Is everything okay?"

"Well, apparently Sally has a kidney stone. She is having a terrible time with it. Teeny had her at the E.R. during the night for several hours before they concluded what's wrong with her. The Doc thinks she may pass it on her own, without surgery."

"Poor Sally. Hopefully she is well soon. We should put together a care package for her and sent it by Teeny."

"Good idea," Art says. "I guess you'll be riding solo until she recovers. How did it go the other day when she went with ya'?"

"Fine. It's Sally," I say. The *do I need to say more* is implied.

"She keeps things as interesting as you do," he chuckles.

When considering Sally's penchant for keeping things interesting, I would lump her with Gertie instead of myself.

Art begins gathering files. He stands and stretches before picking up the documents. As he heads for the door he asks, "Can you hold the fort down? I need to go meet someone."

"Of course," I say. After he leaves, I go back to googling mini cows, which leads me to watching videos of the fluffy miniatures. I spend some time falling in love with the animals while forgetting everything else.

thirteen

"I HONESTLY DON'T KNOW how you keep from vomiting in class after eating those," Mama says, referring to my funnel cake. We have this same conversation every Saturday when I purchase one of the tasty treats at the Farmers' Market. She is impatiently waiting for the day when I do vomit so she can say, 'I told you so'.

"I don't know why you are so concerned about it. Thomas is always my sparring partner so chances are if I do get sick, I will throw up on him."

"He probably is the most deserving person I can think of for such a thing to happen to," she giggles. Then she gasps and grabs the steering wheel as I use my knees to steer, so I can pull apart a bite of the sugary goodness.

"*Relax* Mama. We are going like five miles-per-hour," I say, as my eye spasms.

"It is no wonder you get tickets all of the time," she mumbles. My eye starts twitching again. "What is wrong with your eye? Do you need me to drive?" she asks sounding hopeful.

"No. I don't need you to drive. Have I ever wrecked you

yet?" My eye shimmies once again and I almost run off the side of the road, causing her to release another hysterical gasp. "And I don't know what is wrong with my eye. It's just a twitch."

"I think stress can cause that. Probably from your fight with Jack."

"Jack and I reconciled a week ago, so I'm sure it isn't stress about that." I leave the rest of my thought unspoken— that it is her stressing me out today. "Maybe it's allergies." An allergy to her overreaction to everything this morning.

"Yeah, maybe ragweed. You should get it checked out if it doesn't go away soon."

I tip my head up and down, expressing my agreement. I do not bother disclosing the fact that the twitch started three days ago, first sporadically and now continually.

"See? We arrived all safe and sound," I say, as I pull into a parking spot and shove the gear shift into park.

"Miracles do happen," she says, dramatically.

"What's up with your eye?" Thomas asks. "It's creeping me out."

"Don't try to distract me," I say, circling him on the mat. Finally, I have the perfect opportunity to make my move and I kick out. My left eye jerks. The vision in my right eye blurs due to compensating for the left. The blurred vision causes me to stumble as I force my foot outward. The blow does not land where I intended. Thomas fails to block the hit. My foot, backed by my full weight, plows into his groin area. He doubles over, grunting in pain.

"Damn it, Elle! You know that's a *NO* strike zone!" he exclaims through labored breaths.

"Are you okay? I'm so sorry! I didn't do it on purpose. It's this darned eye throwing me off." He looks at me skeptically as he narrows his eyes, unable to rise from his bent position. "Okay, I'll tell you what, I forfeit. How does that sound? And you can choose anywhere you want for lunch today. I'm buying."

He tries to stand up straight and dry heaves as if he is going to vomit. The whole class is watching in horror. Mama raises a brow at me. I mouth to her quietly, "Still not *me* vomiting." An appreciative smirk appears on her face.

I try to assist Thomas, but he smacks my hand away. "*Uh,*" he heaves, causing me to gag, "*Uh,* you are definitely buying lunch, *uh, uh*"— more dry heaving. "Today and next week, *uh,*" he squeaks out. I choke back my gagging reflex, which is a result of the lurching sound he is making.

"Of course. Anywhere you choose," I say, while rubbing a calming circle on his back. I resist the overwhelming urge to wretch. I do not want to give my mother the satisfaction of saying 'I told you so'.

Scotto appears with an ice pack and a sympathetic look. "Here buddy, let's get you outside for some fresh air," he says. He helps Thomas to his feet and walks him toward the door.

When I exit the studio, I find Thomas sitting on the ground with the ice pack placed to his family jewels. I feel terrible about injuring him. At the same time, I cannot help but thinking that he is planning on taking full advantage of my guilt. He gives me an overly-exaggerated pained look.

Mama emerges right behind me. Between my eye glitch and Thomas's injured groin, she graciously volunteered to drive us to lunch.

When Thomas decides he has recovered enough to leave, we load into the vehicle. I ride shotgun, and he lies in the backseat with his icepack. My mother slides onto the driver's seat.

"Where to?" Mama asks as she pulls onto the street.

"I'm thinking Hibachi," Thomas says.

"Hibachi? You're sure? That's all the way over in Little Justice. You certain you're up for the drive?" I ask. Normally it is a twenty-minute drive, but it will be closer to thirty with my mother at the wheel.

"I'm okay, as long as I don't think about the children I'll probably never have," he says. He exhales a long breath that is meant to sound forlorn.

"Oh, now you're just being dramatic!"

"Dramatic? More like *traumatic*, from my traumatic injury!"

"I'm sure I am not the first person to take a swipe at your balls, Thomas!"

Mama suddenly slams on the brakes, coming to an abrupt stop in the middle of the street. Behind us, a delivery truck squeals to a screeching halt, and the driver blasts his horn. I brace my hands on the dash as I peer over the hood of the vehicle. I am surprised when I do not see a pedestrian or animal in danger of being ran over by the car.

She jams the gear shift into park and yells, "Stop it, the both of you! Thomas, Elle can't help it if she has a twitchy eye and bad aim, so stop being a baby!"

"I wouldn't say I have bad aim...."

"Zip it, Elle! You not only injured Thomas but wounded his pride, embarrassing him in front of the entire class."

"It never occurred to me to be embarrassed until now...."

The delivery truck driver grows more impatient with his continuous horn honking. She ignores him and screeches, "Shush it, Thomas! So help me, I will put both of you out of this car! Understand? And sit in the seat like a normal person and put your seatbelt on!"

"Yes, ma'am," Thomas says.

I mutter "Okay, Mama."

I suddenly realize what life would have been like if I had a sibling....and a *crazy* mother.

She calmly shifts the gear into drive and accelerates. She rolls down her window and flips off the van driver as she mutters something about his horn honking. Her behavior has been unusual lately. She is always the epitome of a classy lady. The snide remarks, yelling and smirks are not personality traits that she previously possessed. My Gran warned me a few weeks ago that she thinks my Mama is going through menopause, and I should buckle up because it will be a bumpy ride. I suspect that my Granny may be correct. I don't know whether to be scared or impressed by Mama-Two-Point-0.

* * *

The Hibachi lunch with my mother and Thomas went well other than a freak accident, in which flames shot out and scorched my hair. I was bent over picking up my cellphone, which I had dropped to the floor. When I straightened up, I noticed a toddler on the other side of the grill staring at me, seemingly mesmerized. It wasn't until Thomas said he smelled something burning that we realized the ends of my hair were scorched. I have no clue how it happened. Neither did Thomas since he was also bent over trying to retrieve the cellphone. My mother was in the restroom at that time and the Hibachi Chef pretended he had no clue of what transpired.

My singed hair seemed to distract Thomas from his injury, and he made a miraculous recovery. It also put Mama in a better mood, because she was allowed to cut the scorched ends of my tresses and style my hair. Although it could have been much worse, losing a couple inches of my hair was worth it for those two to be in a better mood.

After leaving the beauty salon, I arrive at the investigation's office with two trays of steak hibachi for Art and Teeny. I know they will both be there even though the office is supposed to be closed now. They like to spend their Saturdays pretending they are working. Instead, they are sitting around the office, sipping bourbon and gossiping like two schoolgirls. I do not mind their boys club because they include me. It may help that I bribe them with food. The harsh language they use becomes more civil when I am present, which I appreciate.

"Eye still not better?" Art asks, as a greeting when he notices the incessant blinking that is still plaguing me.

"Sadly, no. Mama sent both of you veggies from the Farmer's Market," I say, tossing a bag on each of their desks. They both push the bags aside and grab the Hibachi trays.

"Sweet Annie. Always thinking of others," Art says. I roll my eyes, kicking the twitch into overdrive. *He would not think of her as sweet if he had spent any time with her lately.* He is still in love with my mother, and she still loves him. Why they are not together, I do not know. I refuse to pry or act as a matchmaker. My mother has always had a habit of doing such with my life and I have never cared for it.

"How's Sally?" I ask.

"She still hasn't passed the stone," Teeny says. "If she hasn't passed it when she goes to see the Doctor on Tuesday, they'll do surgery with some type of laser to break it up. She said to tell you thanks for the basket of gifts you sent her."

"Tell her she is welcome. If there is anything I can do to help her, let me know."

"You're a popular girl today," Teeny says, as he dumps white sauce on his rice.

"How so?"

"Pretty boy stopped by here looking for you," he says, referring to Colt. I wonder why Colt did not call or text. "He said it wasn't important. He would catch up with you later. I think

116

maybe he just didn't want to hang out with me while he waited for you." Teeny grins wickedly. "Then a lady stopped by asking for you. She reminded me of a mistress of the dark." He shivers and Art cackles with laughter.

Celeste. His description is accurate enough for me to know who the lady is. "Must have been Celeste Daniels. Did she say what she wanted?"

"Nope. She said to ask you to stop by her gallery this afternoon," Teeny says. I am torn between curiosity and trepidation at the thought of visiting Celeste. "I guess she is the creepy lady that Sally said wanted to paint you?"

"Yep." Why does everyone I know tell everyone else my business? My eye does a double twinge.

"You really need to get that checked out," Art says, pointing at it.

"It's fine," I say, as the eye jumps from side to side and top to bottom.

"Maybe if you cut back on caffeine it would help," Teeny suggests as I slurp my iced coffee. I give him a look that says he is being ridiculous. He raises his hands in defeat.

I prop my jaw on a fist and say, "I suppose I should go visit Celeste Daniels and find out what she wants."

fourteen

THE VICTORIAN HOUSE turned art gallery looks just as beautiful and impressive from the outside as it did the last time I was here. As I walk up the wide steps leading to the broad porch, there is no indication of how eerie the aesthetic is inside.

When I enter, Celeste Daniels is engaged in conversation with a man. Her long hair falls in wild curls. She is wearing what must be her signature red-colored lipstick. She is clad in a belted, white button-up shirt fashioned as a dress, along with black lace tights. The red soles of her almost five-inch Louboutin pumps match the shade of her lipstick. There is a difference in wearing fashionable clothes and in having style. She has style. Style combined with her ability to command a room, makes her a woman people probably don't forget. She smiles brightly when she sees me. "Elle. I'm so glad you got my message."

"Ah the beautiful muse, Elle," the man says. Beautiful is the word I would use to describe him, not myself. Olive skin, the nose of a Greek God, and a smooth voice greet me.

"Indeed," Celeste says. "Elle, this is Jean-Pierre Belanger, an art curator and longtime friend."

"Lovely to make your acquaintance," Jean-Pierre says, as he lifts my hand to his lips kissing the back of it. His French-Canadian accent rolls off his tongue like a purr.

"Likewise," I say, as a blush creeps up my neck and settles onto my cheeks. I am astonished that the two exquisite people standing before me would refer to me as beautiful.

"Mesmerizingly magnificent," he says, lingering over my hand. He is clearly flirting. I resist the urge to whirl my eyes.

"Come along then, Elle," Celeste says, snapping Jean-Pierre to attention. "Follow me and I will show you the masterpiece that is *Elle*."

"*Une belle femme*," he says, on a breath. He kisses the back of my hand once more and then gracefully releases it. I try not to be overly flattered because I can sense by the way he looks at Celeste, he only has eyes for her. I wonder if they are more than just friends.

He confirms my suspicion about his adoration for Celeste when he says, "You are one of very few beautiful things I have seen in this God-Forsaken town. Why she insists on living here escapes my understanding. I must return again and again just to see her."

Impatiently, Celeste says, "Yes, Jean, I know you hate it here and wish I would leave." He cocks a brow at her reply. She turns on her heel and walks toward the dark corridor which leads to the back of the building.

I dutifully trail behind Celeste down the hallway to another room while Jean remains in the front gallery. "Jean is a beautiful specimen, but he can be a petty, little man," she says, in a low voice. "He thinks our friendship should supersede my relationship with Emily and my life here. I sense he has grown resentful of the child because I refuse to leave her. A grown man, jealous of a child— petty."

"What?" she asks, taking in the bewildered look on my face. "Do you think I am oversharing? Come now, Elle, I feel as if we are already friends. Besides, I have told Jean as much to his handsome face."

I do not offer a reply. I look around the room. Several easels are set up with covered canvases perched on them. She makes a show of whipping a black cloth from one of the frames.

"Ta da!" She says, studying my face while I take in the painting. "What do you think?"

For the second time in a week, I am grappling for the right word to describe Celeste's work. "It is beautiful," I say. "And also, *different.*" She has depicted a likeness of me that is stunning. Half of the canvas is opposite of her usual work. However, I take in the half in which my reflection is detailed in a mirror, and I suppress a shudder. The likeness is colored in deeper hues. One eye is stitched shut. The ends of my long, brown hair are as flames. I think of the eye twitch and the Hibachi hair incident and my throat bobs as I gulp. Is this some type of Voodoo?

Celeste has an uncanny ability to make me feel as if she is reading my mind. I seem naked and exposed to her while fully clothed, the same as I did when I posed for her. "You're wondering about the reflection?" she asks, quietly, curiously.

"Yes." I say, a bit breathless. Do I dare mention the twitch and scorched hair? If these occurrences were somehow caused by her, I do not want to give her the satisfaction of knowing they happened. And if they are coincidences, I do not want to sound crazy. Oddly enough, the twitch seems to have ceased since I got here so I cannot even point it out as a reference.

A hint of a smile dances across her lips. "On the exterior you are beautiful even if you are shy about it. You should own your beauty, by the way. On the inside, you have a fire. Or perhaps, it's a darkness that even you probably aren't aware of. I suspect no one knows the real you, not even yourself. You trick yourself into thinking you are average, ordinary, but you are anything but. No, Elle, you aren't ordinary at all, are you?"

I should feel uneasy, maybe insulted but I do not. Many thoughts and instances simultaneously race through my mind. I think of the little rush I get during precarious situations. I am not brave and do not enjoy being in danger, yet there is something about a challenge that intrigues me. I get joy sometimes from disobeying rules. I think of my explosive temper and the love I have for dancing outside the lines rather than conforming like everyone else. Then, I think of the rage that I felt toward Clayton Butcher and the wish that I had killed him while I had the chance. I think of how my views of right and wrong depend on the situation.

How can one person, a stranger, read me like she is reading tea leaves? Perhaps, she is right. But then again, I think we all possess a darkness. If the darkness is not kept in check, people would either explode into madness, or our beings would implode.

No. My soul is no darker than anyone else's. I consider the fierce love I have for people— not only my family but for anyone that I consider a friend. I am loyal to others regardless of their faults. I possess a moral compass, which is the reason I do not act on the hidden thoughts, such as killing the Clayton Butchers of the world.

Still, I am not insulted. Along with my dark side, she painted my lightness, which is much more vibrant and livelier. I look upon the painting with a new appreciation, embracing both sides of myself. "It really is beautiful, Celeste," I say. I cannot help but to wonder once again about the coincidence of the twitchy eye and scorched hair. She seems so amicable toward me that I cannot fathom she would cause me harm, even if she had the ability to do so.

"In case you are curious, it isn't for sale," she says, surprising me. "Now why don't you tell me how you really know Tara."

I look at her perplexed by her question and the sudden change of subject. "I know you aren't friends with Tara. She doesn't have friends. And since you are a private investigator, I must ask what she has you investigating?"

"Someone has been inside Tara's home, uninvited," I say.

Amused, she asks, "And I suppose you think it could be me? Is that why you came to see me the other day? What possible reason would I have to do such a thing?"

"I was trying to get a sense of the people involved in Tara's life and find a possible reason for *anyone* to do such a thing. Could someone have an ulterior motive in the grand scheme of things, such as gaining custody of Emily?"

"Because of the trust," Celeste says. "Let me put your mind at ease. Jacob left me more money than I will ever be able to spend in my lifetime. I have no need to want Emily's trust fund. I love Emily very much. She is a part of Jacob. In fact, she is on fall break from school next week. I will be picking her up this evening. She will spend a week with me. That's how much I love her. However, I have no desire to be a mother. I never have. Tara may have her faults, but she is a great mother."

"Can you think of anyone who would want to do such a thing? Maybe Emily has mentioned someone or something out of the ordinary that her mother didn't know about or recall."

"You looked at me as if I had grown a second head when I told you I thought Tara and Mark were having an affair." She appears contemplative. "I cannot picture Janie or Mark doing such a thing. They have plenty of money and no need for Emily's trust. Janie has her hands full with Maverick. She never wanted more children, so I cannot imagine she would want custody of Emily. Even if Janie suspected an affair between Mark and Tara, she would prefer to keep her head buried in the sand and maintain her perfect life. It's not like he hasn't stepped outside of their marriage before."

"How did you come to have knowledge of an affair between them?" I ask curiously.

"I saw them leaving the motel together. I had a client in town. When I dropped her at the motel after dinner, I saw the pair. I was tempted to confront them but then I thought of Janie. Like I said, she would prefer not to know, or at least pretend she doesn't. I thought of Emily, too. Her cousin Mav is her best friend. I do not want Tara and Mark's bad choices affecting Emily's life. Tara isn't as *good* as people think she is. That fragility and delicateness that men see and dote on— she takes advantage of that. Jacob still did her bidding up until the day he died."

"How did you feel about that? His doing her bidding?"

"I found it rather humorous most of the time. I wasn't jealous if that is what you are really asking. I knew everything about Jacob. He always felt guilty for divorcing her because she always acted so helpless about everything. She certainly knew how to take full advantage of his guilt."

Celeste doesn't sound bitter but rather matter-of-fact. But how much of her perception of Tara may be based on jealousy? When I look at Celeste, past the façade of mystery and the bold exterior, I see a woman standing before me. Just a woman. A woman who may pay more attention to people than what is on their surface, but a woman just the same. A woman who would be capable of feeling jealousy toward another female that she knew her husband loved.

Despite the similarities between my flaming hair and twitching eye in the painting versus reality, it is indeed a coincidence. If Celeste could cause such things, Tara would be experiencing far worse instances to her life and person, other than someone having been inside her home.

I believe Celeste. I do not think she would try to create any type of chaos in Tara's life. If not for her love of Emily, then perhaps she would. But her adoration of Emily is real. She could have easily disclosed an affair between Tara and Mark but chose not to.

I need to talk to Tara again. As soon as I leave the gallery, I call her. If Tara isn't as *good* as people think then perhaps Janie isn't as placative as Celeste thinks. When I call her number, I reach her voicemail. I leave a message, first assuring her I have not found any evidence of who could have been inside her home, then asking if she would be open to meet for coffee to discuss possibilities with her case.

Most families have secrets and skeletons buried in closets. Despite their perfect exterior, their financial security and their seemingly friendly relationships, the Daniels family is no different.

fifteen

WITH JACK PULLING AN ALL-NIGHTER at the office to allow his deputies weekend time off, I have settled into a comfortable evening at home with Buddy. After going on a run with him, I took a hot bath. Now, we are nestled on the couch. Buddy is tired from his daily adventures on the farm, and I am scrolling through streaming services trying to find an entertaining movie to watch, while being thankful the eye twitch seems to be gone.

I have just hit the play button on a quirky rom-com when my phone dings with an incoming text message from Tara.

> Hey Elle, coffee would be great, but I think I know who intruder is. Can you meet at local motel? Explain when you get here. Too much detail, need to show you in person.
> Room 108.

Has she been doing her own investigating? I have a momentary pang of guilt for not doing a satisfactory job. But with no clues and Tara not being forthcoming with information, it is difficult to perform a thorough investigation.

I type a response and hit send.

On my way.

Three dots appear as if she is typing a reply, then disappear with no incoming text. I ponder what she is doing at the motel. Meeting Mark? Am I about to walk into a domestic dispute between Mark, Janie and Tara? I certainly hope not. That would be Jack's department, not mine.

I run my fingers through Buddy's furry fluff and tell him that I will be home later. He does not even budge as he continues his snoring. So much for a relaxing evening at home. Hopefully, whatever Tara needs to show me, will not take much time.

* * *

I pull into the parking lot of the Justice Motel. A parking lot that I am all too familiar with in my line of work. The neon sign blinks between VACANCY and VACA-CY, due to the faulty *N* that they have never replaced. Situated off the highway, the glowing letters act as a beacon welcoming people. In addition to lodging, the staff is willing to keep your secrets if you tip them well enough.

Many of the guests are often locals: teenagers who find someone old enough to rent a room for them to use as a party pad and ladies who want to do DIY spray tans. Then there are those who visit in hopes of getting away with cooking meth. If not cooking meth, selling it out of one of the rooms. And of course, there are the people who frequent the establishment for the purpose of infidelity. More than a few babies have been conceived behind the doors that open onto the exterior of the building. Many marriages have ended as a result of what happens on the other side of those doors.

I have a hard time reconciling myself to Tara meeting Mark here. Most locals with money do not slum it in this place unless it's due to convenience, or part of a kink they may possess. So, what was she doing here on the day Celeste claims to have seen her with Mark?

I have an uneasy feeling as I approach room one-o-eight, noting the door is slightly ajar. A Taylor Swift song blares from room one-o-seven loudly, intermingled with laughter. The shades and curtains in room one-o-nine are open, indicating the room is vacant. I withdraw my gun from my purse and rap on the door. "Tara?" I say, as my knock causes the door to inch open further. There is no reply from within. I push the door open with my foot and point my gun.

Shock causes my feet to become cemented to the floor as I take in the macabre scene before me. I am momentarily unable to speak or move. I try to process what I am seeing.

Tara is lying on the floor at an awkward angle. There is a large stain spreading from beneath her head. Although the carpet is a dark hunter green, there is no mistaking the pool around her as anything other than blood. A white sculpture of a thoroughbred lies beside her, with blood dripping down the horse's mane. And bent over her with blood on his hands, is *Colt*.

His hands are shaking. His face is the pallid, green color of someone ready to vomit. His eyes are unblinking. Clearly, he is in shock. My synapses kick in and I rush into the room.

"Colt! What happened? Did you call an ambulance?" I ask. I desperately place my fingers at Tara's throat to check for a pulse. I exhale the breath that I had been holding when I detect a faint throb.

"Colt!" I snap my fingers at him, bringing his attention to what I am saying. "Call an ambulance!"

Slowly his eyes find their way to my face. He blinks, finally seeing me before him. "Elle. This is not what it looks like." His Adam's apple bobs as he swallows hard.

I fumble with shaking hands to find my phone and dial 9-1-1 to request an ambulance. Colt is now shaking his head, repeating, "This is not what it looks like." Amid the shock, I see panic in his dark eyes. "I didn't do this, Elle. You know I didn't do this!" he says, manically.

"Shhh. I know Colt. Calm down. Let's concentrate on helping Tara. Get some towels from the bathroom."

He stumbles to the sink and hastily grabs towels. Before he can make it back to me, his knees hit the floor, and he loses the contents of his stomach into the small trashcan sitting next to the vanity.

I rush for the towels, and press them against Tara's head, attempting to staunch the bleeding. "Tara? Tara, can you hear me? Help is on the way. Just hang on!"

I can hear the ambulance siren screaming in the distance, while praying they hurry. "What happened, Colt?"

"I found her like this," he says, as if he is speaking through a fog. Then he races for the trashcan, where he vomits again.

I haven't had a chance to call Jack yet. My mind is whirring. What do I need to do? I can hear the siren growing louder. The ambulance will be here soon. Something bad, something criminal, happened here. I need to take photos. When they carry Tara out, crucial clues will go along with her. I raise my phone. I wipe blood from my fingertips onto my pants leg, then open the camera app. With a shaking hand, my finger presses the red button to start videoing.

* * *

After Tara was secured into the ambulance, I called Jack. Tara needs an advocate at the hospital with her. I made the tough decision to stay with Colt. I worried that he would leave, which would make him look guilty. I am not related to Tara. Any decisions that need to be made regarding her medical care must come from one of the Daniels family. I called Celeste. I know she will make the right decisions out of her love for Emily.

I have now been waiting in Jack's office for two hours. Torturous waiting, with no word about Tara yet, and me being unable to speak to Colt. I pace the room like a caged animal. I am in the process of nervously chewing my thumbnail when Jack finally appears through the threshold of his office door.

He has a weary look on his face as he runs his hands through his hair.

"Where is Colt? Can I speak to him now?"

He holds his hands up, indicating I should slow down. "Colt is still in the interrogation room. Why don't you sit for a minute then you can go back to see him."

This is Jack's version of telling me to calm down, something I feel incapable of doing right now. My stomach is tied in knots as I worry about Tara. Why have I not heard from Celeste? I try to remember that no news is supposed to be good news, but it is little comfort. And why is Colt still here? Interrogation room? I take in a deep breath and have a seat across from Jack.

"What did Colt say?" I ask.

"Not much," he says, tersely.

"You believe him, though. Right? You know he did not do this."

He takes a deep breath before responding. "That's what he said. I must look at the evidence at hand though, Elle. You know this. Right now, Colt is all we have."

"You cannot be serious?" I ask in disbelief. He lowers his

eyes, hesitant to meet mine. I know in this instant that he doesn't want me to see in his eyes that he worries Colt could be guilty.

"You know Colt, Jack. There is no way he bashed Tara's skull in. Did you talk to the other guests at the motel? Did you dust the room for prints? Did you double and triple check my video to make sure there wasn't anything you missed?"

"I realize your emotions are running high. That is the only reason I am going to choose not to be insulted that you think I may not be doing my job. Yes, Elle. I did all those things. This isn't a television drama. These things take longer than a minute."

"I realize these things take longer than a minute." I narrow my eyes at him. "I'm not a dimwit. I'm nervous and I was just trying to be helpful."

"You are anything other than a dimwit," he says. "I did not mean to indicate anything of the sort. My emotions are running a little high, too."

"Lawyer?" I ask.

"He said he didn't need one because he has done nothing wrong." Jack says, raising his palms.

Colt *is* being a dimwit by refusing a lawyer. I know he is innocent. I trust Jack and know he will do the right thing. Like Jack said though, his job is to look at the evidence. And right now, that evidence is stacked against Colt.

Colt is sitting at the table. He has bloodshot eyes, disheveled hair, and blood stains on his shirt. Although the sick, green tinge on his face is gone, he still looks as if he could be physically ill at any given moment. He isn't in handcuffs, but the way his hands are locked in front of him on the table, he may as well be.

The room does not boast a two-way mirror like the ones you see on television, nor does it have cameras recording your words and every move. There is a lone video camera sitting atop a tripod in the corner of the room and it is currently turned off.

His eyes cut to me. "Two things," I say, holding up two fingers. "First, get a lawyer." I drop a finger. He starts to open his mouth to say what I assume will be 'He doesn't need one. He did nothing wrong.' I cut him off, saying, "Even if you think you don't need one. Be deciding which attorney you want to call. Second, tell me everything, so I can help you."

He rubs the back of his neck then begins speaking. The tone of his voice is a mixture of anguish, weariness and desperation.

"I was supposed to meet Samantha at the motel. I was happy about meeting her. I stopped by your office earlier to tell you I had reconnected with her. When I got to the motel, I found her the same way she was when you got there."

"Samantha? You do realize the woman in that room is Tara, not Samantha?"

"Whatever her real name is, she was Samantha to me."

"How did you initially meet her?"

"I was working in Lexington. I met her at a bar several weeks ago. She said her name was Samantha. We hooked up. I thought she lives in Lexington, but J.D.— you remember J.D. from my crew?" I nod my head. "He used to do landscaping before he came to work for me. He told me the next day that he thought she looked familiar, and he finally remembered where he had seen her. He had done landscaping at her house here in Justice."

"Which is why I saw you going to Tara's the day I was parked on the street?" He tips his head, indicating yes. "Did she know you were coming?"

"No. I wasn't even sure if it was her. After I saw you that day, I thought maybe I got the address that J.D. had given me wrong. Then I started thinking, why would she lead me to believe she lived in Lexington. Maybe she was married, and I didn't know it. So, I texted her asking why she didn't tell me she was from Justice. Was she married? Because I want no part of breaking up a marriage. She told me, no she isn't married, but that she has a kid and nosy in-laws, so she has to be careful. She asked me to meet her at the motel this evening. When I got there... well you know the rest."

By the end of his explanation his tone has gone flat, void of emotion, and he sounds resigned to his situation.

"Tara hired me because she thought someone was breaking into her house. Possibly stalking her. When you put that into context, you know how your story sounds, don't you?" I ask gently.

He looks into my eyes searchingly. "Good God. You don't think I did this, do you?" he asks with desperation in his voice.

"Of course not! But others may think so. I am reiterating that you need to get a lawyer. ASAP."

"I really liked her. I felt a real connection to her."

"You may want to keep that information to yourself for the time being. Somehow, it makes the situation sound worse." He swallows hard and I realize in that instant that he has already told Jack everything that he has told me.

Jack told me to go home and rest. It's late and there is nothing I can do. I am too close to Colt not to be biased in an investigation, to leave the investigating up to him and his department. He knows I will do none of those things. He is right about it being too late in the night to accomplish much, so tonight I will come up with a plan. In the morning, I will get to work. But right now, I am going to see the one person I know will always give sound advice and their unbiased opinion. Art.

I stop by my house to pick up Buddy, telling him we are going on an adventure to see his Grandpa Art. *Art* is another word in Buddy's vocabulary. He races me to the car in his excitement.

Art lives in an RV camper parked in the middle of the woods on some property he owns. He sold his house a few years ago. He has a nice apartment upstairs from his office, but he prefers to live here. It suits him.

When I pull in, I find him sitting in an Adirondack chair beside his outdoor firepit, listening to Merle Haggard. Buddy rushes over to greet him, almost dipping his tail in the fire.

"Hey Buddy," Art says, embracing the dog. "I wasn't expecting a visit from you." He looks at me questioningly. "Everything okay with your Mama and them?" He asks, referring to my whole family.

"Mama and the family are well," I say, taking a seat in the chair beside him. I grab a blanket that is draped across the back of the chair and pull it across my lap to combat the night chill, then I launch into telling him about what happened. He is unplugged from civilization while he is here, so he had no idea what transpired.

"You know Colt better than anyone," he says. "If you know in your heart of heart's that he's innocent, prove it. Or at least try to that way you can say you did all you could do for your friend."

Art has always told me to follow my gut instinct. He said exactly what I expected he would say, exactly what I needed to hear.

"I realize this isn't a conventional case as far as making a game plan, but I know you can figure things out. If you need any help, just let me know what you want me to do. I'm sure

Teeny would be willing to pitch in, too. Maybe Sally can get some more hours in toward her certification if she ever passes that damned kidney stone," he says.

"You're right. I have no idea where to start. Jack will be a huge obstacle. He doesn't want me anywhere near this investigation."

"Jack has good instincts. Don't go getting too upset with him. He's just looking out for ya. He knows he can't control ya but it's his way of taking care of you. He is as dogged as you when it comes to solving cases. Just because all roads point to Colt looking guilty, doesn't mean Jack isn't considering all possibilities. Even if he ain't sharing them with you," he adds with a wry smile.

Art is correct about this, also. Jack will withhold information from me to keep me in the dark, as his way of preventing me from investigating. He should realize that all this accomplishes is to cause me to work much harder to discover the truth. But the longer that I am busy with seemingly minute tasks, the longer I am out of his hair and in his view, out of danger.

The part of me that considers myself a strong, independent woman could easily become indignant about Jack's behavior. Yet, I am still enough of a romantic to recognize his caring as an endearing gesture. I know he regards my investigation skills highly since he has asked for my aid in the past. Although, he does not always appreciate my methods. He thinks I skirt the edges of rules too much, putting myself in harm's way. I view this as doing what I need to do to get the job done. He certainly does not value my 'better to ask for forgiveness, than permission' attitude, which is what has led to most of our disagreements in the past.

"He definitely isn't an over-sharer about investigative

details," I laugh. Art meets my laugh with his own. "Thanks for the offer to help. I know Colt will appreciate it."

"Sweetheart, I didn't offer for the Ryan boy. Don't get me wrong, I do not want him wrongfully accused, but my offer to help is for you. I know this is important to ya."

When I count the blessings in my life, I always make sure to count Art twice. The man who took on the role of being my father, before, during, and after marriage to my Mama. The man who helped mold me into who I am today. The man who taught me that money isn't everything, if you can help someone, and all it will cost you is time, be certain to do it. The man who loves me unconditionally as if he were my biological father. My own father died before I was old enough to even have a memory of him. I would have loved to have known my dad, to have been raised by him, but it wasn't part of God's plan. I'm thankful that after losing my father, Art was part of the plan.

sixteen

TARA MADE it through the night and seems to be holding her own. She lost a lot of blood from the head wound, but the doctor assured that it looked like much more blood than it really was. There is a possibility that she could have already woken on her own, but at this time she is being kept sedated in hopes that the brain swelling will subside. The first forty-eight hours are critical. Celeste reported the doctors seem optimistic. I am relieved about their optimism. I want Tara to be well. I also know that if she doesn't pull through, Colt will probably be charged with murder.

Jack spent last night at the Sheriff's Office, which is just as well. He would have been kept awake, by my tossing and turning while waiting for sleep that never came. Finally, around four-thirty this morning, I reconciled myself to not getting any rest and arose from my bed.

I spent the early hours researching the people who are closest to Tara's life. Nothing peculiar stands out. Mark, Janie, nor Celest have any sort of checkered past, not so much as a speeding ticket. Their records are more spotless than my own.

Celeste lived in Quebec before marrying Jacob. I had

already guessed that by her French-Canadian accent, but I did not realize how popular her art is in Canada. She was wealthy in her own right before marrying Jacob. She was telling the truth when she said she has plenty of money without needing more. I wonder what type of life she had before settling here. How did she meet Jacob? Surely it was a culture shock moving here. I am a native of Justice and I sometimes miss Boston. I do not miss my life there, but I do find myself craving the liveliness of the city, the restaurants, the concerts and the historic culture. Emily is the only reason Celeste has chosen to remain in Justice after her husband's death.

Perhaps, Celeste has a checkered past that no one could know about. I remind myself that point is moot, considering she has an alibi for the time of Tara's attack. She was at the movies with Emily when it occurred.

Something prickles the back of my mind. Celeste knew about an affair between Mark and Tara. Celeste may remain in Justice to be near Emily, but she seems far too vested in Tara's life as someone who dislikes her. She did not question why someone breaking into Tara's home could result in Tara losing custody of Emily. It's as if she knew how and why someone could have been gaslighting Tara. Could Celeste possess some type of clairvoyancy? Goosebumps swell up my arms as I think maybe she *can* read my mind. I dispel the idea and remind myself that I believe her about not being responsible for the break-ins.

Around seven-thirty, as soon as the first promise of daylight appears, I lace up my running shoes and go for a run with Buddy alongside me. I do not particularly enjoy running. It is penance for my horrible dietary choices. It is also when I do my best thinking.

As my feet skirt around the occasional potholes along the road, I come up with a plan for today. My thoughts come in accompaniment to "Seven Nation Army" by The White Stripes as the song pulses through my earphones.

I would like to be able to visit Tara but with her traumatic brain injury, she was airlifted from the local hospital to one two hours away, which is better equipped to handle such an injury. I need to speak with Mark and Janie Daniels. The couple were in Charleston when Tara's attack happened, but perhaps they have some knowledge that could be pertinent to the investigation.

I should speak with Billy from Justice Security again. Something does not add up regarding the trespasser in Tara's home. It seems a certainty that it is connected to whom her attacker may be.

And I should attempt to retrace Tara's steps from yesterday. Whatever led her to think she had figured out who her intruder was must have happened yesterday. Jack's department would have done a thorough job of speaking to people at the motel, but many people are not forthcoming with law enforcement. Some people who see things occur do not share information. Perhaps, they feel guilty for not alerting someone to circumstances they witnessed that led to a crime. Then there are other people who are not completely forthcoming because of their dislike/distrust of law enforcement.

If someone was entering Tara's home with the purpose of gaslighting her, it is tame play compared to what happened yesterday. What could be important enough for gaslighting to lead to attempted murder? Who would benefit from her losing custody of Emily, or from her death? The problem is that the only people who would benefit from either, have an alibi. It would be easy to confirm Celeste was at the movies with Emily when the attack occurred and just as easily confirmable that Mark and Janie were indeed on vacation when it happened. I ponder once again, the possibility of a stalker.

Who, what, when, where and why? Those are the questions that need to be answered in order to solve the mystery. I know what happened to Tara, when and where. The who and the why are what I need to figure out. Nothing about this case has made sense from the start. I will need to delve deep into Tara's life rather than only investigating the people involved in her life.

Perhaps, it is possible that her attack was random and had nothing to do with whoever her intruder was. One mystery has quickly become two. Hopefully both cases will be solvable. *Fingers crossed.*

seventeen

ALTHOUGH EXTRAVAGANT, Mark and Janie's home is a cookie-cutter house situated amid a whole street of other equally extravagant look-alike homes. The only difference in the exteriors are the paint colors and landscaping.

I park in the driveway at the end of the cul-de-sac, behind a black Range Rover with gold detailing and wheels. It is obviously not a standard edition vehicle. I assume it belongs to Mark. From what I have learned of Janie, she seems like she would be more of a minivan type, like Tara.

I step around two bicycles, haphazardly abandoned on the sidewalk, as I make my way to the front door and then ring the doorbell. Mark Daniels answers the door, looking tired and harried. A sound of chaos echos from behind him. I see a boy, who must be Maverick, jump down from the back of the couch with a plastic sword, screeching, "On Guard!" Emily meets him with a clash of her own plastic weapon.

"Quieter, you two!" Mark yells into the room. "Yes?" he asks, looking to me.

"Mr. Daniels, I was hoping to speak to you about Tara."

Exasperated, he says, "I've already talked to you people twice. What else could you possibly need to ask?"

I assume by 'you people', he means the Sheriff's Department. "I'm not with the Sheriff's department. My name is Elle Riley. I am a private investigator who was working for Tara. I also consider her a friend," I add.

"Oh," he says, stepping onto the porch and closing the door behind him. "Janie is at the hospital. It's best if we speak out here since the kids are in there." I nod my head in agreement. He sits in a chair and invites me to have a seat in the one next to it. "Private Investigator? What did Tara need your services for?" If Janie knows about Tara hiring me, she must not have shared the information with her husband, which seems suspicious to me.

"She believed someone had been inside her home, uninvited. Do you have any idea who it could have been? Or do you know of anyone who could have had the security code to her house?"

"No. Why didn't she mention it to me? I would've gladly helped her."

"Is it possible she could have had a reason to suspect it was you?" His face grows mottled with anger. I realize my question was indelicate, but I am past the point of caring. Tara is lying in a hospital, brushing death, and my best friend may be charged with the crime. It's best to get straight to the point rather than dancing around it. "Were you having an affair with her?" I continue before he has a chance to respond.

He winces. His anger quickly turns to embarrassment. He looks around to make sure no bystanders have appeared. He seems to measure his words when he finally speaks. "I slept with Tara one time. Just the once. It was a mistake. I would appreciate it if it didn't get back to Janie."

"There's a chance your wife knows, Mr. Daniels." His

mouth gapes open. "Do you think Janie could have known and been Tara's intruder?"

"No," he sputters. "That's absurd. And Janie certainly wasn't the one who injured Tara. We were in Charleston when Celeste called to tell us about it. We drove all night to get home and Janie went straight to the hospital to be with her. Would she do that if she knew about the affair," he asks with an air of contempt in his voice.

The thought does cross my mind that a hospital with a person lying on their deathbed would be the perfect place and opportunity for someone to get their revenge. But I keep that thought to myself, instead replying, "No, probably not." After-all, they weren't even in the state when the incident at the motel happened.

"Do you think Tara was seeing anyone else?"

"Look, I don't know," he says, wiping his palms down his trouser legs. "I'm starting to think I didn't really know Tara at all. I have been in love with her for years. Even before she and Jacob were married. I never acted on it. I mean, for goodness sakes, she was my brother's wife."

"How did you come to have an affair, then?" I ask curiously.

"She initiated it. Which wasn't like her, at all. It was just the one time. I broke it off after. It wasn't what I expected. We didn't really talk. I realized after that she probably just wanted me because I reminded her of Jacob. I felt used. It's not exactly a turn on to think someone wants you because you remind them of your dead brother."

No, you covet your brother's wife for years, jumping at the first opportunity to sleep with her, but feeling used is where you draw the line. I recall Celeste saying that Mark had stepped outside of his marriage often and I have zero sympathy for him.

The front door swings open. Maverick and Emily appear,

talking over each other, tattling. Emily spots me and comes rushing over. "Elle!" she exclaims as she wraps her small arms around my neck. "I didn't know you were here."

Mark rises from his chair. With the presence of the children, our conversation has come to an end. "I'm sorry that I cannot think of anything that would be helpful to you. Emily, say bye to Elle in a moment and come back inside, okay?" he says, dismissing himself from the uncomfortable conversation.

"Okay, Uncle Mark," she says.

Maverick trails on Mark's heels as he enters the house and tells him about how Emily wasn't playing fair.

"Did you know my Mommy is sick?" Emily asks as her lower lip starts to quiver.

"I do know that. I'm sorry. Hopefully, she will be well and back at home with you very soon."

"Hopefully," the child replies, with tears in her eyes. My heart breaks for her. What do you say to a child who is all too familiar with the concept of death after losing her father recently? "It is really my Mommy in the hospital, isn't it?"

"Of course, Sweetie. The Doctors are working very hard to make certain she gets well soon."

"It couldn't be someone who looks like my Mommy, like how Uncle Mark looks like my Daddy?" she asks while fiddling with the 'E' on the gold chain around my neck.

"I'm afraid not, Sweetheart. But your Mommy has excellent Doctors taking care of her." How confusing this must be for the six-year-old girl. Her Daddy is gone but Uncle Mark looks like him. Would that be a comfort to the young child or a constant reminder that her father isn't here? I'm uncertain what I should say to her now. There is a chance that her mother may not wake up and come home to her. I would never tell the child this, but I am uncomfortable making a promise to her that she will. Children remember the promises and assurances that adults make to them. Especially when it comes to something as important as this. I am at a loss for words, so I pull Emily close to my chest and hold her in a comforting embrace.

* * *

I sit in my Bronco replaying the conversation with Mark Daniels. My thoughts come in quick succession as I try to put the puzzle pieces in place. I remember the things that I have been told regarding Tara. *She isn't who you think she is*, Celeste said. *It wasn't like Tara*, Mark said. *It was Samantha*, Colt said. Maybe there really is a Samantha and she has been claiming Tara's identity.

There would be no better way to get to know someone than by breaking into their house and going through their things. A person's whole life is inside their home: the style of clothes they wear, their favorite scent of perfume, and their favorite foods in the pantry/fridge. Their mail and calendar could help a stranger to learn their schedule. Footage from old family videos could be watched to learn a person's voice and mannerisms. Their entire being is there on display for the taking.

Clothes in my closet would be hanging in a different spot. I could smell my perfume when I would enter the bedroom, I recall Tara saying.

I discredit the thought of stolen identity. It sounds insane even to me. If a doppelganger existed, she would have needed to be a dead ringer for Tara in order to have fooled Mark. Mark has known Tara and been in love with her for years.

Occam's razor comes to mind. I should choose the conclusion that consists of the fewest assumptions. The simplest solution is usually correct. There are too many hypotheticals to the possibility of a doppelganger. The easiest answer is that Tara has a side that she tries to keep a secret. Perhaps, an alter ego that wants to do things that wholesome Tara would not do. Colt said that she told him she has a child and in-laws that she did not want to know about their affair. That makes sense if she is leading a double life.

But where does her affair with Mark fit into that scenario? He is one of the said in-laws. I instantly disliked Mark. Tara said he makes her uncomfortable. I can see why. If he makes her uncomfortable, why would she initiate an affair with him? Perhaps, it *was* because he reminds her of Jacob. Even divorced, she was obviously still in love with Jacob. Was she able to put aside her revulsion toward Mark in order to find comfort in his arms by pretending he was Jacob. I shake my head at the thought, finding it revolting.

And what about the home intrusions, which she hired me to investigate? She mentioned a mental illness in her birth mother. Perhaps, Tara is suffering from something that could possibly be hereditary and she imagined or invented the whole thing. I need to learn more about her adoption, and what type of illness her mother suffers from.

Still, the question of why she texted me to meet her at the motel stating that she had discovered who had been entering her home, nags me. Maybe her alter ego is very twisted, and no one really knows the true Tara. Perhaps the person who bashed her over the head knows the real her. But who is that person? I do not believe it is Colt.

I file all these thoughts away as I start my Bronco and pull around the circle leading away from the house at the end of the cul-de-sac. When I drive onto the main highway, a black, Dodge Challenger Hellcat rumbles to life from a side street and falls in behind me. I would recognize the vehicle anywhere with its custom forged wheels, and the distinct roar of the engine coming from under the large hood scoops. It belongs to Officer Eli Keith. It's his personal vehicle. I'm not sure why he is not driving a squad car because it is obvious that he is tailing me. There is only one person who could be responsible for that. *Jack*. I suppose I need to make a stop by the S.O. (Sheriff's Office) to see him.

eighteen

JACK'S TRUCK is parked in his allotted spot in front of the station. When I enter, the office is buzzing with the noise of deputies talking on the phone or with each other. It is a scene that is abnormal for a Sunday. Jack ruined everyone's weekend plans by calling them into work when Tara was discovered at the motel. Everyone is too busy to notice me, other than Daphne, who is on the phone. She gives me a smile and a finger wave as I stroll by on my way to Jack's office.

The heels of my shoes click-clack on the ancient green and white tiles as I stride down the hallway. The door to his office is open but he isn't inside the room. I start to turn and make my way in search of him until I notice his normally neat desk is an unorganized mess. Papers and many sticky notes that have been scribbled on cover the surface. I spy photos peeking out from beneath some of the papers.

I take two steps backward, peeking my head out the doorway to make sure nobody is coming down the hallway, then I rush over to the desk. Most of the sticky notes do not make much sense because they were written exactly the way Jack was thinking. Some do, such as the one in which he wrote,

Colt alibi for Tara's break-ins? He either thinks Colt was stalking Tara, or he is looking for alibis for the dates in order to clear him.

I pull the crime scene photos from beneath a stack of papers. I study the pictures, making sure there is nothing I have forgotten about the scene. I have watched the video footage of the motel room from my phone at least a hundred times, enough that nausea no longer threatens to overtake me when I look at the scene. Perhaps that is how emergency personnel cope with the gory situations that they see, by seeing them often enough, they may become desensitized.

I inspect the picture of the statue that was used as a weapon. Although Justice is far from Keenland and horse country, the motel room is decorated in an equestrian aesthetic. The statue was a weapon of convenience, meaning the crime was one of opportunity. If someone went to the motel with the intention of harming Tara then they did not have a weapon with them, or they didn't use a weapon they may have brought.

Perhaps she had another lover besides Colt, and that lover found out about her relationship with Colt and grew jealous. Someone other than Mark Daniels since he was in Charleston at the time. It would be wonderful if I could get into Tara's home to look for clues. I wonder if Jack has already done so.

I spy more scribbly notes along with a couple of receipts. Jack has been retracing Tara's steps from yesterday. There is a debit card sales slip for $42.50 in fuel from the convenience store where Thomas works. Seems a trip to speak with TNT should be on my agenda. Maybe I should try to find out where Tara's van is so I can see how much fuel she used driving around yesterday afternoon. It will not tell me where she went, but perhaps it could indicate if she went on a trip or stayed in town before going to the motel. There is also a ticket for a takeout order from the Chinese restaurant. I file that information in my brain for later.

I hear Jack's voice drifting down the hallway. It is a one-sided conversation. He must be speaking to someone on the phone. I push the photos back under the stack of papers and place the receipts into their previous positions. When he appears in the doorway, he finds me in his chair with my feet propped upon the corner of his desk, scrolling through my phone.

His first instinct is to smile when he sees me as he steps across the threshold. The smile turns to a suspicious frown as he looks at his desk and then back up to me, probably realizing that I have been snooping. I quickly set my eyes back on my phone, avoiding his gaze, while resisting the urge to squirm under his scrutiny.

"Yeah, it would be great if you could just go ahead and forward it to my email. Thanks," he says, before disconnecting the call.

He taps his cellphone into the palm of his hand. "Why do I feel like I missed a coup where you've overthrown me and taken my office over?" he asks while looking at my feet propped on his desktop.

"Well, you do have the most comfortable chair in the building," I say. I drop my feet to the floor then walk over to him. I rise onto my tip-toes to give him a kiss. He embraces me. I run my hand across his cheek, which needs a shave, and let my fingers travel over to his ear where I sharply pinch the lobe.

"Ouch," he says. "Why'd you do that?"

"Why do you have Eli following me?"

"Because you do not listen." He walks over to his desk and takes a seat in his chair. He pushes the papers around to make sure nothing is missing or out of place. "I know you are doing your own investigating." I lift my chin in indifference. "If Colt didn't try to kill Tara, then whoever did is still out there. I must resort to pulling one of my valuable resources from searching for that person to keep an eye on you, and make sure you aren't the next victim."

I scowl at him. "Valuable resource, huh? I lost him within two miles, and he was driving a Hellcat."

"Hellcat or no, not everyone drives like you do."

"Thanks." I beam a sarcastic smile at him then plop down into a chair across from him.

"Not a compliment," he mutters under his breath.

"Maybe I should feel hurt that you chose the one officer who isn't the sharpest tool in the shed to keep me safe."

His eyes crinkle at the corners and he suppresses a laugh. "Give the kid some credit. He's more than a pretty face," he says, referring to Eli, whose social media videos have earned him the name *Officer Sexy*.

It is ironic he refers to Eli as a kid. Jack is not much older than him. This is an example of how people mature at different levels. Jack is the youngest Sheriff to serve the County of Justice. He has a wealth of experiences that many people twice his age have not gone through, making him an old soul. Having been a young Marine during an unpeaceful era and losing a sister to a drug overdose, resulted in Jack mentally maturing sooner than most. On the outside, to the rest of the world, he seems like a simple man. Those who know him best, know that he is very complex. He has taken all the pain and rage from his past and tried to turn it into something positive, rather than becoming bitter and jaded. The anger is what drives him. His moral compass is what keeps the anger from becoming dangerous.

"Of course. You're right. I'm sorry." I feel chastised for the remark. Even if most people think Eli is not very bright, they don't say it aloud. "Can I see Colton?"

"He isn't here. Apparently, he took someone's advice and got a lawyer. I couldn't hold him without charging him." He raises a brow questioningly. He either knows I am the person who suggested the attorney, or he wonders why I did not know Colt is no longer here. I am confused as to why Colt did not bother to call or text to tell me he was released. "I don't want to charge him until I know for certain he is guilty."

"Hmm. That's good. So..." I let out a nonchalant breath while studying my fingernails, "have you made any progress on the case? Have any leads? What are your thoughts?"

He does laugh now without bothering to entertain me with answers. "Fine. I'll show myself out," I say, before he has a chance to point me toward the door.

"Maybe I'll see you at home later," he says. It isn't lost on me that he referred to my house as *home*. Five months does not seem like a long time for a relationship, particularly considering I was not speaking to him a week ago. But sometimes it feels like we have been together forever— like it is meant to be and Jack is home to me. The thought should scare me. Oddly enough, it doesn't. My heart does a little pitter-patter as he comes to give me a goodbye kiss. "Oh, and Elle..."

I interrupt him and say, "Yeah, I know. Leave the investigating to you." The poetic thoughts leave my mind and are quickly replaced by slight annoyance.

"Actually, I was going to say I love you and be safe. But yeah, leave the investigating to me."

"But you know I'm not going to do that, right?"

"Yeah, I know." He rolls his eyes. "But I still love you anyways."

I smile, my thoughts turning poetic again. "Ditto," I say, before leaving his office.

Daphne is still talking on the phone when I return to the front of the building. I stop by her desk, hoping she will be finished with the phone call soon so I can chat with her. I tap the head of her Charlie Brown bobble head to send it bopping. She covers the mouthpiece and says, "Can we do lunch soon? I would love to catch up."

"Definitely. Me too," I reply, realizing that she thinks the call will not be ending anytime soon. I blow a kiss at her and exit the building.

When I get back to my vehicle, I pull my phone from my back pocket to check that I haven't missed any calls or messages. I haven't. I text Celeste to see if there is an update on Tara. Her response is immediate— the type of immediacy that happens when someone is waiting in a hospital with nothing to do but stare at their phone. *Some improvement*, she replies, with a finger crossed emoji. I choose the love reaction to her response before pulling up Colt's name from my contacts and calling him.

He answers on the last ring before the call gets sent to voicemail.

"Hey," he says.

"Hey. How are you doing?"

He blows out a long, exhausted breath. "I honestly don't know."

"I'm glad you took my advice about a lawyer. Why didn't you let me know you were released?"

"About the lawyer.... I'm not supposed to be talking to you."

"Are you joking?" I ask. "I'm the one person who is in your corner trying to help you."

"Yeah, I know." He sounds despondent. "You know I appreciate that, but no, I'm not joking. You were at the motel, so he said it was better if we didn't talk and take a chance on getting parts of our stories mixed up. And..." he hesitates before continuing, "he also thinks I shouldn't communicate with you because of your relationship with Jack."

I try to look at the situation from his attorney's point of view, rather than be hurt that Colt is entertaining his advice regarding me. I should be happy that the lawyer is looking out for him and offering sound advice. But it's the last part that irks me. *Because of my relationship with Jack.* It's perfectly logical for the attorney to think along those lines, but does Colt think the same thing?

I feel as if I have been doing a balancing act during my entire relationship with Jack, trying to ensure that he doesn't begrudge my friendship with Colt. I did not disclose to Jack anything that Colt said to me yesterday while in that box of a room, and Jack did not ask me to. Because Jack knows that it would put me in a tough position. Because Jack knows that I am loyal to a fault.

A pang of guilt squeezes my heart as I think about how deep down, I worried that Jack may want Colt to be guilty, out of jealousy. The guilty grip tightens. I may be loyal, but Jack is the most honorable person I know. He is too noble to let jealousy rule his duties as an officer of the law.

I speak around the lump in my throat and say, "I understand. You should heed your attorney's advice. Take care of yourself." I end the call.

The uncontrollable part of my emotions tells me I should not bother trying to prove Colt did not hurt Tara. I should do as Jack says and leave the investigation to his department. The logical part of my brain tells me I need to follow through. Colt's attorney has one job, to prove Colt didn't do what he is accused of. Jack has the job of trying to figure out for certain who did. I need to do both things— prove Colt is innocent because I believe with my whole heart that he is, and find out who is guilty for Tara and Emily. I do not know what the outcome will be for Tara, but I do know that Emily deserves to know the truth about what happened to her mother if she doesn't come home to her.

Then there is the part of me which is desperate to find out if and what I may have missed about Tara's intruder, and how it fits into the case. So, no, I will not do as Jack says, and leave the investigation alone. I need to find out the truth for myself. I need to know if I could have done something to prevent what happened.

I start my engine and pull my vehicle onto the street. Eli's Dodge Hellcat follows me from the parking lot, sticking close to my rear bumper. I whip onto the side of the street, parking. Eli pulls in behind me. I get out of the Bronco and walk back to his car. He lowers his tinted window. A blush creeps up his neck and settles onto his face. He looks nervous with darting eyes, unsure of where to settle them.

"What, um, what's up, Elle?" he asks, swallowing hard.

I smile sweetly and say, "I figure since you are stuck to me, we may as well save fuel. Scoot over. I'm driving." His red face goes pale. This should be fun, I think, as he slowly swings his door open. He gets out and allows me to slide behind the steering wheel of the Dodge Challenger Hellcat.

I rev the engine and peel out onto the street, squealing tires. The V-8 engine is quick to cooperate with the pressure of my foot. He grips the dash and I giggle before letting off the gas a tad. "Have you ever seen the movie *Fight Club*," I ask.

"Yeah," he says, cautiously. "You aren't going to try to beat me up, are you?"

I give him the side eye. "Of course not. Do you remember 'the first rule of *Fight Club*?'"

"Yep."

"Well, this is kind of like *Fight Club*. The first rule is you don't tell Jack what I am doing."

"Yeah, right, Jack is my boss," he scoffs. "And *he* would definitely beat me up."

"You may be afraid of Jack, but do you know who scares Jack the most?" He shakes his head. "Me."

He tilts his head to the side while considering what I said. His mouth quirks up. "True," he says.

"So, first rule?"

"Don't tell Jack what you're up to."

"Excellent. And if you do?"

"Then you'll probably try to beat me up, and I will have to let you because you are a lady, and I don't hit ladies."

"Exactly." I smile at him, thinking this may be the beginning of a beautiful relationship. "Now, do you think you can find me an address for Billy Johnson?"

Jack will be furious when he finds out I am using his plan of Eli tailing me and reporting back to him, for my own advantage. The thought makes me feel warm and fuzzy with giddiness. Perhaps, I can talk Eli into making a *Tik Tok* video of our ride along and send it to Jack.

nineteen

BILLY JOHNSON LIVES in an apartment above his parents' garage. Hopefully they do not expect rent since his dad fired him for aiding and abetting his criminal friend, Richie.

I knock on the door and Billy is quick to answer. "Hi, Elle. What brings you by? Not that I'm not happy to see you," he adds.

"Hey Billy. Sorry to stop in unannounced. I was hoping I could speak with you again regarding Tara Daniels."

"Sure," he says, then his eyes narrow as he looks behind me. I turn to see what he is looking at and almost bump into Eli, who seems to have made it his mission to be plastered to me. A lady, who I assume is Billy's mother, is peering over the side porch rail of the house. "It's fine, Mom! They're friends. Go back inside!" His face turns a shade of pink as he says, "Helicopter parents, am I right?" He makes a motion of blades whirring over his head.

I dip my head in agreement, mentally laughing, until I remember my own mother. If she lived next door to me, she would be far worse than Billy's mom. She would have already beaten all three of us inside the apartment and started pouring sweet tea.

He steps inside then motions for us to follow. He tosses discarded clothing from the couch and invites us to have a seat. Then he remembers the bong he has sitting on the coffee table. "That, um, that is just decorative," he stammers as he quickly tucks it into a kitchen cabinet.

"Of course," I smile, and Eli gives an exaggerated eye roll. "Billy, this is Officer Keith," I say.

"We've met," Eli says, and Billy nods his head.

"So, what did you want to ask me?" Billy asks as he sits and then shifts nervously in a chair, unsure of what to do with his hands now that they are empty of the bong.

"Tara Daniels was attacked. I just want to make certain I did not miss anything the last time we spoke."

"Oof, that's terrible. I hope she's okay. There really isn't much you could've missed, though. Like I told you before— she called a couple of times, was really rude the second time, but there wasn't much we could do considering her alarm had never even gone off."

"Hmm, right. So, if someone entered her house then they had to have her code," I say.

"Right. She acted like it was my fault and I was like 'look lady, don't be sharing your code with people.' That really set her off. Finally, dad talked to her. He even sent a tech out there to check her system and make sure nothing was wrong with it. Then, he had her change her code for safe measure."

"And same thing after? Her alarm was never triggered?"

"Well yeah, as far as I know. Up until yesterday, anyway. Dad was saying yesterday evening that her alarm had went off earlier. When he called her house, she said that it was her fault and gave him her pin, telling him there was no need to call the law. He was surprised after all the ruckus she had raised before, is why he mentioned it."

"Yesterday? That is when she was attacked." Billy's eyes go wide. "Not in her home," I add. He lets out a huge breath of relief.

"At least you know it wasn't Richie since he is still in jail. And it sure wasn't me. There are cameras all over this place," he says, making a wide range with his hands. "Be easy to prove where I was all day— right here. Even without the cameras, my mom knows my every move. She's been a real pain since my arrest. I can't even go buy my wee..." he catches himself, "wheat. Wheaties. Cereal. Love the stuff."

"I believe you, Billy." *Not about the Wheaties* obviously, but I believe him about being here yesterday. He gives me a grateful smile as Eli makes a "huff" under his voice. I lightly jab him with an elbow. I notice his fingers furiously typing a message on his phone. "Are you texting Jack?" I ask.

"No," he says, laying his phone screen side down on his lap. I give him a look to indicate I know he is lying. "Well, okay, yeah. But I was in Jack's fight club a long time before I joined yours."

"Traitor. It's fine, though. I was going to let him know. It could be important."

"The Sheriff has a fight club?" Billy asks. He seems as if he is considering the possibility. He tips his head appreciatively. "Makes sense." Then he adds, in a panicked tone, "Hey, you didn't tell him about my bong, did you?"

"You mean your decorative *what not*? No," Eli says. Billy leans back in his chair, anxiously glancing toward the cabinet where he stashed the bong. I suspect he will be making use of the *decoration* as soon as we leave.

"Thanks, Billy. I suppose we will get out of your hair now."

"No problem. No need to rush off," he says, bounding out of the chair to open the door for us, his actions betraying his words. His eyes swing to the cabinet once more as we make our exit.

As soon as we get into the car, Eli belts out a laugh. "Not the brightest bulb in the chandelier, that one."

I giggle and say, "Give the kid some credit," echoing Jack's words about Eli. "Sometimes people can surprise you by being brighter than they seem."

* * *

Thomas is behind the counter when I enter the convenience store. "Hey, T. How's it going?"

"Hey, ballbreaker. Better than yesterday. What's up?" He asks while folding his arms over his chest.

Leonard Shipley enters from a back room, carrying a box of cigarettes to stock. This must be his new place of employment. When he sees me, he drops the box onto the floor and sticks his middle finger in the air, flipping me off. Eli steps up to the counter, clearing his throat. Seeing him, Leonard drops the finger to his nose, pretending to scratch the side of it.

"Bodyguard?" Thomas asks looking at Eli, who is now at the Icee machine, filling a jumbo cup with brain freeze inducing blue raspberry flavor.

"Babysitter," I sigh. "New employee?" I ask inclining my head toward Leonard.

"Yep," Thomas sighs in return. He cups his hand over the side of his mouth and whispers, "I'm not sure he's going to work out, though."

I smile, thinking I hope the owner of the establishment is current on his worker compensation insurance payments.

"Who was working yesterday afternoon?" I ask.

"Well, you know it certainly was not me. I was home icing the boys, recuperating from the kick in the gonads you gave me."

His comment causes Eli to get strangled, sending Blue Raspberry ice dribbling from his nose. I slap him on the back, asking if he is okay. He struggles to regain control of his breathing before finally nodding his head. Tears are still streaming down his face, but he seems to be breathing now with only an occasional cough.

"Can we please move past yesterday's *accident?* Or do I need to call my mother?" I ask in a threatening tone. I realize it is a low blow. But it works since she is the only person who can seem to quash Thomas's bad behavior.

"Fine. What do you want?"

I pull Tara's photo up on my phone and pass it to him. "I need to know if whoever was working remembers her being here, if she was with anyone, or can remember who else may have been here at the same time."

Thomas props his elbows on the counter and takes my phone to study the picture. "Pretty lady. If I had been working, I would remember her. Leonard? You were working yesterday. You remember this lady?" he asks, handing my phone off to him.

Leonard grabs at my phone, pretending to have butter fingers, dropping it, and catching it at the last second. A gold crown gleams under the fluorescent light as a malicious grin appears on his face— making me happy about Gertie beating him up. "Nope," he says, tossing the cell carelessly onto the counter before turning his back to us, busying himself. He remembers. I could tell by the split-second look of recognition that crossed his face before he discarded my phone. He could be best friends with her and would not admit it to me. I resist the urge to ask him how his back is feeling.

"Useless," Thomas coughs the word. Then he mouths, "See what I mean?" Eli clears his throat, in danger of getting choked on his drink again. "I suppose you want to look at the camera footage. Come on then," Thomas says, turning toward the back room. "But you," he points at Eli, "need to leave your drink out here. I don't need you spewing it all over the office."

Eli sits his Icee behind the counter and trails after us into the office. I need to remember to suggest he toss the drink and get a new one before we leave. There is a good chance Leonard will spit in it.

Thomas quickly brings up the surveillance video and fast forwards until Tara's face comes into the frame. Leonard was the cashier who waited on her. They spoke long enough for him not to have forgotten her as easily as he feigned.

"She bought gas. Can you pull up footage of the pumps?" I ask.

A few swipes of his fingers at the keyboard and the video of Tara filling her van with fuel comes up. Hers was the only vehicle at the pumps with nobody else in sight. Thomas zooms in on the van and we note there are no other passengers. Whatever she discovered yesterday, did not happen while here.

This is one drawback of an investigation. Spending time chasing down anything that could be a clue, whereby wasting time on things that turn out to seem unimportant. But you don't know until you check. As Art taught me, there is no useless information when working a case. The thing you are looking at may not solve the case, but it can be important in showing who the person is. There is nothing important about Tara fueling her vehicle, but the timestamp on the footage helps piece her day together.

Tara did not seem anxious or hurried in the video, which

indicates whatever happened probably did not occur before her stop here. It appears she was having a typical Saturday. One in which she was child free for the evening, so she decided to run errands and picked up Chinese take-out for an evening at home.

When her van exits the parking lot, she heads North, probably to the Chinese restaurant. That will be my next stop.

twenty

THERE ARE two Chinese restaurants in Justice. Most locals know that the one Tara ordered from yesterday has the best food. The buffet is always piping hot and fresh. Whereas the other restaurant usually has tepid, stale food, along with a rating by the Health Inspector just high enough for them to remain in business— which isn't nearly enough stars to make the fare enticing to me.

Eli parks the car. I decided when we left the convenience store, to let him have control of the driver's seat again. As much as I like driving the car, it's dicey allowing myself that much power at the press of a foot. He seemed very relieved when I admitted him to the driver's side.

The door of the restaurant makes a chiming sound as we enter. We walk past gumball and prize machines along our way to the front counter. The lady behind the register looks up, smiles, and asks, "You want buffet?"

Eli looks to me and says, "I could eat."

"Two please," I say. Eli quickly makes his way over to the line for the hot food. I bring Tara's photo up on my phone, show it to the woman and ask, "Do you recognize this lady?"

She briefly glances at the photo. "You a cop?"

"No, I'm not a cop."

"Sorry, no help."

It takes a couple of waves of my arm to catch Eli's attention and motion him over. In a few quick steps, he is standing beside me, with an empty plate and fork in his hands. "Yeah?"

"Will you show her your badge? She won't answer my questions because I am not a cop." I can see he is weighing his options about whether to do so. Finally, he hands the plate off to me, sticks the tines of the fork in his mouth, and produces his badge.

The lady inspects the badge before turning and opening one of the swinging doors to the kitchen. She yells into the kitchen, in her native language. A young man appears, wiping his hands on a white apron. She speaks to him briefly and then they both walk over.

The young man says, "Her English isn't great, so I will help translate."

"Thanks. Can you tell me anything about this lady? Did you see her yesterday?"

Her words come out in a rush as the young man translates. "She is a regular. A crazy lady. She was here yesterday."

"Crazy lady?" I ask.

"Yes. I asked her if she wanted her usual when she came in. She orders the same thing every Saturday. She acted like I was crazy, but she is the crazy one who cannot remember what she eats every week. Same thing, every week, but usually has it delivered. Then she could not remember where she always has her food delivered." She smacks the side of her head for emphasis. "She orders, not her usual, and leaves. Then a couple hours later, calls, orders her usual and we deliver." She slaps her forehead.

"Can you tell me where you delivered the food?"

"Motel. Always Motel. Every Saturday, Pu-Pu Platter, six-o'clock."

I glance at Eli who does not look the least bit surprised at the information. "Thank you very much," I say, dropping a ten in the tip jar.

We fill our plates and have a seat at one of the booth tables. Eli has gone back for seconds before I have eaten more than a few bites. I take a sip of my sweet tea and say, "You did not text Jack." A statement rather than a question.

He shrugs. "He already knows all this stuff. Other than her alarm going off yesterday." He winces as he brings his gaze to mine, realizing he may have revealed something he wasn't supposed to tell me.

Jack's knowledge of the information is no surprise to me. But Eli doesn't know that. "Hmm. Don't you think Jack is being a little *extra* by not telling me anything. I mean, I just wasted my day and yours."

"Not at all." He places his fork in the stack of noodles on his plate, and then crosses his hands while looking at me. He resembles a parent who is about to lecture a toddler about the reason they cannot have any more sugar to eat. "If you're busy asking questions then you are busy staying out of trouble." I raise a brow at him, roll my hand and urge him to continue. "Let's say hypothetically, you already knew all this stuff. You figure out who tried to murder Tara and you track them down. Now let's say you call Jack. *But* this person is about to get away before Jack can get there, so you dive in headfirst taking matters into your own hands, and land yourself in a dangerous situation."

I wallow my eyes at him dramatically. I do not know which is more offensive— his mansplaining, or him making me sound as if I am an albatross Jack must wear around his neck. He didn't say anything I haven't already discerned on my own.

Still, I press him. "Oh really? Do you realize if Jack would keep me apprised of the case, I would have no reason to investigate on my own?"

He snorts a laugh. "Yeah, right. Even I know you better than that."

"So, Jack doesn't think Colt is guilty?" If he thinks I may encounter someone dangerous then he is obviously convinced Colt may be innocent.

"I couldn't say. He looks guilty to me." His face flushes. "What I mean is if you look at the evidence, it would seem so."

"That's exactly why I am investigating," I say, lightly smacking the table, driving my point home.

"Look, I get it. But, with his fingerprints all over the weapon and everything else about the situation, it's a no brainer." His flushed face goes pale as he realizes he just divulged something that I had no knowledge of— Colt's fingerprints on the weapon. He reaches for his drink while studying my face to notice if I picked up on the piece of information. I avert my eyes and reach for an eggroll.

I'm curious if other prints were found. I know Eli will not tell me if I ask. Daphne would probably tell me, but I would never put her in that position. Calling Colt is out of the question, as I am left wondering why his prints are on the weapon.

Surely, he did not... I cannot even let the thought form without feeling guilt surging through my core. No. I know he did not commit this crime. I can still see the image of him in shock, vomiting over a trashcan at the motel. The only plausible explanation for his prints being on the weapon is he must have touched it when he found Tara, probably while he was in shock and not thinking clearly. Perhaps, he never considered the possibility that anyone would think he was her attacker, therefore he did not think twice about touching it. *"This is not what it looks like. I didn't do this, Elle. You know I didn't do this!"*

His words replay through my memory like a bad song. Through his shock, he knew enough to know it looked bad, even to me. Why would he have touched the weapon?

"I guess you want to go to the motel when we leave here?" he asks, changing the subject, drawing me away from my thoughts.

"No, I don't think so. I mean, it would be a waste of time." I lift my shoulder in a shrug. Besides, Jack is right. I should leave the investigating up to him. Plus, I'm tired from the pointless errands of today. Need to get home to my dog." I take a bite of the eggroll and drop my gaze to my plate. He has the good graces to appear somewhat repentant when I raise my eyes again.

I certainly want to pay a visit to the motel. Just not with Eli in tow. And I want to view the footage from the security cameras that I installed in Tara's home to see what happened when her alarm was triggered yesterday, without him looking over my shoulder. Even if we were partners working this case together, it would seem we would be at odds with our goals. Him, convinced Colt is guilty, and me, who is convinced of his innocence.

It pains me to think Jack may be correct in thinking that I am too biased to see things regarding this case clearly. I will admit the evidence is stacked against Colt. If I looked at the situation from a stranger's viewpoint, I would think him most likely guilty. Which is why I need to keep digging. I seem to be the only person he has on his side who believes him.

Eli pulls in behind my Bronco to drop me off. I can tell he is relieved to be finished with our ride along. Our exchange resembles the ending of a very awkward first date.

"So... you know how you mentioned *Fight Club*?" he asks.

"Yeah."

"Do the same rules apply, as far as you not mentioning to Jack anything I may have let slip that I shouldn't have?"

"Of course," I smile. His breath of relief is audible as I open the door, tell him goodbye, and make my way to my vehicle.

I wait until his car is out of view before starting my own engine and pulling onto the street. I head in the direction of the motel.

twenty-one

I MAKE sure that I have money in my pocket before walking across the parking lot. I know from previous experiences that information from this establishment will cost you. When I step through the glass doors and make my way along the geometric patterned carpet, I am surprised to find Jared Rose behind the front desk. Jared is Gertie's grandson, who up until she went to live at the assisted living community, occupied her basement, getting high on weed and playing video games. Judging by the glazed eyes and Nintendo Switch in his hands, it looks like he is still high and still playing video games, just in a different location. He looks up from the handheld device and hops down off the stool he is sitting on.

"Sup, Elle? Fancy seeing you here."

"Hi Jared. I had no idea you work here. When did you start?"

"A few months ago. Sure does seem longer. Dad said I had to get out and get a job or get out of his house." I do not feel sorry for him. He is thirty years old. He's well past the age of joining the workforce. "You need a room?" he asks. The question sounds loaded with innuendos.

"No. Actually, I was needing to ask you some questions," I say, as I slide a twenty across the counter.

He pushes the faded green bill back in my direction. "Your money is no good here. What do you need?" His bloodshot eyes slide down and linger on my breasts.

I place my finger in front of his face and use it to guide his eyes back up to mine. He has the good grace to look embarrassed. "Were you working yesterday when Tara Daniels was attacked?"

"Yep. Stuck working every weekend."

"Did you see or hear anything?"

"Nope. Didn't even know anything happened until I saw the ambulance zoom in."

"Was she a regular? And if so, have you ever seen anyone other than Colt here with her?"

"I've seen her here plenty. When I first started, she rented the room by the week. Always paid in cash and tips very well. Hadn't seen her in a while until yesterday. She seemed off yesterday. Like her cornbread wasn't done in the middle, if you know what I mean. Came back in a while after checking in, saying she forgot which room number was hers. You'd think she would remember since she always gets the same room."

"Hadn't ever seen Colt here, though," he continues. "Some other dude used to come by. Never got a good look at him. He always tried to be incognito, ball-cap pulled low, walking all slouchy with his head down. I could tell it was a dude. Oh, and he drove a sic Range Rover. Nothing incognito about it."

"Black with gold detailing?"

"Yep."

"Did you tell the Sheriff all of this?"

"Nope. Gary, the manager sent me home before they got here. Said he'd handle it." He shrugs.

"Did he not think his employees might need to speak to Law Enforcement considering a crime had been committed?"

He laughs. "Nah. He wanted to be the one to talk to them, *especially* because a crime had happened. They don't call this place a *No Tell Motel* for nothing. Money's the only thing that does talking around here." I nod my head in understanding.

"So, I guess you're in debt to me for a favor now?" he asks.

"Sure," I say, cautiously. "But nothing weird!" His gaze begins lowering to my chest again. I snap my fingers to gain his attention and his eyes swing back up to mine. "And nothing perverted!" His mischievous smile falters slightly. "On second thought, why don't you just take the twenty and we'll call it even."

He shrugs, picks the money up from the counter and mutters, "Harsh. Just so ya' know, I'd never ask you to do anything perverted. I mean," he places his forearms on the counter, leaning casually on it, "unless you wanted to." He winks. I pierce him with a withering glance, and he raises up. "Just kidding. Besides, I keep all my naughty thoughts of you locked up here," he taps the side of his head.

He isn't kidding. I find the thought of him having naughty thoughts of me clunking around in his skull cavity, repulsive.

"How many twenties to make those thoughts disappear? Or should I just knock them out of you?"

"No need to be *aggro*," he says, taking a step back in case I make good on knocking him on the head. Then he places his hand over his heart as if he has been wounded.

* * *

Every conversation I've had with someone about Tara makes her behavior seem more and more perplexing. I am left with more questions than answers, and led to think perhaps she does have some type of personality disorder. I pressed Jared further before leaving the motel. The other peculiar thing he mentioned was that one of the girls in the party room next to Tara's claims to have seen her leaving the room, not long before Colt or I arrived. The girl was at the door to her room, arms loaded with pizza boxes, while she waited for one of her friends to let her in. She noticed Tara leave her room, seemingly in a hurry, without so much as glancing at the girl. The girl did not pay attention to her getting into her vehicle or driving off. Other than that, no one heard or saw anything that afternoon. Where did Tara go? Why did she leave the motel and when did she return?

Why did she lie to me about her affair with Mark? Why did Mark lie about how many times he and Tara slept together? I have no personal connection to either one of them. I am nobody. Simply an investigator she hired to do a job. Perhaps it is as simple as the pair being ashamed of the affair.

When I pull in and park in front of my house, my thoughts are still tumbling through my mind. I open the voice memo app on my phone and make a recording of everything before forgetting. Then, I jog up the front porch steps and notice a small cooler sitting in front of the door with a note taped to the top.

I know you are working a big case and sometimes forget to eat when you get busy.
Enjoy.
Love, Granny

Then in different handwriting below Gran's words, Uncle Mike wrote, *don't forget to thank your favorite Uncle Mike for dropping it off. He's the best.*

I giggle after reading Mike's note. I pop the lid of the cooler open, revealing chicken and dumplings, along with dressing and all the works. That's my Grandmother, always thinking and worrying about others. This is the second Sunday that I have missed family dinner.

I open the door, swinging the cooler high into the air before Buddy can tackle me. "Hey boy," I say, catching him in a hug as he licks my face. "I've missed you. You want to go for a walk?" I ask. He jumps down from me and starts twirling in excitement. I set the cooler on the floor, open the door, and race Buddy up the gravel road.

twenty-two

BUDDY and I are now nestled on the couch after our lengthy walk and my shower. I pick up my MacBook from the coffee table and open it as I pull a cozy comforter over my lap. I click on the icon for the app bringing up the footage for the cameras that I installed in Tara's home. I promised her that she would be the only person to view the footage but considering the circumstances, I think she will forgive me.

Trying to put the pieces together is like working a puzzle without all the shapes. I have matched the edge pieces but everything in the middle seems to be missing. For a person who seemingly led a boring, mundane life, Tara's life is a paradox. It is hard enough to figure a person out based on their face-value, but when you throw well-kept secrets and hidden agendas into the package, it's nearly impossible.

I watch the footage from both her home and the motel several times. I notice a pair of gold hoop earrings on the bedside table in the motel room that I had not previously noticed. Tara was wearing her usual diamonds when she was attacked. The gold hoops seem odd and out of place but then again, perhaps the hoops are what Samantha would wear.

I slowly fast forward until my eyes grow heavy and I feel like a fog is settling over my brain. My eyelids droop closed, and I force them open. I finally give up, shut the MacBook and lie back on the couch, settling in for a nap. I am not certain how long it has been since I drifted off when I am awoken by Buddy. His excited barks as he jumps over the side of the couch and tramps toward the front door, tells me Jack must be here.

I make my way to the door, turn the deadbolt and let Jack in. He doesn't have a key for the new lock, and he may never muster the courage to ask for one. I will eventually give him a replacement key but for now, I feel it is best to keep this arrangement. I may have forgiven him for his showdown in my kitchen/yard with Colt, but I still haven't forgotten the incident.

He is greeted by Buddy's dancing and joyous howl of "whoo-whoo". He drops to one knee, giving the dog the petting and attention that he is craving, quickly following with a hello kiss for me.

My neck is stiff from the odd angle at which I was lying on the couch. I rub at the tightness then tilt my head to the side. Jack takes the opportunity to place a kiss on the exposed column of my neck. He then rids himself of his holster and belt. He places them on an overturned box that is temporarily serving as a pitiful excuse for a sofa table. I did not have much furniture when I purchased the house. I am taking my time and being choosy in accumulating pieces to fill my space.

"What did you get up to today, other than carjacking Eli?" he asks as he sinks down onto the sofa beside me.

I toss a throw pillow at him. "As if you don't already know."

He smirks proudly, causing me to feel indignant. That feeling is short lived as he pulls my foot onto his lap and starts massaging the arch. I am tempted to purr like a kitten as his fingers work their magic. The stress of the last couple of days temporarily melts to the back of my mind.

I should remain indignant. I should be offended often and thoroughly at Jack's overbearing protectiveness. It isn't only Jack. Art and Teeny are just as guilty of the same behavior. Before my abduction by the Butchers, I would become enraged thinking that they considered me incapable of taking care of myself. After, I became more forgiving. If not for their watchful vigilance, I would most likely be dead. I learned it isn't that they consider me inept, it is because they consider me reckless. I suppose I can be reckless. I don't mean to be. Sometimes things just happen. Opportunities and circumstances present themselves. Things seem like a great idea at the time but quickly spiral out of my control.

"I can't stay long. I just came to take a shower and catch a nap."

"Uncle Mike dropped off leftovers from Gran's. Do you want me to heat them for you?"

"Do you even have to ask? You know if your Granny cooked it, I want to eat it."

I smile as I make my way to the kitchen to warm up a plate of chicken and dumplings, dressing, mashed potatoes and green beans.

He washes his hands at the sink then slides onto a stool at the island, the only seating in the kitchen. The room is the only one that has been fully remodeled. The custom-made island is new yet looks like it is original to the home. The massive brick hearth on the other side of the room that was hidden away behind layers of sheetrock is now exposed; the bricks that were in disrepair, lovingly restored. An emerald- green, double oven Hallman gas range is a showstopper and is my only modern splurge. I consider the range an investment.

I purchased the home from Tom Barnes, a state trooper who is a close friend of Jack's. He had big dreams of becoming like Chip Gaines when he bought the property. But with three children under the age of five and a wife who grew tired of him spending every off-work hour at the property remodeling, he realized it was causing discord within his own home. When the interest on his loan came due, he decided to cut his losses and sell. Jack knew I would jump at the opportunity, and I was able to purchase for a fair price before the property was even put on the market.

One look at the kitchen when I viewed the house was all it took to make me fall even more in love with the home and property. I remember dancing with my Gran in her kitchen when I was a child to Van Morrison. And then with my Mama in our kitchen to Tom Petty. I knew this was the type of kitchen made for dancing in and I can picture myself doing so with my own children, someday.

The microwave dings. I retrieve the hot plate and slide it across the island toward Jack. "I spoke with Billy's dad. Looks like Tara must have accidentally set off her alarm yesterday," he says.

I'm surprised he is offering any morsel of information. First a foot rub and now this. He knows this is information that I am already aware of, but still. "I know. After speaking to Billy, I watched the video footage from her house," I say.

"How did you... you know what, I don't want to know." He raises his hands, absolving himself of guilt for having knowledge of something I may have done that I should not have.

"Relax. I installed the cameras. I have access to the footage. I would like to show you something from the video after you eat." I grab a bowl of coleslaw from the fridge and scoop some onto his plate.

"Okay," he says, blowing on a dumpling. "Get the video. I'll watch it while I eat."

I retrieve the laptop from the living room, bring up the footage and spin the MacBook around until it is facing him. We watch as Tara enters her house carrying reusable shopping bags, and rushes to sit them on the kitchen table. Her alarm goes off. She ends up on the phone with who we can confirm is William Johnson at Justice Security. She then tosses a few refrigerator items into the otherwise pristine fridge and makes her way back out the door. She does not reset the alarm as she leaves.

He gives me a look of confusion. "Is that it? What am I supposed to be seeing?"

"Okay, hear me completely out before you say anything." He nods his head in agreement as he scoops mashed potatoes into his mouth. "Celeste picks Emily up around two-thirty. Tara goes shopping, fuels her vehicle then goes to pick up her food order— where the lady tells her she orders the same thing every Saturday and has it delivered to the motel at six-o'clock. She then rushes home in such a hurry that she just tosses her items into the refrigerator haphazardly— her normally orga- nized fridge, and she leaves without even setting her security system. Then she rushes to get to the motel well before six, where she claims to have forgotten her room number." I take a deep breath before continuing. "I think someone has been pretending to be Tara and she figured it out. Probably this person who Colt knows as *Samantha*. That would explain everything, including the text saying that she figured out who her intruder was."

He looks skeptical. "Or— now hear *me* out," he says, holding up his fork. "She was having an off day. Everyone has days that they just cannot think straight. She was in a rush to get to her lover at the motel. Maybe she was nervous because she has more than one lover and one found out about the other. Identity theft happens all the time, usually from behind a computer. I mean, someone would have to be spot-on to physically pull it off and what are the odds of that?" He shrugs, as if his explanation much simpler than my theory.

"I knew you would think it's crazy," I say, disappointment evident in my voice. I should have kept my theory to myself.

"I do not think it's crazy. But, Elle, how many people have someone walking around who looks enough like them to fool even the people they know? In a town this small? You said her mother had a mental illness. Maybe it is something hereditary that is affecting Tara now and that explains why she could have been pretending to be Samantha."

"Split personality?" I perk up slightly. "That has entered my mind, but I don't think dissociative identity disorder is hereditary. But maybe she has some type of psychotic disorder that is? " I open my mouth ready to mention the girl claiming to have seen Tara leaving the room in a hurry when he interrupts me.

"Or..." he says, drawing out the word before wiping his mouth with a paper towel and walking around the island. He places his hands on my shoulders, gently forcing me to focus on him. "Maybe she just gets off on it."

I pull back slightly. "That still doesn't explain why she hired me. Why go through the trouble if someone truly wasn't inside her home without her knowledge?"

He drops his hands and leans back against the counter. "Attention? Or you said someone had referred her to you. Did she ever say who? Maybe she has a reason to want to mess with you. Or maybe she has been getting a thrill from it. Seems like the whole family has issues. They hate each other but they love to be around each other. They cannot stand each other but they sleep with one another. They turn a blind eye to each other's affairs. Who knows what else they may be hiding. I think Tara is Samantha and she gets a weird kick out of being her, but she knows exactly what she is doing. So no, I don't think you are crazy. But no matter what reason she had for being Samantha, if that's the case, someone *else* still tried to kill her. I do think that perhaps you may be overreaching in order to try to prove Colt's innocence."

"I am not overreaching." I measure my words, controlling my temper. "I'm trying to make sense of everything, not just for Colt but for Tara, too."

"You are not responsible for either one of them," he says, with a level of patience in his voice that he reserves for when he doesn't want me to misinterpret what he is saying and become angry. His hands come back up to sit on my shoulders before he softly places them on the sides of my face. "Tara was having an affair with Colt. Maybe she had another lover who attacked her. But Colt and *only* Colt's prints are all over the weapon." Mentioning the prints without my bringing it up is another surprise. "If someone else is responsible, they cleaned up after themself. Or maybe it really was Colt, and you don't know him as well as you thought. Did Tara know about your friendship with him?"

"No. Why would she?" I could argue that I do know Colt as well as I think but the reminder would only make Jack think of how I know Colton in every aspect. Aspects that neither one of us wants to think about. Or perhaps he would think of our conversation when he insisted that we should talk through things— Me telling him Colt is the person I would call if I needed to get rid of a body. I was joking, of course. Mostly. But he may remember and wonder if Colt really is a person that nobody knows with a secret identity hidden under the easy-going persona. A secret identity like he thinks Tara has. The same faint twinge of guilt from earlier shadows my mind as I think of how for a split second, I questioned my certainty about Colt's innocence. No, it wasn't Colt, I remind myself. I know deep down in my heart that it wasn't him.

"It's a valid question. Perhaps, she found out Colt has been stalking her, and wanted to show you in person so you would believe her because she knows you are friends."

I am confused. Earlier, I convinced myself that Jack thinks Colt is innocent. I suppose I was wrong. "Are you serious? Don't you find it odd that his prints are the only ones on the weapon? I mean, come on, it's a motel room. We both know the cleaning staff isn't *that* thorough." I look at his expression intently. He breaks eye contact. "My God. You are going to arrest him, aren't you?" That explains the foot massage and the generous offer of information without my asking for it. He has been trying to create calm before the storm arrives that he thinks his words will cause.

He turns his face away from me before swinging his gaze back. "We are hoping Tara wakes up tomorrow and can tell us what happened. If she doesn't then I must do my job, Elle. I haven't arrested him yet, because I want to find the truth as badly as you. Once I do arrest him, it starts a clock, legal wise."

He expects me to be angry. He has braced himself for my reaction. "Of course. I understand," I say, surprising him. I am disheartened by the situation but not disillusioned enough to be oblivious to the facts.

"You do?" he asks. His voice is laced with suspicion. Disbelief flits across his face.

"I do. I know you will do everything to find the truth. Just as you know, I will also." He starts to open his mouth, but I quickly replace his words with a kiss. He draws me in, forgetting whatever he was on the verge of saying.

He deepens the kiss, distracting my mind from everything troubling it. It is a welcome relief from the thoughts of Tara battling for her life, Emily's tear-filled eyes when speaking of her mother, and Colt being arrested. He moans softly as I sink into his embrace. I can feel his heart beating steadily against mine. That's Jack, steady like the heart beating in his chest. Steady enough to love me despite my faults. I yearn for him to make me forget the bad things for a while longer.

He does.

twenty-three

I MISSED the morning dawning by a couple of hours, an unusual occurrence when I am stressed about something. Perhaps, it was my subconscious relaxing as a result of giving up hope for Tara's case. All the questions have been asked, people profiled, and timelines worked out. There seems to be nothing left to do other than wait for Tara to wake up.

I chafe against the thought of not finding the truth. There comes a point when you must be honest with yourself. You must remind yourself that doing the same thing repeatedly and expecting a different outcome, may make you seem crazy — or at the least, cause you to drive yourself insane. I reached that point last night. I have gone over everything again and again, yet I am still at a loss. Some cases are unsolvable. There are storage rooms all over the world, filled with boxes containing cold case files. Up until now, I have never experienced such, so perhaps, I am due a loss.

Unless something new emerges such as a detail forgotten or someone coming forward with the truth, Tara is the only person with the answers. Even if she wakes, it is unpredictable what her mental state will be. She may not be in a condition to disclose the truth. She may not even be able to remember what happened.

I have yet to check into Tara's birth mother and learn of her family history. It seems rather pointless to do so now. Even if Tara imagined an intruder or has some type of mental illness, it was impossible for her to self-inflict the injury that she sustained. No, someone else did that. Someone other than Colt.

Last night, I tried to think as a stranger would when looking at this case. The evidence proves Colt's guilt. But I know something a stranger doesn't. Other than knowing him incapable of committing the crime, I also know he is smart. If Colt was responsible for hurting Tara, he would not have gotten caught. He would have had enough wits to wipe his prints from the weapon and flee the scene. One could argue perhaps he would have if I had not shown up. But when I got there, he was in shock, cradling Tara's head. The only way Colt could have committed such an act is if he were in a blind rage. And if that was the case, he would not have cared enough to stay with her.

He may have a history of getting into a drunken brawl or two, but he isn't violent. He never has been. And life has given him plenty of reasons to be angry. He just doesn't possess the meanness that makes someone a violent person.

I have known him since we were children. For so long that I can remember when we were both too young to think of being boyfriend and girlfriend as anything other than gross. There was always a connection between him and I, even at such a young age. It seems like the universe planted us in the same town because we were meant to be a part of each other's lives.

Colt's father was a long-haul truck driver. His mother was a beautiful woman who liked to step out on his dad while he was gone for a week at a time, hauling goods across the country. One day, she stepped out and decided she wasn't coming home again. She left young Colton with his dad, got herself a new husband, and started another family. It must have been devastating for Colt to see his mother in town later with his half-siblings after she abandoned him. It was as if that was a past life for her, one she wanted to forget. Colton being part of that life was forgotten by her, too.

His dad checked out after that. Even when he was home, he was absent, by being passed out drunk in his recliner. By this point Colt was ten years old and basically raising himself. His dad made sure the bills were paid, and Colt had money for food and things that he needed. Other than that, there was no parental guidance. His dad wasn't a bad man. He didn't abuse Colt in any way. He just wasn't present. He was neglectful due to his own sadness.

Colt could have easily taken the wrong path in life. He could have gotten himself into trouble during his unsupervised years. He didn't, though. Neither did he become dark and broody. Instead, he hid his sadness behind a mask of smiles and jokes. He was the daredevil, fun-loving kid that everyone wanted to be around. Everyone except the two people who should have wanted to be there— his mother and father.

It was my mother who made sure Colt had a decent, home-cooked meal to eat. My grandmother who made sure he attended Sunday School often enough that he wouldn't forget God. His mother may have forsaken him, but Jesus never would. When he was old enough to play football, it was my uncles who showed up to cheer him on from the stands.

I suppose this is the reason Mama has always had a soft spot for him. Either that or because he has the type of personality that makes you love him. She was disappointed when I married Liam, hopeful when Colt and I started dating after my divorce, then disappointed again when we broke up. Being in a relationship with Jack has helped to ease the letdown she felt when she realized Colt and I would never marry and make beautiful grandbabies for her.

Now, Mama's disappointment lies in the same realm as Jack's. Much like him, she wishes that I would sit home behind a keyboard all day as a journalist or spend the entirety of my time publishing books. I am stuck working local cases while Art stays busy tracking down things for lawyers in Louisville. There aren't many horrific crimes that take place in Justice, at least not many that people know about. I could probably solve most of my investigations by hanging around my mother's salon. Much of her clientele are more than happy to share the gossip about everything they know. The one time of getting abducted and almost murdered was all it took for her to wish she had never allowed me to be Art's protégé during my formative years. Possibly, Art is starting to wish the same. He doesn't like being on *Sweet Annie's* bad side.

I take a sip of my coffee and glance out the kitchen window. The sun is finally making its display from behind a mountain in the distance. I rinse my mug out at the sink and place it in the dishwasher before opening the back door to call Buddy inside. He barrels into the room, leaving muddy footprints across the floor in his wake. I grab my mop and set to work, quickly cleaning the mess. I am supposed to meet Mama for breakfast this morning and I do not want to keep sweet, menopausal Annie waiting.

* * *

I pull in and park next to the diner, eight minutes late, preparing myself for a lecture regarding punctuality from my mother. To my surprise, her Buick isn't here. I know she did not park at her salon and walk to the diner, because I drove past there on my way here.

Finally at sixteen minutes past nine, she pulls in. "Have you been waiting long?" she asks.

I debate on lecturing her about punctuality, but I decide against it due to the mood swings that seem to come upon her out of nowhere. She has a pleasant look upon her face, so I won't take a chance on ruining her seemingly decent mood, even for the sake of a joke about her running late.

"No, not at all."

"Good. However, if you had, it would be payback for all the times you have kept me waiting. Your birth included."

Don't antagonize her, I remind myself. I reply, "I am sorry for all of those times, Mama." This response seems to satisfy her. I silently let out a breath of relief. Lately, when she has been in these moods, it is for the sole purpose of picking an argument. The wrong reply will send her off on a rant, with sweat dripping down the sides of her forehead causing her hair to stick to her face and neck. I can't say that if I was dealing with hot flashes that I wouldn't be brewing for a fight either.

I always thought I must have inherited my temper from my dad, but lately, I think it was probably passed down from her. Apparently, she must have been a late bloomer in the temperament department due to hers not showing up until her late forties. But it's here now and has a very short fuse most of the time. I have been googling menopause, wondering how long it lasts. The answers are disheartening. Years. Sometimes up to fourteen years. And the symptoms are horrible. This research has made me more empathetic of her plight. If I am being honest, empathetic, mostly because I know what goes around comes around and I am not looking forward to insomnia, night sweats and brain fog.

She began carrying a small, battery-operated fan in her

pocketbook, wearing waterproof mascara, and pulling her hair back into a ponytail. The ponytails confirm that the heat demons assailing her are serious business. She has always fussed at me for choosing to wear my hair pulled back into a ponytail or a messy bun, instead of taking the time to style it to its full potential. Her theory—the only time you should wear your hair so casually is during a workout or other activity where you need your tresses out of your way, and if you are blessed with hair, you should show it off as your crowning glory.

I hold the door for her, and we enter the diner. Out of habit, I head for the usual booth that Thomas and I occupy most every Saturday. She tugs on the back of my Free People shirt, and I can hear the seam threaten to rend as she yanks me in the opposite direction. The top is supposed to look worn, comfy and lived in, not ripped by her aggressive pull.

"Let's sit here," she instructs. "I don't like that booth. The duct tape always sticks to my clothes."

I wordlessly slide onto the bench across from her, bringing the menu up in front of my face, as if I do not have every item memorized.

Jennifer saunters over to our table, looking much more relaxed than she does during my visits with Thomas. "Morning, Annie. Hey, Elle."

"Good morning," Mama and I both reply.

"You ladies know what you're having today?" she asks as she sits two coffee cups on the table and fills them.

I nod to my mother to order first. "I'll have scrambled eggs, whole wheat toast, turkey bacon, and a fruit bowl on the side."

"And for you? The usual breakfast?" Jennifer asks, looking in my direction, pen poised.

"I'll have the same as her." I say, playing it safe, not wishing to get my mother started on nutrition this morning.

Jennifer's brows furrow in confusion at my refusal of the stack of pancakes that I usually order with a side of bacon. She doesn't say anything about it though, as she leaves the table to hang her order slip on the carousel for the cook. She's probably just happy I am not changing my order up like Thomas does.

"No pancakes?" Mama asks. "Are you on a diet?"

"No. Just trying to take a lesson from you and eat healthier."

"Hmm. I give that until lunchtime." She has no idea how right she is. "How is the lady in the coma?" she asks, changing the subject.

"Still in an induced coma. They plan on trying to bring her out of it this afternoon. Hopefully all goes well."

"Amen to that. And poor Colton. I cannot imagine what he must be going through. For anyone to think that angel could do something like this, is unfathomable to me." The soft spot she has for him is coming to light in this conversation.

"Yes, unfathomable," I say, but I would never refer to him as an angel. He is far too mischievous to be considered angelic.

"Oh, I forgot to tell you, my friend Donna, the nurse practitioner, you remember her?" I nod my head. "Well, she is going to start doing Botox parties at the salon once or twice a month. You should really consider getting some as a preventative. The way you frown sometimes, you're sure to wrinkle early. I'm planning on getting some to tackle these pesky wrinkles I am starting to notice. I can't believe you hadn't told me I am starting to look old."

"Okay, first of all, I do not frown as much as you think. Certainly not enough to cause premature wrinkling. Second, you don't have any wrinkles for me to have needed to point out," I say, as Jennifer sets our plates on the table. She smiles, tops off our coffee and wordlessly disappears.

"You can't tell me you hadn't noticed," she says, pointing

to the area around one of her eyes. She ignores her food as I slather ketchup on my scrambled eggs, spread butter on my toast, then top it with strawberry jam.

"Again, I don't see anything," I say, around a bite of toast. She rolls her eyes then points out her imagined fine lines and wrinkles again. This goes on for several minutes— Her scooting closer to the light of the window, turning her head this way and that, as the shadow of a corndog painted on the window falls across her profile— Me, squinting at her as she tries to show me something that isn't there. I lean across the table to get a closer look, telling her, "no, I still don't see it." Finally, I grow exasperated. "Gee whiz, Mama, there is nothing there. No fine lines. No wrinkles. Maybe you need to get your eyesight checked. If you were to google the *Fountain of Youth*, it would probably show a picture of you." As soon as the words leave my mouth, I'm on high alert. It's okay to tell her she looks young but to tell her that her eyesight may be faltering, could be a different story.

"You really think so?"

"Absolutely." And I mean it. She is a gorgeous woman who looks years younger than her age. She stays in great physical shape, eats healthy and was blessed with good genes. I can only hope those same genes are dominant in my DNA. Her eyes gloss over with tears, and she becomes weepy. The waterproof mascara is a smart idea, I suppose. This is a new mood swing that she has not experienced in front of me, until now. I am uncertain of how to proceed. I swallow hard, forcing the turkey bacon down my throat, hoping this isn't my last meal.

"Oh, Elizabeth, my baby girl. You always know the perfect thing to say." She covers my hand with hers and gives it a loving squeeze. "I'm sorry for being so emotional and moody lately."

Now, I am even more confused. "You haven't been that

bad," I lie. Sometimes I think a little, white lie is necessary. I look at her plate of untouched food, wishing she would eat quickly so this mommy and me time would come to an end. Not that I do not enjoy spending time with her. I always look forward to it. Just not as much lately. It is like having someone blindfold you and place you in front of two big boxes. One of them is full of fuzzy, lovable puppies to pet. The other biting spiders and mouse traps. Choose wrong and it is going to hurt.

For the rest of our meal, she is back to being the normal, pleasant, lovable mama that I know. This causes me to not wish our breakfast time away quickly anymore.

twenty-four

"I HAVE time to walk to the coffee shop for an iced coffee before my first client. Want to join me?" Mama asks.

"Sure," I say, always agreeable to iced coffee, and wanting to spend time with her while she is her normal self. She loops her arm through mine and down the sidewalk we go, admiring the fall decorations.

The man is back on the ladder this morning, with the lady directing him "higher" today, rather than left to right.

He backs down the ladder with excessive force, stomping on the rungs, causing the ladder to clang and sway. "Maybe you should do it yourself since you know exactly what you want!" An argument ensues and I wonder if the next time I walk past, it won't be his corpse that I see hanging from the side of the brick building in place of the skeletons he took down last week.

We amble down the street, giggling when we get out of earshot of the theatre. Coming up on the barber shop now, I see the group of men sitting outside, participating in their daily ritual. More than a few raucous laughs drift up the street. They are probably telling dirty jokes then going through the farce of acting like perfect gentlemen when someone comes within earshot. Among them, I see Leonard Shipley. He came and went at the diner this morning before I arrived. I was grateful for that. If someone is shooting the evil eye at you during your breakfast, I feel certain you will have digestive issues that day.

The men wearing hats on their heads, tip them as we walk by, greeting us. "Mornin' ladies." All except Leonard. He is no gentleman. He smiles at my mother then sticks a middle finger in the air as a greeting for me. Mama sees it from the corner of her eye. She unloops her arm from mine and walks backward three steps as if she is preparing to do the moon walk. *Uh oh*, I think. He has kicked a hornet's nest and is about to be stung by Mama-Two-Point-0.

"Did you just shoot my daughter the bird?" she asks him. His jaw goes slack. I can tell he is not sure of what he is supposed to say— Confess to the angry lady and take his licks, or confirm he is a liar in front of everyone by saying he did not.

"It is fine Mama. Let's go." I say, tugging on her purse. And it is fine. I am not offended by Leonard's gesture. He is harmless. My mother has never had to deal with issues such as slashed tires and phallic images drawn on her car, or she would realize this is nothing to sweat. Besides, if him greeting me with a hillbilly howdy each time I see him is the price to pay for witnessing Gertie, the geriatric warrior, opening a can of whoop ass on him, I will happily endure it.

"No, it isn't fine, Elizabeth," she says, huffing and yanking her pocketbook away from my hand. "Maybe you should have some of these other fellas teach you that is not the way a gentleman acts. Your mother is a fine lady, and I know you weren't raised to behave like that. You should be ashamed of yourself." I guess we are going to pretend she didn't hold up traffic while repeatedly giving a delivery truck driver the one finger salute last week— Something her own mother did not raise *her* to do. "You listen to me, Leonard Shipley, if I ever see or hear of you disrespecting my daughter again, you will find yourself in a mess that no lawsuit can help you with."

The men are acting nervous. She has put them in an awkward position, especially by referring to them as gentlemen. They are probably wondering if they should intercede on their pal's part, or if they should take up for the lady. They are watching, mouths hanging agog, some of them trying to suppress a laugh. One of them seems mesmerized as he pinches tobacco from his snuff can and stuffs it behind his lower lip.

Leonard's face is now the motley shade of red that a person's countenance becomes when they are torn between indignation and embarrassment. He starts to open his mouth then he just as quickly clamps it shut again. Smart move.

"In other words, I will kick your ass," she says, enunciating each word. "Now, apologize like you should."

It is a moment before he says anything. I can tell there is a wrestling match going on inside his head between what he wants to say and what he was told to say. Finally, he mumbles, "Sorry," insincerely. She narrows her eyes at him, slicing him with a dangerous look. "Sorry, *ma'am,*" he says, almost choking on the words.

I can see she is not satisfied but decides to let this pass as an apology. "Thank you," she says. "Now was that so hard?" She smiles sweetly at him before turning and continuing her path toward the coffee shop. The *gentlemen* wait until we are a respectable distance away before they start cackling with laughter.

When we leave the coffee shop, I try to convince her to walk up the other side of the street back to the diner, but she was having no part of that. We parade past the barber shop, her head held high, and my face slightly flushed with embarrassment. The men tip their hats once more as we pass. Leonard has vacated his spot on the bench and is nowhere to be seen. He is probably checking into getting a restraining order against my mother, to make himself look like a victim at some future time.

* * *

I arrive at the office around ten-thirty. Art had to make an impromptu trip to Louisville. If not for the out-of-town cases, his business would be struggling, much as it has in the past. Not too many residents of Justice can afford such things as private investigators. Many people prefer to handle their problems on their own, creating a whole slew of issues for Jack and his deputies. It is never fun to get in the middle of a domestic call, such as a scorned woman burning her husband's belongings on the front lawn. If she is angry enough to do that, there is no calming her down.

Teeny is occupying one of the desks, holding down the home front while Art is away. I have never been a person who likes to sit still in the same place for too long, so the addition of Teeny to the office has been a Godsend to me.

"Good morning," I say, as I deposit a half a dozen of chocolate chip muffins from the coffee shop on his desk.

"And a very good morning to you," he says, as he quickly scoops up a muffin, peeling the tulip shaped parchment paper from the side of the treat.

Sally peeks her head around the doorway of the small kitchen. "Morning, Elle." Her eyes land on the muffin Teeny is cramming into his mouth. "Teeny Tulane! That is not diet approved."

He scowls, continuing to shove more in his mouth. "It'd be

rude not to eat it after she went through the trouble of bringing 'em." Sally throws her hands up as if to say, *I give up.*

"Sorry. I did not know anything about a diet. How are you feeling, Sal?" I ask, changing the subject. Teeny seems grateful for the distraction. She focuses on me, and he reaches for a second pastry.

"Good as new. Well, as good as the old-new was for me to start with," she giggles. "I thought I would keep him company today, maybe get some shadowing in."

"I'm sure he appreciates that." Teeny averts his eyes. I'm sure he would appreciate it more if she did not have him on a diet.

"How is the Daniel's lady?" he asks.

"No better, but no worse. I spoke with Celeste before coming into the office. The swelling of Tara's brain hasn't reduced enough for her medical team to feel comfortable trying to bring her out of the induced coma. They are hopeful that in a couple more days, they can move forward with the plan of waking her." I got the sense that although this is not the best news, Celeste was bittersweet about it not happening today. Janie is at the hospital with Tara. Mark claims to be under the weather, leaving Celeste with the task of tending to Maverick and Emily today. Janie being the only person present at the hospital would not be an ideal situation, if anything went wrong while they tried to bring Tara out of her coma, and Celeste realizes that.

"Which means Jack will possibly arrest Colt today," I continue. Jack is under a lot of pressure concerning this case. He has the general public wanting him to make an arrest. But most of the urgency is coming from Mark and Janie Daniels, who are convinced of Colt's guilt. Combine that with him wanting to be certain he is arresting the right person— Well, I would not want to be in his shoes.

Once he makes an arrest, the clock will start ticking on burden of proof. Right now, the means, motive and opportunity all point to Colt. Jack should be more appreciative of my efforts to work on finding the truth, however stalled I may be at the moment. Instead, his insistence that I abstain from anything involving this investigation, remains steadfast. I must tread carefully, because I would not disregard the possibility of him locking me in a jail cell for interfering with his case. He would view it as his way of keeping me from harm's way, or more probable, as a means of keeping me *out of the way*.

"That's a shame. Pretty boy didn't do it," Teeny says.

I peer at him questioningly, confused by his response. He has never been a fan of Colt.

"I don't think he has it in him. I'm pretty good at reading people," Teeny says. "Pretty boy may have his faults but being a stone-cold attacker or killer, ain't one of them. Besides, the theory would be he was some sort of jilted lover. Let's face it, if he was into bashing ladies on the head who broke his heart, you would have already been a goner."

Sally's mouth is pulled to the side, contemplating, as she nods her head in agreement with Teeny. "I am happy to hear you think Colt is innocent but just so we are clear, I did not break Colt's heart. He was ready to settle down. I wasn't, so he broke things off and moved on." This is old news. I do not understand how they don't see our breakup as anything other than what it was. "He is the one who started seeing someone new."

"Or he was trying to put you in the position of wanting to settle down, by making you jealous," Sally adds, holding up a finger. "Either way, it's water under the bridge and you're still above ground."

Teeny says, "The only person he loves more than you, is

himself. And he likes himself too much to know how bad he would fair in prison. Like a lamb to the slaughter..."

I swallow hard as I hope soap on a rope isn't on my Christmas list for Colt this year, then shake my head in disagreement about Colt being madly in love with me. I decide to move on and change the subject. "What are both of your thoughts concerning the attack?"

Sally and Teeny look at each other, gauging who will speak first. As usual, Teeny is happy to present his theory. Most people take in his appearance and do not see past the rough exterior, ex-con. There is so much more to him. He is a literary junkie who knows no bounds of genres. He is particularly interested in psychology, criminology, or anything that helps him learn what makes people tick. He doesn't look like a scholar but if there is such a thing as reincarnation, I'm certain he was one in a past life.

"Well, everyone assumes this is a crime of passion since it took place somewhere where passion usually takes place. It's seeming like a crime of opportunity, considering the weapon. Perhaps it has nothing to do with a lover, but an argument that went wrong. Or maybe, a wrong place, wrong time scenario. Maybe a burglary that went awry. Was anything of hers missing that you could tell?"

I think back to Saturday in that motel room. "I don't think so. She was wearing her diamond studs that she seems to wear all the time. Her expensive watch was still on her wrist. Her purse and phone weren't in the room. I'm assuming they were in her van but would have to ask Jack to confirm that, which I would rather not do. If it was a robbery, her jewelry would have been taken."

"I get the sense her attacker might have been a woman," Teeny says. "I think if it was a man, he probably would have choked her or something along those lines."

"Hmm. That's an interesting theory. What if..." I say, wanting to mention my suspicions of identity theft, or the possibility Tara may have been leading a double life that could've led to her attack. I stop before continuing, worrying another person may think it sounds as ridiculous as it does to my own ears. "Never mind."

"No. Let's hear it," he says, rolling his hand, urging me to continue.

"Spill it," Sally says.

"Tara told me she was adopted, and her biological mother has some type of mental illness. What if it's hereditary. Obviously, she did not harm herself at the motel, but maybe her illness could have led to the people in her double life she seemed to be living. Or, and trust me I know this sounds unrealistic, what if someone has been impersonating her? That would explain everything, her odd behavior from Saturday, and the things that led up to her attack."

Teeny says, "Either way, you need to find out more about her biological mother, and Tara's own medical history. Maybe multiple personality disorder? I don't think it's passed down to children, but it may help you to have a better idea about Tara if you know her familial history. If you knew more about the reasons that she could've been leading a double life, it could help you figure out who she may have been involved with. And, as someone who had their identity used for something illegal, I don't think identity theft is a far stretch, at all. I have some contacts in San Francisco. Let me reach out and see if we can find out anything about her birth mother."

I am not surprised to learn he has contacts there. He seems to know people in every state of the country. People capable of retrieving information for him. I never ask about his associates or their methods of garnering info, because I'm not entirely sure their techniques are on the up-and-up. I feel his contacts will be going on a fool's errand. Adoption is something that is difficult to dig into, with sealed records and family secrets. It's easier to do today with the advances in technology, but still usually a dead-end road.

"Thanks, I appreciate your help," I say, as my phone buzzes with an incoming text from Jack.

> Wanted you to be first to know. Brought Colt in. And, yes his lawyer was here too. He could probably use a visit from a friend.

I send a reply, telling him I will be there shortly.

Sally has been quiet for the last few moments but finally she asks Teeny, "What makes you think it was a woman? Do you think men are smarter about their crimes?"

He shrugs. "Not at all. I just figured a man would probably be more hands-on. I feel like a woman would be more apt to lose it and commit a crime of passion. Ya know— hormones, fits of rage.... Probably from being on a diet."

I decide it is time for me to go before Sally has her own fit of rage. I wave goodbye to them as I step toward the door.

Colt has been arrested. It's official. Tick tock. The clock is ticking. Time for me to attempt to restart the engine on my stalled investigation.

twenty-five

ALTHOUGH IT ISN'T a long walk, I opt to drive to the Sheriff's Department, giving myself private time to sit in my Bronco and gather my thoughts before entering. This is such a mess. Where does this case go from here? The evidence hangs Colt for the crime. The only hope he has is for Tara to wake up and be capable of telling what happened. But what if she does wake up and can tell, but decides not to tell the truth? If she has been leading a double life, would she want to conceal who attacked her in order to hide what led to the attack? This is something that had not occurred to me, until now. It is a new worry to add to the list. Frustration brews inside me. I take a few deep breaths to calm myself before exiting my vehicle and heading inside.

The office is eerily quiet this morning. Almost as if a somber tone has settled over it. Colt is well liked by most people, and I am sure many are not happy about his arrest. Least of all, Daphne, whose eyes are pink rimmed as if she has fought back a few tears.

She steps around her desk when she sees me. She rubs my forearms and says, "This is terrible. I always thought if Colt ended up in jail, it would've been for tipping cows, and it would have happened while we were teenagers."

I smile as the memories spring to mind of the instances of harmless mischief our group of friends got into growing up. Colt was always the ringleader or the instigator. It usually started out with a dare by one of the other guys in our group. I always went along with an *that sounds like fun* attitude. Daphne was always the voice of reason and still is. She has a way about her, gentle, yet firm, supportive, yet truthful, and fun-loving, yet polished. She has always had the ability to solve problems, often before they even arise, which is why we always looked to her to be our voice of reason. And, why she runs this office without a squeak in the wheel.

"It's a lucky thing Fordy was sheriff back then and not Jack."

"True," she giggles. "Let's go to the kitchen and get something to drink before you talk to Colt."

I follow her converse clad feet across the tile floors to the kitchen at the back of the building. The smell of someone's leftovers having been heated in the microwave, mixes with acrid coffee and Mrs. Meyer's cleaning spray. If not for Daphne keeping the kitchen clean, I would refuse to drink anything from here. Ford's coffee cup looks like it hasn't been cleaned since his last year in office. She produces a couple of flavored coffee pods from a cabinet, pops them one at a time into the shiny Keurig, and brews two cups of fresh coffee.

"How is Colt?" I ask as she pulls the sleeve of her black and white polka dot blouse up her forearm.

"Angry. Understandably, but not helping matters any. At least he has the best lawyer. John Jessup."

"Wow. John. That is great news. My last conversation with him did not go well, and I had not thought to ask Jack who his attorney is." If I am ever in legal trouble and had to choose representation, it would be John Jessup. He is called J. J. by everyone who knows him. He is tenacious and a formidable opponent in the courtroom. He is esteemed by judges, his peers and law enforcement. He is one of very few lawyers that Jack respects.

"Jack is even angrier than Colt. Apparently, the Daniels' family has put their money into making this arrest happen. Jack was hesitant about arresting him to begin with, and you know he doesn't like having his hand forced. Words like bias were tossed around by higher ups, making him even angrier. Now he is going at this investigation a hundred miles an hour. He has half his staff interrogating the employees from the motel again. The other half scouring every half-brain idea they can think of for a lead."

I can imagine how insulted Jack became, being accused of partiality. Alleged favoritism because of his girlfriend being best friends with the accused. As if that would stop him from arresting Colt if he thought he was guilty.

"I would not have imagined Mark and Janie Daniels as being so adamant about Colt's arrest. I am not entirely sure about those two. They were out of town when the attack happened, but I cannot help but suspect they know more about things— at least Mark. That family has their secrets, to be sure," I say.

"No doubt. Maybe they have some secrets they want to keep hidden," she ponders. "Jack will find the truth."

"If at all possible," I say.

"Have you ever known of him not accomplishing what he sets his mind to? You and he are similar that way," she laughs. As usual she is a voice of reason.

Jack is out of the office, probably questioning Jared or another motel employee. Eli leads me down the hall. I glance over to him expecting to see a *I told you so* look on his face. Instead, he has a look of nervous regret.

"You can go ahead and have a seat in there. I'll go fetch him," he says, before going to escort Colt up from his cell located in the basement.

"Thanks." I step into the drab room, turning my back away from him, and prop a hip on the table. My foot starts tapping with impatience. Tap. Tap. Tap. The minutes creep by on the caged clock hanging from the wall.

Finally, Eli opens the door and Colt appears. He has a handcuff around one wrist, but the other bracelet hangs loose. I suppose officer Keith doesn't deem him a threat and is playing it loose with the rules. Perhaps, he had a change of heart about Colt being guilty. Or more likely, he knows Jack thinks Colt is innocent, and he agrees because of the hero type worship he has for Jack.

"Y'all know the rules," he says, without waiting for us to respond as he shuts the door. More, fast and loose with the rules. I appreciate the fact that he doesn't seem to think I would smuggle in illegal contraband or slip Colt a shiv.

Daphne was not exaggerating when she said Colt is angry. He seems to be enveloped by a shroud of fury. Gone is the shock and pallor of Saturday. In their place is righteous indignation that the rest of the world doesn't just take his word about his innocence.

"You know you don't have to sell me on your innocence," I say, after he finishes with a tirade. "What happened to taking John's advice and not discussing case related things with me?" I ask before he has the chance to start running Jack down for arresting him. I love Colt and I understand his frustration, but that would be an end to my visit.

He buffs his eye socket with the heel of his hand. "Yeah, I know. But who else am I supposed to talk to? J.J.? He just keeps saying trust the process. I have been and look where I am." He lifts his braceleted hand. "I always thought if you did nothing wrong, you would not have to worry about being accused. How stupid was I? That's not the way the world really works. Unlucky bastard that I am to be in the wrong place at the wrong time." He is beginning to appear spent.

The wrong place at the wrong time, I think about the conversation with Teeny earlier. I wonder if Tara was also, simply in the wrong place at the wrong time.

"Sorry, Elle. I know you understand. I just feel so... helpless." He turns his palms up, an indication he is empty of words.

"I know. J.J. is right. You need to trust the process. I know it must be hard to do, but I'm sure he and Jack are working hard to find out who really attacked Tara. As am I. Jack's not too happy about that, but..." I tilt my head to the side, squinching my nose up, and finally get a smile from him.

"Lord help the man who tries to tame you," he laughs. I am glad to have gotten the reaction from him.

"I'm not that bad." I roll my eyes.

"No. Not bad at all," he says, with a tenderness in his tone. He reaches across the table and takes my hand. "I know I must have hurt your feelings the other day when we talked. I shouldn't have listened to J.J. I know you would never do anything that wasn't in my best interest as far as my case is concerned."

I squeeze his hand. "It's okay. J.J. is great at what he does, and you did the right thing by listening to him. I would never compromise you, but people make mistakes. Maybe I could let something slip to Jack that I shouldn't. I believe you are innocent, and I would never intentionally betray you. Let's just leave it at that and follow John's advice about not discussing the case. Okay?"

He nods his head in agreement and applies pressure to my hand again. "I do have a couple of questions about Tara though," I say.

He pulls his hand away and nods again. "Okay."

"If it makes you uncomfortable, I don't have to ask."

"No. It's okay. I guess it is just still hard for me to wrap my head around her being *Tara*. Again, how stupid was I?"

"People lie, connive and trick others all the time. If they didn't the world would be closer to perfect." His mouth quirks up, attempting to smile, but he doesn't quite pull it off. "Did Tara, er, *Samantha* usually wear diamond stud earrings when you would see her?"

"Maybe. I'm not sure." He rubs his head, searching his memory. "Shit. Sorry. I can't remember."

"That's okay. Did you ever notice if she had a scar on the wrist of her watch hand?"

"A scar? Not that I ever saw. I do remember her having on her Apple Watch every time I saw her though."

Apple Watch. Perhaps that is significant. A smart watch is not the expensive gold watch, which I suspect is a Cartier, that I have seen on Tara's wrist each time. Maybe the smart watch is part of Samantha's persona. But Tara was wearing her gold watch when she was attacked. Again, the expensive timepiece remaining on her wrist, dispels the idea of a robbery.

"Why is that important? Was her jewelry missing?"

"No," I say, calibrating my words. "It was just something I was curious about. I noticed Tara always wore the earrings I mentioned. She was wearing them when she was attacked, but I noticed a set of gold hoops on the nightstand in the motel room. She was probably planning on switching earrings."

"And the scar?"

"I noticed it the first time I met her. I just wondered if you had seen it, too. If she wore a watch, you probably would not have. Seems like she tried to keep it hidden." I do not want to mention the idea of someone impersonating Tara. It sounds far-fetched and he is desperate enough to cling to any possibility.

"As intimate as I was with her, how could I not have noticed the scar? You did even if she tried to hide it. And the scar being on her wrist? Seems like she may have had a lot of problems I didn't know about."

"It does seem that way. I am stumped, too. I have a difficult time reconciling the Tara I know and the Samantha you know, as being the same person. Perhaps, there are some people we never truly know, no matter what. I just can't wrap my head around all of it," I say, arching my arms to indicate the whole situation. Usually if you search hard enough, answers come. The only thing this case leads to, is more questions, never answers.

"Sometimes I wonder how things could be different, if I had made different choices," he says.

"You cannot go down that path. You had no way of knowing what would be waiting on the other side of that motel door."

"No. Not that. Well, yeah that, too, I suppose. But I mean, how would my life be different if I hadn't given up on us. You and me. Do you ever think about it?"

I won't pretend it didn't hurt when Colt and I broke up. It stung to think he had started seeing someone else before our relationship ended. But I understand why. We had drifted apart, both of us realizing we wouldn't have a future together. If I am honest with myself, any hurt I felt was a result of feeling that I had failed at one more thing.

Suddenly, the thing other people have been telling me that

I have refused to see, is staring me in the eyes as I look at him across the table. I clear my throat, before answering. "I don't think you gave up on us. I think we both realized that *us* isn't something that should be. I love you, Colt. I always will. But in a different way than what soulmates are meant to love. And I think you feel the same way. You are just being nostalgic right now because you are in a terrible predicament, with too much time and your own thoughts."

"Of course. Yeah. Yeah, no, you're right. Things worked out the way they should. I'm glad to see you happy with Jack." He gives me a small smile.

I should pursue the conversation. I should get it all out into the open. I should find out if Colt is in love with me, or if he has any type of false hope about a future reconciliation. I should do a lot of things. But I won't. This is not a conversation I ever wanted to think about having with him. It was better to go about my days thinking everyone else was mistaken in their view of how he sees me. Now, I know deep down in my heart, no matter how he will try to play it off lightly or never mention it again, Sally and Teeny were right. When this ordeal is over, I need to pull back from our relationship to a safe distance. For both our sakes, and for the sake of my relationship with Jack.

I am beginning to see things from the outside— from Jack's perspective. It's like someone has wiped the fog from a mirror and I can see a reflection of Colt and myself, vividly. My admiration for Jack grows. For him to understand my friendship with Colt and support it while he might have known Colt's true feelings for me, is something I would never have been able to do if the roles were reversed. If it was a female version of Colt involved in Jack's life, I would rather claw her eyes out than allow her to crowd in. No wonder Jack was so easily provoked the morning they had their boxing match at my house.

I open my mouth prepared to respond but no words come, so he continues, "There was a time I wasn't happy about you being with Jack. But then I saw the two of you together one day. You were unaware of me or anyone else who could have been paying attention to you. He leaned over and said something into your ear. You smiled— A genuine smile. The kind that makes your eyes sparkle and your face light up. You kept looking at him like that, even after he turned away. That's when I knew, he makes you truly happy. I have never made you smile like that. Sure, I'm good at making you laugh. That smile though, that's something else."

"Colt, I...."

He holds up a hand, interrupting me. "If anyone other than me is going to make you happy like that, I'm glad it's Jack."

I wish I could have made myself feel for Colt, the same way I feel toward Jack. But just like with a tangible object, if you apply too much pressure or force, it will break. If I had lied to myself and to him, we both would have ended up broken.

"You will find your someone who makes you smile like that someday, too," I say.

"Maybe. After you, they have all seemed to turn out crazy," he grins and rubs the whiskers on his jaw.

I smile in return, trying to lighten the mood. "Oh, I almost forgot. I smuggled you in some contraband," I say. I produce a can of Dr. Pepper from the back waistband of my jeans and slide it across the table.

"You wouldn't happen to have something stronger, would you?"

I give him a mischievous smile and reach back again. I bring forth a small bottle of Jim Beam. "What type of friend would I be if I didn't?"

twenty-six

MY PHONE VIBRATES as I am opening the door to my vehicle. I fumble, pulling it out of my back pocket. The screen is lit up with Teeny's name.

"Hey, what's up?" I ask.

"No luck with my contacts about Tara's birth mother. I was able to get eyes on Tara's bank statements for the last couple of years, though. Nine months ago, she had a payment go to a P.I. office in Berkeley, California, where her family is from. Abel Investigations. Frank Abel is the P.I.'s name."

"Gee, and I thought Art of Investigations is clever."

"I know, right. Apparently, he is supposed to be one of the best in the greater San Francisco area. Or as a review put it, 'Frankly, he is able to solve any crime.' Kinda cheesy, but I dig it." I chuckle at the review. "Anyway, I called his office. His secretary said he is out in the field on a case. She will get the message to him, and hopefully I'll hear something back."

"Thanks, Teeny. Good job."

"Hold up, I'm not finished yet. Sally was able to track down a long-lost cousin of Tara's. A guy named Matthew Greene. He is younger than her and hasn't seen Tara in years, but Sal was able to charm him into telling her everything that he knows about Tara's past."

"Do tell," I say, anxiously.

"It seems Miss Tara got herself into some trouble during her college years— for possession. It was swept under the rug discretely when her parents sent her to a posh rehab. No small feat on her father's college professor salary. Matthew said the rehab seemed to take, but not long after that, Tara took her dad's straight razor to her wrist, and she ended up in a different kind of rehab. She seemed fine after that. Dropped out of college and enrolled in nursing school."

"Thanks, Teen. You and Sally are as handy as pockets on a shirt."

"Well, I wouldn't exactly call it the discovery of the century, but the slit wrist could point to issues other than just depression. If she has a history of substance abuse, maybe there's some type of substance induced psychotic disorder. I don't know, I'm just throwing ideas."

"You could be right." I don't bother mentioning that I already knew about the scar and had considered the reasons for it. But the attempted suicide in combination with a history of drug use, could point to some mental health issues. Maybe some issues that would explain why Tara wanted to play the part of being *Samantha*.

"If I learn anything else, I'll reach out," Teeny says.

"Appreciate it."

"Don't mention it, Five-Foot," he says, referring to me by the nickname he gave me— short for five-foot-five (my height).

Perhaps, Tara had some type of substance induced disorder in the past, but she doesn't seem like she is involved with drugs now. Or could she be? If she was able to maintain a secret life, could she have also kept drug abuse hidden. If she was involved with drugs, maybe that led to her attack. Could it have been a deal gone wrong? No, that doesn't make sense. She would not have invited me to the motel if she was there to meet a drug dealer.

None of these things feel right to me. I don't think Tara is mentally ill or abusing controlled substances. And I honestly do not think that she has been pretending to be Samantha. What else could have led to her attack?

I still feel that Samantha really exists. I could be overreaching, as Jack suggested, not only to prove Colt is innocent, but to make Tara into the person that I hope she is. *Tara isn't as good as people think she is.* When I think of what Celeste said about Tara, it makes me question if I have gotten any better about not being manipulated by people.

At what point will I decide to let things play out, and wait for Tara to come out of her coma? When will I grow tired of the same questions running circles in my head, and simply give up? I think of Colt reaching across the table to take my hand earlier, and about how Mark and Janie pulled strings to make his arrest happen. The answer is clear. I will not stop until the truth comes to light.

I think I should pay another visit to Mark. My intuition tells me that he is hiding something. It could be the fact that he was having an *ongoing* affair with Tara. But I feel that he may know something else that could be useful in discovering what was going on in her life. He may know about her troubled past, and it could be relevant to her state of mind recently.

I text Celeste, asking for Mark's number. She is quick to respond. I debate on whether to have the element of surprise or just show up at his house. I decide it's best to give him a heads up, in case he is truly ill. I tap my finger to the contact link in her message and the phone connects his number.

After three rings, I think my call will go to voicemail, then he answers. "Hello?" he says, sounding winded.

"Hi, Mark. This is Elle Riley. We spoke a few days ago at your house."

"Oh yeah, sure, the Private Investigator."

"Yep. I was hoping I could stop by and speak to you."

"Now is not the best time. I'm sick." He forces a cough that sounds much too fake. "I would hate for you to catch whatever I have."

"I'm sorry to hear you aren't feeling well." I roll my eyes while thinking Celeste is correct in her assumption that he is faking an illness. "I've had my flu vaccine and have a healthy immune system. I'm sure we will keep our distance enough that I won't have to worry about catching whatever you have. I would rather talk in person than by phone. I have some important things that I wish to speak to you about."

It will be much better to speak in person, so I can gauge his reactions and facial expressions. It is harder to figure out if someone is lying over the telephone. The *important things* that I mentioned speaking to him about seemed to pique his curiosity, because he suddenly agrees to allow me a visit. "Alright. If it is important then I suppose it will be okay." He coughs again, this one sounding more forced than the last.

"Great. I will see you soon," I say, disconnecting.

I take note there is no Dodge Hellcat in sight as I drive down the street toward the Daniels' residence. Eli is still at the Sheriff's station. More than likely, he is trying to figure out why Colt smelled like whiskey and Dr. Pepper, and how I managed to smuggle it in. He looked confused when I whispered, "Fight Club," and gave him a fist bump on my way out. Or maybe, he was just happy Colt was in a better mood when he escorted him back to his cell. Either way, I will most likely be getting a pat down if I visit Colt again. I groan when I think about listening to Jack's tirade if he finds out. I am almost certain Eli will not mention it to Jack though, because he will not want to listen to his tirade either.

I pull in and park next to the curb at the end of the cul-de-sac. Mark's blinged out, gold Range Rover is parked in the driveway. I make my way up the sidewalk, past the bicycles that are lying in the same spot as my last visit.

I ring the doorbell and Mark is quick to answer. The pallor of a sick person is missing from his face. Instead, his cheeks are flushed. He is the picture of health; other than the pained expression he is wearing. It is the appearance that someone assumes when they are trying to evoke sympathy from another person. He covers his mouth, emitting another fake cough. It comes out the wrong way, almost causing him to choke.

I step back as he swings the door open. I expect him to join me on the porch, but he holds the door, beckoning me to enter. He guides me into the living room, where he kicks toys out of the path leading to a chair. He crosses the room and has a seat on the couch. I make myself comfortable in an oversized chair.

He gets straight to the point rather than leading with any small talk. "You said you had something important to discuss with me?" I detect worry in his voice. What I assumed was curiosity on the phone, could instead have been fear of something I may have discovered.

"Yes. Celeste has been keeping me informed of Tara's status. As I'm sure you may have assumed, I am still investigating and trying to piece together what may have happened." He nods and whirls his hand impatiently. "I think it's possible that you may know Tara better than you thought you did. You may know her better than anyone else. Afterall, your affair was ongoing and not just a one-time fling like you said."

"And. So?" He crosses his arms over his chest.

"So, why lie about it?" My reply to his smartass demeanor is out of my mouth before I can bite it back. I do not like this man.

"What does it matter?" he lifts a shoulder, nonchalantly. His eyes shift around the room rather than making eye contact with me. He seems nervous.

"It doesn't, I suppose. I was just curious if you do know her best, maybe you would be privy to things that were going on in her life. Other associates she may have had. Affairs she could have been involved in that could have led to someone wanting to harm her."

He laughs bitterly. "Do you honestly think if she had other lovers, we were discussing them?"

"I wasn't exactly insinuating other lovers." I raise a brow. "Associates and affairs can have other meanings." I smile sarcastically. Of course, if you are a philandering, sleazy man with shifty eyes, naturally your mind wanders to affairs of the carnal nature.

"My mistake. I just assumed since you were so interested in our affair...."

"I could care less about your affair, Mr. Daniels. I do care about whatever led up to someone attempting to murder Tara."

"I wasn't even in Justice when it happened." His eyes roam around the room once again as he avoids me. Something is seriously off with his behavior. There is a reason he is not interested in being helpful with the investigation to find out who attacked Tara. I would think he would care more. Perhaps, he does have an inkling about someone she may have known who would have hurt her. Maybe he feels scorned and thinks she deserved it if it was another lover who harmed her.

"I'm aware. I know you didn't attack Tara. I am not trying to indicate you have done anything wrong. I was just wondering if perhaps Tara has mentioned someone or some type of situation that could be pertinent. Perhaps, something you would never have given a second thought until now. Something to point to who really attacked her. Despite your insistence of Colton Ryan's arrest, I know him well enough to know he is not guilty."

"He seems guilty to me," he smirks. He sarcastically taps his finger to his cheek, pretending to search through his memory. It isn't lost on me that he doesn't seem to be angry about thinking Colt hurt Tara. It may have been Janie who pulled the strings for Colt's arrest, and not Mark. "Nope. I cannot think of anything."

"Did you know she was adopted?"

"Of course. What does that have to do with anything?"

"Did she mention any biological relatives that she may have discovered?"

"Nope. She did not know who her biological parents were, and she didn't want to know." He seems certain. For the first time, he makes direct eye contact. Whatever Tara's reason for hiring a private investigator in Berkeley, it must not have been to search for her birth parents.

His phone chimes with an incoming text. He doesn't bother picking it up. He raises his wrist and reads the message on his Apple Watch. I wait patiently as he picks up the phone and types a lengthy reply. "Sorry. An issue that was time sensitive," he explains, although I was not interested.

My small smile tells him I understand. "Do you know anything about Tara's past before she married Jacob? Any problems she may have had?"

"Nope. Tara and I haven't exactly been besties over the years," he says, snidely.

"Right," I say. I am certain he has answers to my questions, but I am going nowhere fast by trying to get information from him. "I should go and let you get back to recuperating. Thanks for speaking with me. If you think of anything, please give me a call." I feel the desire to get away from him before I say or do something I may regret.

I arise from the chair and turn in the direction of the front door, when he stops me. "Wait," he says, rather rushed, almost as if there is a note of desperation in his voice. He hesitates. "I just thought of something. Not long before Jacob died, he gave me a box of papers and things to put away for safekeeping. I have never looked in the box. I thought it was odd at the time. Maybe you could look at it and see if there is anything helpful there."

His sudden willingness to be helpful confuses me. How could he have forgotten such a box? Why would he not have checked the contents after Jacob passed away? What could possibly be in the box that could have anything to do with what happened to Tara? I feel uneasy but push the feeling aside. Instead, I say, "Okay."

"I have it somewhere in the garage." He leads the way to the door off the kitchen that opens to the attached garage. He glances around, seemingly at a loss as to where to look. "I know it's here somewhere." He starts rummaging through items on shelves. "Where did I put it?" he says, to himself while clucking his tongue.

I check my watch, wondering how much longer this will take. "I can come back later if you need more time to find it."

"No. That's okay. I know it's here." He rummages through more items, then takes his time retrieving a step-ladder from the other garage bay. Finally, he says, "Well, would you look. There it is," he smiles, pointing to a box on the top shelf.

I catch a whiff of black cherry and jasmine wafting through the air. It is the unmistakable scent of Tom Ford Lost Cherry. I wonder if it is the same scent as Tara's perfume, which is a Tom Ford scent, and if perhaps Janie wears it, too.

He turns in my direction, but he appears to be peering past me at something beyond my shoulder. Maybe Janie is here and that is why I smell the perfume. A shadow passes over my own in the reflection of the fluorescent garage light. Yes, Janie must have come home.

I start to turn but I am stopped by a sudden pin prick to my neck. "What the hell?" I slap my hand to my collar, unable to shift my body. My knees feel like a bucket of water that someone has splashed onto the ground, as they buckle. My vision becomes blurry. There are three of Mark standing across the garage, rather than one. I feel a sharp, biting pain to my head as if someone has hit it with a hammer. I crumple to the hard floor. My words sound slurred as I say, "I knew there is a reason for me not liking you," before slipping into a landslide of darkness.

twenty-seven

I AM JOSTLED to consciousness by a feeling of being bounced. I attempt to open my eyes and experience a stabbing pain in my head. I squeeze my eyes shut again. My thoughts are swimming in a pool of sleepiness. One of them breaks the surface telling me to open my eyes and pay attention. I struggle against the pain and slowly crack them open. I am in the back of a vehicle. That explains the jostling. But why? I try to reach out, but my hands are bound. I feel nauseous. I close my eyes again to fight against the sickness.

I hear voices. Another thought floats to the surface of the dark pool, telling me to listen. I take a deep breath and open my eyes again. The voices sound like they are coming through a tunnel. I study my surroundings. I am in the back of some type of SUV. But why?

"You sure you got the right dosage?" A man's voice. I know the voice, but I cannot put a name to it. Dosage? Am I in an ambulance? No. Your hands aren't bound, and you are not tossed in the back of an ambulance like a sack of potatoes. The waters of my thoughts are murky. I know where I am, but the knowledge is stuck in the mud, unable to wade to the shore.

"Yes, I got the dosage right. I am a nurse, after all. I know how to administer medication. It is the head injury that caused the problem," a woman's voice says. I do not recognize her voice. Head injury? Are they talking about the blonde woman I know?

"Really? Cause it seemed as if she was passing out as soon as you stuck her. Now I have blood in my garage where she hit her head, and it's probably in the back of my vehicle! What the hell am I supposed to do about that?"

"Maybe needles make her woozy. I don't know, but the dosage was correct. We should have had at least thirty minutes after I injected her. I didn't know she was going to go down like a stack of bricks. You agreed it's what we needed to do, so stop acting like this is all my fault!"

"Of course, I agreed. She knows! What else were we supposed to do?" he asks.

I think they are talking about me and not the blonde woman. But what is it I know? I shift my eyes and see the trees whiz by. The acrid taste of bile rises up my throat, and I tightly close my lids again. I can feel myself starting to sink. I try hard to concentrate on their conversation.

"There wasn't much blood and we got it cleaned up, so stop fixating and worrying about it. We'll tend to her head, and everything will be okay."

"I'm happy that you are so confident about it, because I am not so sure everything will be okay!"

"Well, it has to be," the woman says, with resignation in her voice.

Concentrate, I remind myself as I attempt to make sense of my jumbled thoughts. The task takes its toll on me. The stabbing pain in my head continues, and I must keep my eyes closed to ease the sickness that is roiling in my stomach. My mind urges me to stay awake, but my body no longer cares. I let the blackness overtake me. I am once again drowning in the deep pool of sleep.

twenty-eight

THE NEXT TIME I AWAKEN, consciousness comes quicker, yet just as painful. I'm no longer in the back of the vehicle. Now it feels like I am lying on a hard, cold surface. Unable to raise up, I roll onto my side. Something heavy pulls at my left foot. A chain, I realize as I slowly pry my eyes open. I am on a concrete floor with my foot tethered to a cinder block wall. I roll onto my stomach and vomit.

"Oh wonderful, you're awake," I hear the man's voice that I recognize, but his face is blurry. I twist back onto my side, shielding my eyes from the glare of the light. "She's awake," I hear him yell. Who is the man behind the voice? Is it Jacob Daniels? No, that doesn't seem right. I rub the back of my head. I wince from the pain of my touch. Dried blood is congealed in my hair. I remember being in a room with shelves along a wall. I must have hit my head. Or rather, *someone* hit me on the head. It had to be the man or the woman from the SUV.

Then, I hear the woman's voice. "Oh, I'm so glad you're awake!" I remove the cover of my forearm away from my eyes as she rushes over to me. Tara. No, that doesn't seem right either. "Let's get you situated." I am pulled into a sitting position with my back placed against the wall. She wipes at my face with a cool cloth.

I lean forward and wretch again. "Any chance if we drug her again and drop her off outside of a hospital, she won't remember any of this?" the man asks. I open my eyes and his face is a little clearer this time. Jacob Daniels. No, not Jacob. Alike but different. Mmm... I grapple trying to recall the name.

"I'm afraid not. I wish we could. I'm sure she has a concussion but chances of her not remembering anything are slim. We can't take the chance. Especially with her boyfriend being Sheriff."

Jack. His name is the first lucid thought I have. I can see his face vividly as it stirs in my mind's eye. Jack will find me. I know he will.

I reach for the cool cloth, wiping my mouth. "Tara?" I ask, glancing around. My vision is double. All I see is her in front of me, blurring into my periphery.

"No. I'm Samantha," she says. Her name sounds familiar. I should know her. It's as if consciousness is ransacking my brain, rummaging through my thoughts and tossing them aside before I can process them.

"Why?" I ask, pulling weakly at the chain connected to my foot.

She lifts a bottle of water and some tablets to my mouth. "Shh. Take these. They will help with the pain and nausea. Don't worry about talking right now. I'll explain everything after you rest." I gulp down the large tablets. She may very well be feeding me poison for all I know. The promise of help for the pain is so enticing that I will happily go to my death.

I close my eyes and when I awake again, I am alone, this time lying on a cot.

* * *

It's hard to say how long I have been here. It could have been hours or days. This time when I start to come to, I keep my eyes closed. I must go through steps to prepare myself, like climbing a ladder. Take a few deep breaths, swing a foot onto the first rung. Swallow down the bile, second rung. Ignore the drumming pain in my head, third rung. Wrestle back the fear that threatens to overtake me, slowly make my way to the top and pull myself out of the pit.

How many times is a person allowed to cheat death? How often do they get a second chance at life before the Grim Reaper no longer knocks at their door, but kicks it in? These are the thoughts that I have as I become lucid and clock my surroundings.

I have no way of knowing how long I slept. I have had moments of being awake before drifting back off again, painfully sick moments when the man or woman have roused me. Their names come to me now, Mark and Samantha.

I am still on the small bed, which is much more comfortable than the floor was. The chain connected to my ankle is longer than I thought when I first got here. The chain seems lengthy enough for me to reach the portable toilet across the room. There is a basin of water, towels and toiletries that sit atop a plastic crate, which has been upturned next to the commode. I suppose I should be thankful to be afforded such luxuries as a prisoner. However, it makes my heart sink because I realize this means my stay here will not be a short one.

There is a sandwich and a bottled water sitting on another overturned milkcrate next to the bed, along with a bottle of medicine. I avoid the food. My stomach still feels queasy. I avoid the tablets, also. I do not know if they cause drowsiness. I am aware enough now to know that I need to stay alert.

The space seems to be underground. Despite the whirs and

hums of what must be an air purification system, I can smell an earthy scent that reminds me of moss. The scent mixes with the aroma of citrus air freshener. I vaguely recall Tara telling me Jacob and Mark Daniels had built a bunker. I am certain that the bunker is where I am now. I can see into a space beyond which looks like a living quarter that has been beautifully designed— unlike the space where I am, which seems to be used as storage for supplies.

I am wearing a clean shirt. I touch the back of my head. Although still tender to the touch, the blood is no longer there. My hair has been washed, and the gash on my skull seems to have been glued together to stop the bleeding.

My shoes are missing. I glance around the room. They are nowhere to be seen. If I do find a way to run, it will be in nothing other than socks. I pull at the chain on my foot, testing it. It is too tight to slip my foot out. I stand slowly, steadying myself as I sway, then I follow the links to the wall. The anchor is secure. I am spent from the task and fall back onto the cot. I rest for a moment before mustering the energy to walk across the room. I check the extent of the chain length. As I suspected, it is just long enough to reach the toilet.

I hear the heaviness of what I assume is the door to the bunker opening. The sound echoes along the corridor. I stumble back to the bed and sit. Mark's voice comes from the doorway. He seems surprised to see me awake.

"You look much better," he says.

"Disappointed?" I ask. My voice sounds croaky and odd to my own ears.

His mouth turns up in amusement. "Not at all. Sam and I were really worried about you."

"Where is Samantha?"

"Not here."

"How long have I been here? Why am I here? What are your

plans for me?" I ask in a rush, anxious to know the answers to everything immediately.

"Whoa," he says, holding his hands up. "One thing at a time. Why don't you get some food on your stomach first?" he nods to the plate that is resting on the overturned crate.

I have no desire for the food, but I know I will need to build my strength up if I want to get out of this predicament. I pick up the peanut butter and jelly sandwich from the plate. "You first," I say, tearing off a piece and extending it.

"Do you honestly think I would poison you?" he laughs.

"Perhaps not poison, but *definitely* drug." I scowl at him, yanking my foot causing the chain to scrape against the concrete floor. He laughs again. He comes over to take the food from my hand, and pops it into his mouth, humoring me.

"You've been here since yesterday," he says, disappearing into another room. He comes back with a chair, sets it across from me, and takes a seat in it.

"Why?"

He waves a hand of dismissal toward me. "Because you started asking questions that made me think you knew about Samantha." There is only one reason he is indulging me with answers; he knows I will not be leaving this bunker, so he will not have to worry about me telling anyone.

"Are you going to kill me?"

"That's not my plan. I know you are confused and probably think I am a monster. I am not. I just need some time to decide what to do next. When it's safe to do so, I plan on letting you go. You probably don't believe me, but that's the truth." The look on his face seems convincing, but I can tell it is fake— the same as his man-cold was.

"You're right. I don't believe you," I say, as I pull on the chain. I could beg and plead. All that would accomplish is to give me false hope and exhaust my energy. Instead, I resort to a veiled threat. "You do know there are people who will move heaven and earth to find me, don't you?" I can imagine how frantic Jack, Art and Teeny are knowing that I am missing. They will leave no stone unturned while searching for me. Although, I do not feel an immediate threat from Mark, neither do I feel secure enough to know if I will still be alive and well when Jack arrives. If he finds me and I'm not alive and well, there will be hell to pay for Mark and Samantha.

"Yes. I do know. I may not be a monster, but neither am I stupid. Let me paint you a picture. You see, you weren't at my house long, due to me being too ill to talk to you. When you left, you stopped on the side of the road. Maybe, you wanted to make a phone call before you crossed the mountain and had to worry about losing cell service. From there, who knows what happened. They have probably already found your Bronco abandoned miles away. Someone torched it, along with your phone, watch and purse inside of it. At least, that is what they will piece together. But they'll never find the truth. It will always remain a mystery. You appreciate a good mystery, don't you?"

Now I know that he does intend to kill me.

"I suppose I have no choice but to patiently wait and see if you are a decent human being. One who won't murder me in cold blood— despite the fact that you drugged me, tried to bash my brains in, and chained me up down in a hole in the earth."

With a chuckle, he says, "I see why Tara likes you so much. I wish we had met under different circumstances, Elle." He stands to leave. "I'll be back later to bring you dinner and check on you."

"Wait. I'm assuming you have this bunker locked and sealed like Fort Knox. Is the chain necessary?"

He cocks his head to the side, studying me. Finally, he says,

"Like I said, I'm not stupid." And he isn't, which is very unfortunate for me.

* * *

When Mark is gone, I set to work trying to figure out a way to release myself from the chain. Even though the space is comfortable, it is still underground. No matter the generous size, the thought of feeling like I am trapped in a tomb causes me to feel claustrophobic. I grapple with the panic that is on the brink of rising.

I still have many questions that I need answers to. Why don't they want anyone to know Samantha exists? What are they hiding? Why did they harm Tara? Why did Samantha have a short-lived affair with Colt if she is obviously involved with Mark? I do not have the time or energy to allow my mind to enter a rabbit hole to try and sort it out. The stabbing pain is back in my head and the nausea threatens to overtake me. I need to concentrate on finding a way out of here before I am forced to rest from the sick feeling.

Think Elle. If my hair was still in the messy bun, I would have a hair pin that I could use to try to pick the lock. When Samantha washed my hair and doctored my wound, the hairpins disappeared. Along with the lessons Jack gave me on reading people to tell when they are lying, he also taught me how to get out of handcuffs. He found it amusing when I asked him to teach me, neither one of us thinking the skill would ever actually come in handy.

I run my hand along the chain, checking for a weak link, finding none. I check the cot for anything useful. There are no pins or screws to be found in the steel frame. The legs and tubing of the bed are connected by pieces that snap together.

Everything about the portable toilet is plastic and useless to me as a tool.

I test the length of the chain again, wishing I could reach the opposite wall of shelves stockpiled with supplies. I scan the walls and along the floor searching for something I could use to unlock the chain. Finding nothing, I have a momentary feeling of despair before I remind myself that all is not lost, and I am not a helpless person. I will figure a way out. I will have to think of some other way that doesn't include picking the lock. Then I come up with the only plan that is possible. I will have to incapacitate Mark and search his pocket for a key to the lock. Sounds like a simple plan, but like he said, he is not stupid. I will have to bide my time and earn his trust to make my plan work.

twenty-nine

WHEN I HEAR the door open, I strain my ear trying to hear if the heavy door locks. I hear nothing to indicate that it does. The footsteps echo through the cavernous space. I'm not sure if it is Mark or Samantha.

It is Mark who enters the room. He greets me cheerfully as if he is a husband coming home from work and I should say, "Hi honey, how was your day", rather than this being an abductor/hostage relationship. I wonder how he finds so many opportunities to be away from home and come here without anyone knowing what he is up to. Janie is probably still at the hospital with Tara, and someone else must be tending to their son due to Mark being *ill*.

He leaves the room and heads to the living quarter, where I can hear the familiar sounds of a meal being prepared. When he returns, he sets a small table in front of the cot, pulls his chair over, then exits the room again. He re-emerges with a bowl of spaghetti along with two plates and utensils. He stirs the bowl of pasta, dips some onto both of our plates and then takes a bite. "Making sure you know it isn't poisoned," he smiles.

Surprisingly, my stomach growls at the aroma of the food, and I dig into the meal. "This is good. Have you always known how to cook?" I ask, deciding to make the most of the time to get to know and win him over. Samantha may not return. It's Mark's trust that I will have to earn if I plan on getting out of here.

"Not really. After Janie gave birth to Maverick, she had postpartum depression, and I was forced to learn to cook if I wanted to eat."

"I am sorry to hear that. I understand postpartum depression can be very bad for some women."

"Horrible, actually. It went on for a year or so before I finally convinced her to get help. She still takes medication. She hasn't really been the same since. She went from caring too much, to not caring about things at all. Including me."

And there it is. A glimpse into his explanation for his extramarital affairs, and the reason why Janie seems to want to remain oblivious to them. It isn't that she is unaware. She probably just doesn't care.

"That must be hard. Divorce isn't an option if you are unhappy?"

He laughs bitterly. "Sounds simple enough. But no. It isn't." I expect him to end his explanation here, but he continues. "I had to quit my job to take care of Maverick because she couldn't that first year. We moved here to be close to her family so they could help. Her family is loaded and footing the bill for our household. I signed a prenup before I married her, so I get nothing if we divorce."

"No desire to go back to work, and not have to depend on her money?"

"Why should I, after taking care of her all these years?"

He sounds impassioned as if he expects me to jump on the pity train for him. Poor, pitiful Mark who doesn't have to work because his in-laws are wealthy. Sad, little Mark who must have forgotten his wedding vows declare the words *In Sickness* as well as *In Health*. I don't sympathize, empathize, or pity him. I may be trying to win his trust, but the best I can do is keep disgust from twisting my face while he talks.

"Besides, when Tara wakes up, I won't need Janie's money."

"I'm confused. What does Tara have to do with your finan-cial situation, and why did you or Samantha try to kill her if you want her to be alive and well?"

"We did not have anything to do with the assault on Tara." My brows knit together in skepticism. "How about we change the subject before we end up arguing?" he asks giving me a tolerant smile. He stands and begins clearing the dishes away then he leaves the room. He returns with a deck of playing cards. "Up for some rummy? I have a couple of hours before I need to be home."

"Sure," I say, ready to manipulate him into thinking that I trust him and am at ease with remaining in my prison. I have gotten all the answers I will get out of him for the time being.

Over the course of the next hour or so, we play cards and talk. More importantly, *he talks a lot*. He seems to enjoy me acting as if I am interested in him and his life. He has a big ego and likes to boast himself.

I steer the conversation in the direction of learning what I can about the bunker. I start out by asking about how the Daniels brothers decided to become preppers. From there, the conversation evolves into one about the specifics of building such a space, which he doesn't seem to know much about. Jacob had plenty of money, and that affords the luxury of not having to learn about such things. Instead, he hired others who were experts. But I do learn that there are no cameras on the inside, however there is security and constant monitoring of the outside world. My best hope is to be alone in the bunker if someone comes to my rescue.

That's if anyone could even find this place. It's located in the middle of the woods in nowhere. The door is obscured, and the spot is soundproof. Afterall, you would not want intruders stumbling upon your safe space during the apocalypse. Who knew that the safest place to be when the shit hits the fan, would turn out to be the most unsafe place for me to be.

"Tara said you also have a cabin on this property. Do you have to walk far to get from it to the bunker? You must be getting plenty of exercise by bringing my meals?" I inquire innocently.

"Yes, Jacob had the cabin built first. It's a bit of a trek to the east. I'm surprised she told you these things. They're supposed to be a family secret," he says, lightheartedly. "We do a lot to cover any tracks from the cabin to the bunker. I mean what good does it do to have a bunker if anyone can stumble upon it?" He continues to talk until my eyelids grow heavy and I suppress a yawn.

He glances at his wrist and realizes he isn't wearing his watch. "No wonder you are yawning. I'm not sure what time it is, but probably far past time for me to go. I guess you should get to bed." He scoots the table and chair out of my reach and walks to the door. He turns before leaving and says, "It was nice to be able to talk to you, Elle."

I feel a momentary compassion that is fleeting when the chain makes a rattling sound, as I settle back on the bed. I promised myself that I would never be manipulated by people again. Regardless of how nice a person Mark may be starting to seem— he is desperate enough to hold me prisoner. Desperate people justify doing desperate things. It could be that he is trying to gain my trust and manipulate me, the same way I am trying to manipulate him. I make a new resolve not to fall for his nice act.

* * *

There is no window to see if it is daylight or dark outside. I will have to gauge the number of days by the meals that I am brought. Yesterday, Mark said I had been here since the day before. So, today when he brings a bowl of oatmeal and a magazine for me to read through, I say to myself, "Day three."

He is very talkative again today, if I do not mention my situation or Tara. He immediately shuts me down if I do. So, I listen intently to him and remain quiet for the most part. I want him to notice my silence and the sadness in my eyes. I want him to think I may be giving in to my current situation. I would love for him to think I was becoming somewhat depressed. It would work into my plan for escape.

He does notice, and he turns on music that flows through the sound system before leaving, in hopes it will lift my mood. I start counting songs to keep up with hours. I figure each song is an average of three minutes. After twenty songs, I know it has been at least an hour, probably longer. I eventually lose count of the number of songs around the fourth hour. I have read the magazine from cover to cover twice and taken a nap before he returns.

His footsteps echo through the space. He enters the room with a pizza box and a soda. It is the type of pizza with a crust that tastes like cardboard and can be bought at a drive-thru window for six-ninety-nine. He doesn't bother pulling the table over, instead he places the pizza on the floor in front of my cot and slides a Diet Mountain Dew in my direction. The drink almost makes up for the pizza.

"Sorry, I know it isn't much, but I am in a rush. I can't stay long."

"It's fine. I honestly do not have much of an appetite. I am happy to see the caffeine, though." I smile wistfully at him.

"Shit. I'm sorry. I never thought to bring you coffee or a pop before."

Look at him, acting like a considerate psychopath. I remind myself not to fall for his nice act. "No worries. Thank you," I say, as I open the lid of the plastic bottle and bring it to my lips. It tastes splendid on my tongue. "Bad day?" I ask as I blot the greasy pepperonis with a napkin.

"Nothing to concern you with. I just have a lot going on and can't stay. Are you good?"

Am I good? I would have to struggle to think of a more ridiculous question to ask someone chained to a wall in a dungeon. "Sure, I'm good. You can go ahead and leave," I say, with a note of sadness to my voice.

"How about I make sure you have some coffee in the morning? I bet that would put a smile on your face?"

"That would be great. Thank you for being so thoughtful." He nods his head and smiles, pleased with my response. I suppose I will be here for a day four.

"Be back soon," he says. I smile in return, until he turns his back to leave. The smile on my lips quickly skips into a grim line.

He may be sincere and have a pleasant side. I would be more inclined to consider his nice qualities, had he not had me drugged, whacked over the head and chained up in this hole. Instead, the tight cuff cutting into my ankle makes me hopeful that I will have an opportunity to throat-punch him.

I toss the slice of pizza back into the box. I know if I eat it, the result will be stomach spasms and visits to the plastic commode. "Day three," I say to myself again, as I lean back against the wall and take a swig of the drink, savoring it.

thirty

I HAVE BEEN awake for what seems like forever. The growls from my stomach have grown increasingly louder and longer in protest of not eating dinner. So, it must be morning, or close to it.

I have spent the time daydreaming of the things I will do when and if I get out of this predicament. I will hug everyone I love tightly, ideally at the same time. I will laugh, run and play with Buddy. I will make up for lost time with Jack. I will ask Gran to make me something scrumptious for supper and spend the afternoon with her and my Mama. *When* I get out of here. *If* I get out of here. No, when. I cannot think of the ifs.

I begin pacing the floor. Nine steps to the toilet. Nine steps back. Nine steps forward, nine steps back. Two-hundred and twenty more round trips will get me to a mile. I wish I could break free of this chain and run. I long to feel the pavement under my feet and music blasting into my ears. I yearn for that freedom.

Finally, I hear the door opening. Day four. The footfalls patting down the hall do not sound as heavy as Mark's. According to him, he has kept Samantha away because she is far too tender hearted to see me here. He fears I could manipulate her into setting me free. I remember her refusal of allowing him to dump me off at a hospital. That did not seem very compassionate to me. I did not share my opinion on the matter with him. He seems totally enamored with her and would have become angry. Instead, I suggested to him that she must have gotten the dosage deliberately wrong on the drug she injected me with. I was trying to create doubt in his mind toward her. I don't think he bought it.

She enters the room, seemingly surprised to see me standing. "Good morning. Mark said you were much better, and I see now you are. I hope you like bacon and eggs. And of course, coffee. Mark insisted." She smiles nervously and sits the food on the table before gently pushing it in my direction.

She tucks a strand of hair behind her ear, in the same manner as Tara. I am amazed at how alike they are. Not just their appearances, but also their mannerisms. They are identical. Not like Mark and Jacob, who were twins, yet had differences.

She reaches for the bottle of tablets beside the bed. "I guess you don't need these anymore."

I gently reach for her hand, staying it. She appears alarmed at my sudden movement and closeness to her. "Leave them, please. My head still hurts terribly."

"Sure. Just be careful with them. They can be habit forming." *No shit.* A large portion of Justice's population have collapsed into the habit. I nod my head in response and take a seat on the cot. I'm sorry about your head, by the way. You hit it pretty hard when you fell in Mark's garage." I absently reach back and run my fingers across the tender spot. My stomach rumbles at the smell of the food. "Someone seems hungry this morning," she smiles again.

I give her a shy grin in return. I am hungrier for answers to my questions. Perhaps she will be more forthcoming than Mark.

"Well, enjoy your breakfast." She hesitates, then turns to leave.

"Wait." She halts, swiveling back at me questioningly. "Can you please stay a bit? I am desperate for some company."

"Of course. Just don't tell Mark. He doesn't want me spending too much time down here."

"Our secret." I trace my finger and thumb across my lips, making a zipping motion.

She makes small talk, asking me questions that a nurse would ask a patient. I answer carefully. It is better to make them think I am still on the mend. If they do not realize that I have regained strength, their guard will be lower. I study her, taking in the doe-like brown eyes, the tilt of her nose and shape of her lips— all so much like Tara. They even pursued the same professions as nurses. "I'm sorry, I don't mean to stare. It's just that I have never seen two people who are more alike than you and Tara. Have you always known about her? Were you adopted, too?" I ask before biting into the bacon.

She pushes a blonde lock behind her ear again. "I have known about her for a while, but I didn't know *who* she was until recently. She hired an investigator to find my mother— our mother. No, I wasn't adopted. My grandmother raised me." She waves her hand. "It is a long-drawn-out story."

"I would love to hear it."

"Okay." She clears her throat. "The man who raised Tara was our biological father. He was an English professor. He was married. Our mother was his student. They had an affair which resulted in pregnancy. My mother suffered from episodes of schizophrenia. When his wife found out about the affair and pregnancy, she used my mother's mental disorder against her to force her to give Tara up. They did not know about me. My mother and grandmother kept the fact of twins from them. My mother lost her mind not long after that. She remained in a facility for the mentally ill until she died a couple of years ago."

"Wow. That is a heartbreaking story." I reach over and pat her hand.

She continues. "I never knew the truth growing up. I had no family other than my mother and grandmother. Everyone assumed my mom was a crazy lady, babbling on about someone stealing her baby. When I graduated from nursing school, I got a job at the facility where she was, in order to be close to her. That's when I started to listen to her. *Really* listen to her. My grandmother had already passed away by this time. It was hard for me to put the pieces together, but I eventually did. I was never able to get our father's name from her, though. When she passed away, I left the facility and went to work at a hospital. I had no clue how to look for my sister. I certainly couldn't afford an expensive investigator like she ended up hiring."

"Then one day, the Director of Nursing at the facility called to tell me an investigator had been there asking questions about my mother. I was overjoyed. My sister was trying to find me. I contacted the investigator and he said, 'his client no longer wished to pursue the matter'. She no longer wanted to even know her birth mother's name, so she didn't know about me, either."

I decided to be clever, and I hired him on the spot to find Tara. He couldn't exactly refuse since she was no longer his client. He did not even have to investigate because he knew who she was. For two-hundred and fifty dollars, he gave me her name."

I am on the edge of my seat, waiting for her to continue, completely enthralled by the tale. She excuses herself, offering to go to the kitchen and brew another cup of coffee before she finishes her story. When she returns, she sits the two mugs on the plastic table and takes a sip. "I came here with the intention of introducing myself to her. I sat outside her house one day and watched her while I tried to work up the courage. I failed that day and kept returning, but never could muster the courage. I eventually stopped doing that after her daughter saw me one day and confused me for Tara."

I remember Emily asking if it was really her mommy in the hospital and not someone who looks like her. If only I had known to probe more about her question. I am surprised Samantha wasn't harassed by Elaine of the neighborhood watch for lurking on the street. Chances are if Elaine saw her, she thought her to be Tara. Possibly another reason she thinks Tara is odd. Who just sits in a car on the street outside their own home repeatedly for long periods of time?

"Then Mark saw me at the ATM one day and he also confused me for Tara. I decided to play along. It didn't take him long to figure out I wasn't her, but he let me continue the farce for a while before telling me he knew." She smiles like it is a fond memory and I suppress an eye roll. "Then we came up with a plan. I would pretend to be Tara and we would get access to her money, and then we would leave together. He said it wasn't fair that Tara and Jacob were dealt everything so easily, and we should have our turn. And I decided he was right. She hadn't even cared enough to follow through with finding our mom. I would have made sure to leave enough money for her and her daughter, though."

"Is that why you tried to kill her? To assume her identity and take her money."

"What? No. I didn't try to kill her. I had nothing to do with it. I did see her at the motel, but she was alive and well when I left."

Perhaps she fell and hit her head too, I think sarcastically.

255

"You don't believe me?" I do not bother with an answer. "Why do you think we had this room set up the way it is? We planned on putting her here until we were safely away, and then she would be freed."

Perhaps, the hurt she felt turned to rage against Tara, because Tara did not have to watch their mother wither away in a mental hospital. Or maybe it is as simple as she panicked because Tara saw her, and she bashed Tara over the head. Or maybe she really did not attack Tara. I do not want to believe her, but her explanation seems plausible. Tara being found dead would prevent Samantha from posing as her and gaining access to her money.

If she is being honest about not hurting Tara, then perhaps they do plan to let me go. I study her face and decide she is telling the truth about not attacking Tara. What reason would she have to lie about it? And, if she didn't hurt Tara, who did?

"What about Colton? Were you just toying with him?" I feel angry thinking of how she has caused him so much hurt.

"You truly must think I am a terrible person."

Why do both her and Mark seem to care what I think of them? Whether I see them as monsters or bad people. The fact that they have me chained up here, should speak volumes about how much weight my opinion carries. And it certainly tells the story of if their characters are questionable.

"No, I wasn't toying with him. I really liked Colt. I asked him to meet me at the motel that day so I could break things off with him. I had tried to distance myself when Mark and I started to get serious. Ignoring him did not work, so I decided I would rip the Band-Aid off in person."

"He is a big boy. He could have handled a break-up text." I say, coldly. How I wish that is what she had done. She may not have wielded the weapon that hurt Tara, but she is the reason Tara and Colt were both there that day. If not for her, Colt

256

wouldn't be in jail, and Tara would be safely home with her daughter.

"Oh, I see," she says, with an enlightenment dawning on her face. "You must be close with him. No wonder you sound angry."

"Close enough to know he didn't hurt her and should not be in jail, standing accused of it."

"If I didn't do it and Colt didn't, then who did?"

"That is exactly what I was trying to figure out before I came to be locked up here."

thirty-one

I MAKE the most of my time after Samantha leaves by getting in a workout. At least, as much of a workout that a person can do with a heavy chain attached to their foot. Although I am better than either one of them know, I am still not recuperated to a hundred percent. Dizziness overtakes me if I move too quickly and results in the nausea returning. And there are still times when my head pounds so intensely that I must close my eyes. I have forced myself to drink plenty of water to stay hydrated. I will need to be at my best when I make a run for it.

They need Tara to live so they can pull off their scheme. She now knows of Samantha's existence, but she isn't aware of her involvement with Mark or their plan, so they still have a chance to succeed. Tara will assume Samantha left Justice. And, if Samantha wasn't the person who attacked Tara, no one will have a reason to look for her. Except for me, nobody knows what they have planned. Me. I am their problem. I would like to think they will leave me safely here until they make their escape, the same way they planned to do with Tara, but I am too much of a liability to them.

I have been here for four days now, and nobody has found me. If Mark and Samantha are clever at covering their tracks, then I may never be found. I lie back on the cold floor, my thoughts exhausting me more than the exercises. I close my eyes. My breathing steadies and I start to drift off when I hear the door opening.

I can tell by the heaviness of the footsteps that they belong to Mark. I am disappointed. I hoped for Samantha to return, so I could start trying to manipulate her into releasing me, as Mark feared I would be capable of doing.

Something is different about him. His demeanor seems frigid. He avoids making eye contact with me. When he finally does meet my eyes, his face is sorrowful, almost pitying. I know in that instant that something has changed, and he has reconciled himself to killing me. For the first time, I am truly scared of him. I must prepare to act sooner rather than later.

"Is Tara, okay?" I ask. I try not to let my voice betray the fear that has set in.

"She still hasn't woken up. But there is still hope," he says.

"Oh," I say, feeling confused. Maybe Samantha told him about her time spent here this morning, and he is upset about that.

He starts to leave the room, but he stops suddenly by placing his hands on either side of the door jam. He does a quick turn about. I resist the urge to flinch as I think he is going to head for me. He turns to leave the room a second time then once again swivels back around. His elbow comes up in the air as he tugs at the hair on the back of his head. Finally, he says, "Any tips on how to get your boyfriend to back off? I can't even go home because he is at my house again. This time questioning Janie or putting thoughts into her head."

And there it is. The reason he is agitated. I resist the urge to smile thinking of how Jack will find me soon. I almost feel sorry for Mark when Jack finds out what he has done. The urge to smile quickly fades as another thought comes. If he thinks Jack is on the cusp of discovering what he has done and where I am, he will surely kill me before that can happen. My mind races as I think of a reply. Jack is one hell of a detective but telling that to Mark would not be in my best interest.

"Not really. He is headstrong when he gets an idea in his brain. I don't think you should be too concerned. He's a good sheriff but if he hasn't found me after four days, I think you're safe." He narrows his eyes at me, sensing that I am lying. "You know the first forty-eight hours are the most important. After that, most disappearances don't have a chance of being solved." I try to seem sad so that he will believe me. He doesn't seem convinced.

It may be too late by the time Jack gets here. I need to execute my plan to escape. I shrug, "Besides, Janie doesn't know about Samantha. She doesn't know about your plan. She doesn't even have a clue I was at your house, so why are you worried about Jack talking to her?"

"Yeah, maybe." He rubs his jaw, then tilts his head back and loudly exhales. When he drops his head back down, he claps his hands together and says, "Right. Of course, you're right. I am just being paranoid. How about a tuna salad sandwich?"

"That sounds great," I lie. When I think of what I want my last meal to be, it isn't tuna salad.

"Great. I'll be back in a jiff," he says.

Take your time. I need to prepare for my escape.

* * *

I lean forward, putting my head between my knees, taking slow, deep breaths, to keep from hyperventilating. When I raise up, I set to work quickly. I open the bottle of medication that Samantha left, hiding most of the pills inside the pillow-case. I strategically place the bottle and a couple of the tablets on the floor to make it look like I have dropped them. My hope is that Mark will come in and think I have taken the pills, rush over to check on me, and I can then incapacitate him. With any luck, the key to the locked chain will be in his pocket.

I have thought long and hard about this plan. I've considered that he may realize I do not seem like I am a suicidal person. Maybe he will think I became desperate and took an easy route out. My expectation is that he will panic and react without thinking.

So many things can go wrong. What if he thinks *Oh well, she saved me the trouble and turns to leave?* What if I am too weak to overtake him. Samantha would be easy to overtake, but Mark is stronger. He is smaller than Thomas, and I have had great success taking Thomas down. Thomas is trained at kick-boxing, so tackling Mark should be a piece of cake compared to him, right?

Then there is my problem of vertigo. I become extremely dizzy if I move too quickly. I must move fast if I am to render him incapable of thwarting my escape, and moving fast may cause me issues.

What if the key isn't in his pocket? If that is the case, maybe I can render him unconscious, and Samantha will come to check on him. She will eventually come, right? When and if she does, I have no clue what my plan will be then. I suppose it will be time to start begging for my release.

The plan isn't perfect. I would not even say it is a good plan. But all I need is the element of surprise to make a move on him. I say a silent prayer that I will be able to overtake Mark, the key will be in his pocket, and I can make it to safety. I am no saint. I would not even consider myself a well-behaved person at times, but I am a praying person. A miracle from God is what I need to get out of this predicament.

thirty-two

I HEAR the sounds coming from the kitchen as the meal is being prepared. I can smell the tuna preceding Mark's entrance into the room, and I bite back the urge to gag. I lie very still, trying to slow my breathing— a hard task since my heart feels like it will pound out of my chest.

"Time to wake from your nap, sleepyhead," he says. I do not dare to open my eyes. A silent pause ensues, and then just as I had hoped, he rushes over. He shakes me hard. Still my eyes remain shut, and I hold my breath. "Elle! What did you do?" He assumes I have taken an overdose of the pills, as I hoped he would think. I can detect anguish in his voice. Was I wrong to think he is planning on killing me? No. I know deep down inside that I am right to be scared and I need to stay the course.

He pulls the cover back. My eyes fly open as I squirt him in the face with a bottle of water. It isn't exactly a lethal weapon, but it does have the desired effect of momentary shock, allowing me the element of surprise. He pulls back, wiping at his face, as I spring up from the bed. I jump onto the edge of the cot, get behind him and lock him into a choke hold.

The element of surprise is gone. In its place is the desire to fight back on his part. He stamps at my foot, catching the chain, causing the tight cuff to tear roughly along my ankle, ripping it open. I groan in pain but refuse to release my hold on him. He frantically searches with his foot, trying to trample the same spot. He succeeds. Not only do I feel my ankle being torn, I'm also certain he has broken it. I fall back onto the cot, arm still locked around his neck, with his thrashing weight upon me. Tears of pain run in rivulets down my cheeks. I wrap my undamaged leg around his waist to help hold him down, and I tighten my hold.

Finally, thankfully, I can feel his weight sag against me as he passes out. I release my hold, shoving and kicking at him until he is off me. He crumples to the floor, slumping against my injured limb. I scream out in pain.

I lie back upon the bed catching my breath between sobs, knowing that my escape will not be swift. That is if I can walk upon my foot at all. I take one last shuddering breath before making myself begin to search his pockets for the key.

Sometimes, miracles do happen. I yank the key ring from his pocket, fumbling to open the lock. After dropping the keys twice, I am finally able to free myself. I click the cuff into place on Mark's foot and stick the keys into my pocket. I hurriedly search his other pockets for his phone, with no luck. He isn't wearing his Apple Watch either, so calling for help is not going to be immediate. I crawl to the other side of the room out of his reach where I slump against the wall, saying "Thank you, God."

I scoot toward the towels and grab one of them. I use it to make a binding for my ankle, as I glance around the room seeking something, *anything* that I can use as a crutch. Not seeing anything useful, I force myself to stand. Putting all my weight upon my right foot, I hobble to the wall then use it for support, as I make my way out of this room to search the others.

It is a slow journey. By the time I make it to the living quarter, I can hear the chain clanking as Mark starts to stir, coming to himself. He yells my name repeatedly. I have a split second of panic when I worry, what if he has another key in his pocket. I brush the thought aside, knowing that it would not make sense. Why would he need two keys? And I would have seen it when searching for his phone. Still, I let the paranoia drive me to hurry.

The room is spacious. Open living concept, with what appears to be two bedrooms off to each side. Enough space for both Jacob and Mark's families to hunker down comfortably during a crisis. The eighty-six-inch television mounted on the wall has security footage from the outside playing in real time, lending a sense of gazing out a big window at the great outdoors. All the creature comforts and more are present. It is exactly what you would expect a millionaire prepper's bunker to be.

His yelling has grown louder, and he is enraged. "Elle! Unlock the fucking chain!" he shrieks, then adds in a softer, desperate tone, "I promise, I won't hurt you."

Fat chance. I have every intention of checking out of Hotel de Daniels, and I do not plan on doing it in a body bag.

I find a small broom closet off the kitchen area. A mop is not an ideal crutch, but it will have to work. I unscrew the mop head from the end, and stumble back out into the corridor.

The room across the hall is a wall of security cameras and electronic devices. Green, red, blue, and white lights all blink in sequence. The room feels at least ten degrees warmer than the rest of the bunker, from the heat of all the electronics. I do not find a phone here, so I start pressing buttons on keyboards. Of course, everything is locked and is password protected. I would expect nothing less from a tech guru. I take one last glance around to ensure there is nothing that I can utilize to contact someone to come to my rescue, before making my way back out into the hallway for the outside.

Mark's shrieks have grown quieter, then suddenly loud again, as he alternates between begging and anger. I head for the door without looking back.

thirty-three

I HAD EXPECTED steps leading to the outside. Instead, I find a ramp after opening the first door that leads to some type of decontamination room. "Please, don't be locked," I say as I see the exterior door. The door beeps but the handle does not resist when I turn it. Another miracle. Although not locked, this door is much heavier and hard to heft open, with its thick seal acting as a sort of vacuum. I brace myself against the wall the best I can and pull the handle with all my might. The door gives way and I stick the mop handle between it and the opening, to keep it from slamming shut again. I hobble across the threshold, careful to not let the door smash me. I retrieve my makeshift crutch, scramble on my hands and knees up the slight incline, then through the brush that was intentionally put there as a camouflage.

Once at the top, I gulp in the fresh air as tears of joy stream. Now what? I clock my surroundings. There is nothing but forest. I have no idea where I am or which way to go. The weather has turned much cooler in the last four days. It is almost dusk, which means I have limited daylight. I could go back inside the bunker to search for a flashlight, but I decide against it. I need to hurry. There is still the possibility that Mark could get loose. If it wasn't a certainty that he was going to murder me before, it is now.

I force myself to focus. I assume there is water nearby. If you follow water, you will always eventually come upon some type of civilization or people. The telltale sound of a creek garbling as it flows over rocks isn't present. There is no well-worn path upon which the Daniels family have trodden back and forth to the bunker. They must park somewhere, though. Somewhere close enough to pack in supplies and such. I close my eyes to engage my senses. I shiver against the coolness of the evening. The open air that I was so happy to breathe, will not be nearly as pleasant if I must spend the night outside in it.

I almost let fear and hopelessness creep in. But then I recall Mark saying the cabin was to the east. If I remember correctly, the wind usually blows from west to east in this region, so I focus on the slight breeze. I head in the direction that the wind is blowing toward and hope I am walking the right way. There is a possibility that Mark's vehicle will be there, and I have his keys in my pocket.

The journey isn't as far as I had anticipated, albeit slow due to my injury, before I come upon the clearing surrounding the cabin. My heart skips a beat of joy when I spot Mark's Range Rover parked beside the house. I do not bother with entering the cabin to search for a phone, out of fear Samantha may be there. Instead, I slide the keys from my pocket and head toward the SUV.

I am halfway across the leaf carpeted lawn when head-lights swing across my body. I shield my eyes, noting there aren't any blue and red flashing lights atop the vehicle. It isn't Jack coming to my rescue. I stand frozen in place as Samantha parks. She cautiously exits a minivan that is the same make, model and color as Tara's. If you are going to steal someone's identity, it's better for everything to be exact, I suppose.

I prepare to wield the mop handle as a weapon. Under normal circumstances, I would have no qualms about my ability to overtake Samantha, but with my injured foot, I may not stand much of a chance. She doesn't appear to have a weapon in her hand. I can only hope there isn't a syringe of Rohypnol in her pocket. I am prepared to die on this lawn rather than return to the bunker, where they will end up killing me anyway.

She is as frozen in place as I am. Her eyes drop to my hands, which are gripped around the mop handle, and she sees the keys dangling from my finger. To my shock, she says only one word— "Go," as she points to the Range Rover.

I hurriedly hobble toward the vehicle before she has a chance to change her mind. I make my escape down the gravel road that leads away from the cabin.

The tires skid along the gravel, as I take the curves much faster than I should. I remind myself I am safe and force my foot to ease from the accelerator to a safe speed. I haven't driven far, perhaps a couple of miles, when I see flashing lights coming toward me on the one lane road. I put the Range Rover in park. Jack is out of his truck, gun drawn, pointing it at the SUV. When he sees it is me behind the wheel, he holsters his gun. He rushes around to scoop me into his arms before I have a chance to get out of the driver's seat.

"Are you okay?" he asks as he releases me to stand so he can do an examination of me.

I wince as my left foot touches the ground. "I'm okay," I say, as his eyes find the damaged limb. His face grows dark with anger.

Everything becomes chaos. I am loaded into Art's car to be

taken to the hospital. Jack and his team of deputies take off in search of the bunker.

thirty-four

WHEN JACK ARRIVED at the cabin, he found Samantha sitting on the front porch steps, waiting. She had not been to the bunker where Mark was still chained up. She had resigned herself to giving up, and she knew Mark would try to talk her out of it.

My Bronco was found burned in an isolated spot, as Mark said would happen. I am still upset about that. *Bastard*. I loved my Bronco.

After I went missing, it took a couple of days for Jack to obtain my cellphone records from the company. Finally, he became frustrated and reached out to his contacts at the F.B.I. They managed to help him get the records. My cellphone had pinged from a tower near Mark's house, too long for me to have been there and left quickly, as Mark had feigned. Based on the information, Jack was able to get Judge Evers to sign off on a search warrant of the Daniels' residence.

Mark and Samantha did a decent job cleaning up my blood. Just not as superb of a job as they thought. It doesn't take much for a forensic search to show blood is present. When they discovered blood in the garage, Jack applied pressure to

Janie Daniels, who up until that point thought Jack was on a fool's errand, and her husband was innocent of any wrongdoing.

Mark was at the bunker with me, making tuna salad after the blood was discovered. Janie had no clue where Mark was, but revealed he liked to spend time at the cabin. She also told Jack about the off-grid bunker located on the property. Jack wasn't aware of the property, because it technically belongs to Tara and is in her name. As soon as he learned of it, the calvary was on its way.

Everyone was surprised to learn of Samantha's existence. Everyone except Teeny, who had believed my crazy theory, even though he is still waiting on Frank Abel to return his call. Everybody else had thought that the odd coincidences were just a result of Tara acting peculiar. Perhaps, she was distracted and had too much on her plate as a single parent. Maybe, she had suffered some type of mental break after Jacob's death, they thought.

After Samantha met Mark and he presented his scheme to her, she no longer had the desire to meet her long, lost sister. He convinced her she deserved all the things Tara's money had afforded her to have in life. It wasn't a hard sell for him to persuade her, considering Tara did not seem to want to know about her birth mother or any other family she may have.

Jacob had given Mark the security code to Tara's house, in case there was ever an emergency. Tara was unaware of this. Jacob never disclosed that he had given Mark the code, because he knew Tara would object. Mark shared the code with Samantha. That is how she was able to enter the house. When Tara changed the code, Samantha's intrusions stopped. So, Tara did indeed have an intruder. No one, including her nosy neighbor, Elaine, knew or suspected. All they saw was who they thought to be Tara coming and going from the residence.

It was Samantha that Celeste saw with Mark the day at the motel. When I asked him about the affair, he played along about her being Tara, to keep me from discovering Samantha. Even Tara's love of Jacob did not override her dislike of Mark enough for her to seek comfort in his arms.

Samantha was able to learn Tara's style and interests from her visits to the home. She started dressing like her, wearing the same perfume, and even using the same make-up and hair products. If Tara had not been attacked, the couple could have pulled off their plan without a hitch, and they would have already absconded to their getaway spot.

Do I think Mark and Samantha are monsters? No, I do not. They are not like the Clayton Butchers of the world. Do I think they are bad people? No, not really. I think they are human. Greedy, jealous and desperate. Do I think they would have killed me? Yes. Like I said before, desperate people do desperate things for love. Especially for their love of money.

Colt was released from jail on bond. His bail was posted by Art as soon as the judge set the amount. Without a doubt, I know Art did this for me, not Colt. With the knowledge of Samantha being at the motel coming to light, the charges against Colt will likely be dropped. I believe she was telling the truth about not hurting Tara, though. Her real attacker still needs to be discovered.

The swelling of Tara's brain has improved, and the doctors hope to wake her in a couple of days. I plan on being there when that happens. Hopefully, she will be able to say who her attacker was, and the guilty person can finally be arrested.

thirty-five

"ARE you sure you don't need a wheelchair?" Jack asks as we step out of the elevator from the parking garage.

"Positive."

"Will you at least let him give you a ride?" He motions toward the driver sitting in the golf cart type trolley, who is preparing to transport people from the garage to the hospital's interior.

"Nope. I can walk." I swing the crutches out in front of me, keeping my casted foot from touching the ground, and take off across the floor of the breezeway.

"Want me to carry you?" He asks jokingly, although I suspect he may be serious. The injured foot makes going from point A to point B, slower. But I know he asked out of concern rather than impatience.

I shift my head toward him. "That's sweet, but I could use the exercise." I will not be running or attending kickboxing for a while, according to the orthopedic surgeon that I spoke with yesterday at my appointment. There is a possibility that I may have to have surgery on the foot. If I can avoid that, I will gladly follow Doctor's orders and avoid my usual physical activities.

But I refuse to be laid out on my couch for weeks on end with my foot propped, as Jack would like me to do. That type of inactivity could cause other parts of my body to become weak. I have worked too hard trying to become tough, to throw it all away during the course of a few weeks. The Doctor's instructions were to keep weight off the foot and give it plenty of rest, which is what I intend to do.

What I do not intend to do is take any of the pain medication that he prescribed to me. I will not lie and say that the pain does not make it seem tempting, but then I remember my time in the bunker after Samantha had given me medicine. I never wish to feel that way again. Nor do I want to become dependent upon the tablets and reach a point when I *do* wish to feel that way. I have seen too many people go down that road, and it is one I don't want to travel. I prefer to have all my wits about me.

We turn to the right, making our way past a small seating area toward a bank of elevators. We do not have to wait long after Jack pushes the button before the doors of a carriage swing open. He presses the button to the fifth floor, and we shoot upward, watching the numbers of the floors light up as we speed past them.

We exit the elevator, walk past the nurse's station and rooms with beeping monitors, until we come to Tara's room.

Janie is sitting in a chair beside the bed. She is not at home fretting over Mark's predicament or proclaiming his innocence. She is gently holding Tara's hand. It turns out, Mark must be wrong. She does care about things and people— just not him.

She glances up when we enter the room and tells the nurse it is okay for us to be here. Emily is in Celeste's charge and

Maverick is with Janie's family. With Mark in jail, that just leaves Janie to be here when they try to wake Tara. I expected awkwardness. Perhaps even anger from her directed toward Jack, but she seems relieved we are here. I couldn't imagine the stress of thinking you will be alone, if things do not go well when they attempt to wake Tara.

"They have slowly lowered the sedatives that are keeping her under. Now we just wait," she says, giving Tara's hand a gentle squeeze. "I am confident she will come back to us."

Tara is pale, fragile looking. Her already thin frame has become gauntly. Her head is bandaged, and her hair hangs down her neck, limp and greasy rather than bouncy like it normally is. Her nails are ragged and dirty. The room smells of antiseptic and human waste. My eyes tear up as my heart breaks for her.

"Vitals are good," the nurse says. "Anytime now she should start coming around. I've called Doctor Ahmed. He should be here soon."

We wait. Painfully, patiently wait. Time passes by excruciatingly slow. We talk about the weather, recipes and our hometown. We talk about everything except Mark, Samantha, my abduction and Tara's attack. Janie is talking about the cooking show that is playing on the TV, when she stops midsentence. "I just felt her hand twitch!"

The nurse rushes over from the other side of the bed. Tara's hand is still. "I swear I felt it," Janie says.

The nurse pats her shoulder and says, "It's a slow process."

Dr. Ahmed enters the room, doing a once over of Tara. He studies the monitors and then says, "Tara? Tara, it is time to wake up now. He takes her hand from Janie. Squeeze my hand if you can hear me." The seconds tick by. He is ready to pull away when Tara's thumb moves on the back of his hand, and she gives it a light squeeze. He looks at the team of medical students that trailed after him into the room. They have been watching intently. He smiles, as if to say, watch and learn.

Her eyes flutter slowly open, and Doctor Ahmed shines a light into them. He then begins asking questions and conducting a thorough examination. The nurse ushers us from the room, saying she will come get us when the Doctor has finished.

We stand outside of Tara's room, peering out a big window at the end of the hall. Down below, life goes on. Pedestrians do not glimpse up at these windows wondering who is being born, who is taking their last breath, or who is in between those two things.

After ten minutes, the nurse appears, smiling brightly, an indication that the doctor is pleased. She motions for us to follow her back into the room.

"Be patient with her," Dr. Ahmed says. "If answers come slow, or her mind seems a bit hazy, it's normal. Overall, I am astonished at how well she is doing. Her motor skills seem to be intact. She can fully communicate. She remembers why she is here. Keep in mind, she is still healing, but she is out of the woods. I have ordered a swallow test and some scans, so she will be taken for those later. She will most likely need some physical therapy. Overall, things look great. She is on the mend and will be going home before you know it."

"Thank you, Dr. Ahmed," Janie says, as she wipes tears from her face. She rushes to Tara's bedside, speaking softly to her and leans down to give her a kiss on the cheek.

"Emily?" Tara manages to squeak out.

"Emily is fine. She is anxious for her mommy to get well and come home," Janie says. This seems to satisfy Tara. Her eyes flutter shut as she decides to rest. Jack and I step out to get lunch and allow Janie some privacy with her.

When we return, we offer to sit with Tara while Janie takes

a break and gets something to eat. The smile is slow when Tara sees me, but it comes. She reaches for my hand. "Thank you," she whispers. "Janie said you saved me."

"All I did was call an ambulance. You were tough enough to hang on and save yourself."

"For...Emily," Survival skills often show up when people are faced with death, as Tara's probably did. I know it was the thought of Emily losing her in addition to having lost her father, that would have made Tara hang on.

"Samantha?" she asks.

"We know about your twin sister," I say. I do not disclose all that has happened for fear of upsetting her.

"I want to know her," she struggles to get the words out. Her words reassure me that it was not Samantha who hurt her. I want to ask who attacked her, but I do not want to upset or agitate her. "I want Emily to know her." Her words are coming slower and quieter now. She is tiring and her voice is getting weak. "I saw her at the motel." I nod my head to let her know that I am aware of their meeting.

"You should rest your voice," I say, trying to encourage her to take a break. She shakes her head no, anxious to tell me more. She seems to be struggling against the weight of her eyelids.

"I was mean to her because she was my intruder. She became upset and left. I wanted to follow and tell her I was sorry, but then he showed up."

He? It must have been a man who attacked her. So much for Teeny's theory of the attacker being a woman. My heart sinks. Colt? A sick feeling swells in the pit of my stomach and I feel as if I could vomit. A fever pitch of emotions threatens to overtake me. If I was wrong about Colton being incapable of doing such a thing, then I will never trust anyone or anything again. I can no longer quell the urge to know. "Tara, did Colt hurt you?"

She struggles against the weight of her eyelids. She seems puzzled. I wonder if her memory is spent and fading due to exhaustion. She looks straight into my eyes and shakes her head "no."

I glance at Jack, who has vacated his chair. He is now standing at rapt attention beside the bed. My gaze swings back to her. "Do you know who did hurt you?"

She nods her head, "yes." She tries to speak, but her voice cracks and her words are inaudible. I stand and lean over her, putting my ear close to her mouth. She whispers a name faintly into my ear, and I wonder if she is confused or mistaken.

thirty-six

"I DO NOT LIKE THIS," Jack says, as we stand in the hallway outside of what serves as an interrogation room at the Sheriff's Office. His arms lock across his chest as he takes a stubborn stance.

I shrug. "What other choice do you have? She insists. I am the only person she will speak to."

"Let's see, I could strangle her and try to force her to talk to me."

I'm certain he could be serious. "You aren't a fan of police brutality."

"Hmph. Maybe not, but if you come out of there with your eye twitching or something catches on fire, I am locking her in a padded cell and throwing away the key."

I giggle, trying to hide my nervousness at the thought that those things could possibly happen. I lightly tap his leg with my crutch, urging him to move aside and let me enter the room. Finally, with a sigh, he opens the door, and we step in.

Celeste Daniels greets us with an amused smile. Her chair is pulled away from the table and she is sitting with her legs elegantly crossed.

"I was beginning to wonder if you were going to show up," she says. I expect her to insist on Jack leaving the room, but she doesn't.

I take a seat in a chair on the opposite side of the table. Jack leans against the wall, with a hard expression on his face. I prop my foot in the remaining chair, since he is choosing to stand.

"Why did you wish to speak to me? You could have answered Jack's questions and been on your way by now. As you can see, it is not as easy for me to get around now," I say, not bothering to hide my annoyance, as I raise my casted foot and place it on the table for emphasis.

"Because he was rude," she swings her head up to leer at him.

at him. His expression doesn't change. The five-hour round trip to the hospital and the long day have put him in a cranky mood. Having to deal with Celeste after getting back, has almost sent him to the edge of his patience.

She is the only woman that I know, other than Cammie Parker, who would not instantly fall under the spell of Jack's handsome looks and answer his questions. "Besides, I feel like you and I have become friends," she says, swinging her eyes back to me.

Being friendly and being friends are two different things. I am friendly with Celeste, but I would not consider us friends. Her idea of a friend seems to be like having a pet. Someone she can toy with. For some reason, she has decided I am her new pet. She enjoys trying to get reactions from me, and it always feels like she is staring straight into my soul to gauge what those reactions may be.

"Speaking of friends, tell me about Jean-Pierre," I say.

"What about Jean-Pierre? You met him. I thought I was

284

here to talk about Tara's attack. Which by the way, you know *I* did not perpetrate."

"Perpetrate? No. Orchestrate? Still unknown. Where is Jean-Pierre now?"

"He is in Canada. What does this have to do with Tara?" She is quickly growing exasperated.

"We believe he was the person who attacked her. Did you know about it?"

She laughs. "That is ridiculous. I suppose you are running out of people to add to your list to accuse. Scooby and his gang would have better luck."

Jack pushes away from the wall and takes a step forward. I give him a face to remind him strangling her isn't an option. He braces his feet in a determined stance and crosses his arms over his chest. He nods his head, indicating he will let me continue to be the one to speak with Celeste.

"According to Tara, it was him." I say, without preamble.

For the first time her face falters. "She was able to tell you that?"

I dip my head. Up until this moment, Celeste had no clue how well Tara was doing. After Tara told me it was Jean-Pierre who attacked her, Jack urged Janie to be vague when she communicated with Celeste regarding Tara, to tell her she was sleeping and probably would be for a while. The hospital was instructed not to give Celeste information if she called. We had no way of knowing if Celeste was involved with the attack. Even if she wasn't, we did not want her tipping Jean-Pierre off.

"She is doing remarkably well. Even her doctor is amazed."

She briefly closes her eyes and draws in a deep breath of relief. "I want nothing else than for Tara to be well. But Jean," she says his name lovingly, "could never do such a thing. Tara is mistaken. Her memory is probably foggy and should not be trusted."

I gauge her intently. I believe her when she says that she wants Tara to be well. Jean-Pierre attacked Tara, but I am not convinced Celeste had any knowledge of it. "We checked. He had a room at the motel the same time the attack occurred, and he left town right after. Don't you think that's odd?"

"Not at all. He makes frequent trips here. He stays at the motel often." She studies her red, manicured nails, trying to dismiss the conversation.

"But this time, he left earlier than he intended. According to the airline, his return flight was scheduled for Monday. He changed the flight and left Saturday evening." Her eyes flicker up. I register the acknowledgment of her knowing he left sooner than expected. "Are you protecting him or were you involved?"

"Neither! I would never hurt Tara, and neither would he," she says, her voice suddenly not sounding as confident.

"Fine. Prove me wrong, then," I say, challenging her. She looks at me intently. Her piercing stare sends a small shiver from the nape of my neck to the small of my back. She would indeed need to be able to see into my soul to sense it, as I do nothing to betray my discomfort.

She taps her nails onto the table, considering. At last, she presses her lips together and thrusts her chin out. With a small nod of her head, she accepts the challenge. "Fine." She smiles coyly and narrows her eyes. "What do you want me to do to prove it?"

* * *

Jean-Pierre has called Celeste daily, asking about Tara's health status. As of now, he thinks the medical team was able to wake Tara, but she still isn't fully conscious. He has no clue how well she is doing, or that he is in danger of being arrested.

Celeste called him saying things seem bleak for Tara, and she needed her friend to come aid her with Emily, because she was not sure how to explain such things to a child. Celeste can be very convincing, but it did not take much persuading for him to agree to come to her as quickly as possible. It is as if she has a spell cast over him. I suspect he is madly in love with Celeste and has been for a long time.

True to his word, he made it here in record time. He pulls the rental car into her drive-way and then he bounds up to the door. Jack, Eli, Fordy and I sit in the back of a surveillance van parked up the street, listening to the audio coming from Celeste's wire.

"*Mon ange*, I came as quickly as I could. Please tell me I can stay with you and not that horrible motel," he says, his voice pleading.

"Of course. Emily isn't here this time. She is with Janie's parents. I am glad you came so quickly."

"What news of Tara?" he asks anxiously.

"The most wonderful thing has happened! Since I last spoke to you, she has made a miraculous recovery. The authorities are there now, trying to find out who attacked her." Celeste says, deciding to go rogue and veer from the script. She isn't supposed to say or do anything to clue Jean-Pierre to the fact that he has been discovered as Tara's attacker.

He stumbles over his words. "That is wonderful news. I suppose you don't need me, and I can go home now?"

"Don't be silly, *mon amour*. You owe me some time after rushing away quicker than you should have during your last visit. What was it that called you away unexpectedly?" She veers further off script asking him questions that should be reserved for after he is arrested.

Careful Celeste, I think, hoping she doesn't tip him off. Jack looks over at me, and I can tell he is thinking the same thing.

He is hoping for a confession before arresting him. If Jean-Pierre knows we are onto him, he will be trying to figure out a way to cover his tracks or attempt to flee.

"Nothing for you to concern yourself with, *ma belle*."

"You know you can tell me anything, *ami*," she says, practically cooing.

"*Oui*. But a man does deserve some secrets," he says, tsking his tongue.

Jack scoots back from the equipment. "That's it. I'm calling it. She is not going to get anything out of him, and he is starting to sound suspicious."

I think he should give her more time, but he slides the door of the van open, and jumps down before I can convince him. He directs Eli to go to the back of the house in case Jean-Pierre tries to run. He and Fordy walk up to Celeste's front door and ring the bell.

Celeste acts shocked about what is happening, and Jack pretends she would not have a reason to know. Jean-Pierre needs to think she is clueless so that he will keep trusting her. There is a chance she may be the only person who can convince him to confess.

I am standing on the street as Jack leads Jean-Pierre away from the house in cuffs. The only word Jean-Pierre says is, "Attorney," as he looks down his nose in contempt toward Jack.

thirty-seven

JEAN-PIERRE BELANGER'S attorney caught the first available flight from Canada. Even so, it still took a while for him to arrive. Money can buy the best of things, but it still takes them longer to reach Justice.

The lawyer, Max Tremblay has perfectly slicked back hair and a disdainful look on his face. He keeps his head tilted up in a proud poise, allowing Jack to see his distaste every time a question is asked. Then, he instructs his client not to answer each one.

"You have nothing but the word of Tara Daniels," Max says to Jack. "And that cannot be trusted until she is evaluated. Until that time, I suggest you release my client." The suggestion sounds like a threat. Jack does not deal well with threats.

I am sitting beside Officer Eli Keith watching the video of the interview in real time. We look over at each other thinking the same thing— this is not going to go well for Max Tremblay.

"Tara Daniels is under the care of an esteemed neurologist who says her memory can be trusted," Jack says.

"Hmm. We shall see," Max says, looking at his watch with impatience.

"That isn't all I have." Jack decides to drop the bomb. "A witness at the motel has come forward, just today. Well, I guess it's yesterday now, since it took so long for Jean's legal representative—you, to show up," Jack says, trying to needle the lawyer. "A young lady who works at the motel remembers Jean-Pierre. She can place him rushing from Tara's room right after the time of her attack."

Bailey Jenkins told Jared Rose that she thought she knew who harmed Tara. Jean-Pierre has stayed at the motel on numerous occasions. She remembers him well, because not only is he a frequent visitor, but a very flirtatious one. That Saturday afternoon, she saw Jean-Pierre rushing from the direction of Tara's room. He brushed past her, bumping shoulders and did not even apologize. Her ego was somewhat stung that he didn't act like Peppy Le Pew when he saw her.

Gary, the motel manager, sent Bailey home before Jack could speak with her that day. He also conveniently left her name off the list of employees working, when he finally produced the list to Jack. Jean-Pierre gave Gary several hundred-dollar bills upon his early departure, as recompense for checking out early. Gary accepted the money, suspecting it was to keep his mouth shut. Bailey has been ill with the flu and had not been back to work, until yesterday. When she and Jared Rose shared a pot-brownie on their break last evening, she told Jared what she remembered from the day of Tara's attack. He immediately called me.

With Tara pointing the finger at Jean, Jack could most likely figure a way to prove Jean-Pierre's guilt, but the addition of Bailey's statement will make the task easier.

"I would like to confer with my client privately for a moment," Max says.

Jack turns off the video recorder and leaves the room. When he re-enters, he presses the record button again.

"Against my sound legal advice, Mr. Belanger would like to speak to you now." Max nods to Jean-Pierre. Jean picks up a water glass and gulps down a drink, then he sits in silence.

"Any time you want to begin," Jack says, urging him to speak.

"I was sitting in my car, preparing to leave to get an evening meal, when I saw Tara enter the motel. I thought perhaps she had taken a lover. Marvelous for her!" He stops to take another mouthful of water before nervously continuing. "When I came back, I heard an altercation coming from the room as I walked by."

I think he is preparing to plead his innocence, until he continues. "I went to my room, minding my own business. Then I decided I should go check on her. Afterall, she is Emily's *Maman* and Celeste loves Emily." He clears his throat and reaches for the water again. I have a strong desire to enter the room and take the glass from him, so he will get on with the tale.

Finally, the glass is empty of water, and he has no distraction to keep him from talking. "What happened next?" Jack asks as he slides the glass out of Jean-Pierre's reach.

"The door was slightly ajar. I found her sitting on the bed crying. I stepped into the room and asked if she was okay. She said she was fine. I could see she clearly was not. I sat beside her on the bed."

"She was rude and told me to leave. I told her I would love to, and I would love to leave this place but Celeste's love for Emily holds her hostage here, so I must keep returning. I told her she should release Celeste from any obligation she feels toward Emily, so she can leave this God-forsaken place," his words rush out.

Jean-Pierre pauses, fidgeting his hands together on the table. "And then what happened?" Jack asks.

"She got up and paced to the sink. She was looking at me behind herself in the mirror. She laughed, maliciously. Then she turned and walked toward me. She told me that I was a stupid man, and did I really think Celeste would ever want to return home to be with me? She said Celeste was not in love with me like I was with her."

"Her words wounded me. She was so callous and mocking. Not at all the lady I knew her to be. I turned to leave. But then she said, 'why would she love you? You are not half the man Jacob was, and you never will be'."

He drops his head into his hands. When he raises to look at Jack again, tears have sprung forth into his eyes. "I did not go there to hurt her. I acted out of rage at her words. I picked up the statue and hit her on the head as she turned to walk back toward the mirror. Then, I panicked and ran."

"I did not mean to harm her. I just became so angry." Tears are falling from his eyes, running in rivulets beside his perfect nose. He drops his head in shame. Max Tremblay looks at him in disgust.

When Jean meets Jack's eyes again, he says, "I can still see the look of shock on her face when she saw my reflection in the mirror, preparing to hit her. It haunts my dreams."

Jean-Pierre was well-meaning when he stumbled upon Tara's private moment. She was shocked, upset and angry. She had just found out that she has a twin sister, and that Samantha was breaking into her home. Then he told her that she should force Celeste out of Emily's life. Tara is very protective of her daughter. She doesn't want Emily to lose another person who is important to her. So, she lashed out in anger.

There was no creepy stalker in Tara's life, lying in wait to prey upon her. It was simply a man, who became enraged when she wounded his pride and ego. Jean-Pierre has been in love with Celeste for years and resented her marriage to Jacob.

When Jacob died, he thought he finally had a chance with her. But she refused to leave Justice and Emily. He blames Emily for his lost chance at happiness with Celeste. He refuses to acknowledge that Celeste does not love him the same way he loves her. Even if he had not hurt Tara— he still would not have a chance at happiness with Celeste.

Tara and Jean-Pierre were both in the wrong place at the wrong time, as far as letting their anger cause them to lose control.

I think about Celeste's initial insistence that Jean-Pierre was innocent. It was the same as my insistence about Colt. I think about Jean-Pierre's undying love for Celeste, and how it was the catalyst that eventually sent him over an edge. Then I think about how Colt may love me in a way that I do not love him. I know I must release him from any spell that he feels I hold over him.

I will always love Colt and consider him my best friend. It is time for me to pull back from our relationship, but I feel the bond between us will never be broken, regardless of time and space. I understand how selfish it would be to continue the way things were. My heart hurts from the absence of him in my life, and it has not even happened yet.

It is also time for me to consider that perhaps Jack and my mother are right about my line of work. I still plan on being an investigator, but if there is the possibility that a murder may have occurred, or a creepy stalker is involved... I'm out. I have grown tired of being kidnapped. I no longer want to think of myself as a survivor. I want to consider myself, normal and average. The problem is, normal and average are so boring....

epilogue

TWELVE WEEKS LATER

Christmas came and went. I spent the holidays snuggled up with Jack and Buddy, watching Christmas lights twinkle on the live Christmas tree, which took up most of the space in my living room. We binge watched classic Christmas movies and drank hot chocolate. It felt like I was living in one of the holiday movies. Indeed, I did have all the warm, fuzzy feelings that those scenes seem to evoke.

Jack excitedly gifted me with a necklace; a black diamond, which he knows are my favorite, hanging from a delicate chain. Perhaps, he really is crazy for me. The warm, fuzzy feelings intensified.

I jokingly gifted him with a GPS tracker to put on my vehicle. He thought it was great and no laughing matter. He raced outside and placed it under the back bumper of my new Ford Bronco. He said he plans to make me start wearing one on my person. I don't think he was joking. When he came back inside the house, I gave him his real present, concert tickets to see Zach Bryan.

One of the best presents that I received, came several weeks after Christmas. After three months in a cast, I graduated to an orthopedic boot without having to undergo surgery. In my opinion, that is great cause for celebration. When Jack asked where I wanted to dine, I told him— anywhere other than the Hibachi restaurant. So, we had dinner at a lovely farm-to-table place.

After dinner, we decided the night was too young to end our celebration, so we made our way to The Troubadour. I am now pulling him onto the dance floor, insistent that I can dance with the boot on and that I will not be dangerous. Unless, I hear him say one more time— *I told you I had a bad feeling about this case.* Then, I may re-break my foot by stomping *his.*

He was right about his bad feeling, but I was right about Samantha existing. I may have gone about things the hard way, but I did find her. In some ironic twist of events, I managed to finish the job that I was hired to do. I will take the win.

Some things have changed over the last three months, and other things never will.

Tara is doing well. She still has physical therapy sessions to help regain some lost muscle strength, but overall, she has astonished everyone. She is planning to testify on Jean-Pierre's behalf at his trial. She feels that she played a part in her attack by provoking him. Although, I agree her words may have provoked him, I am not comfortable with the thought of a person being so easily provoked into doing something so heinous, being free.

With no one to bond Mark and Samantha out of jail, they are still in lockup. Tara now knows of the couple's plot to steal her fortune and escape. She still chooses to visit Samantha in jail, but she thinks she should pay for her crimes against me. If it was a crime against herself, she would have already bailed Samantha out. She feels a sense of loyalty to me for aiding her after her attack, so Samantha will remain in jail until her trial. I was correct in thinking Tara really is a good person. She is much more forgiving than I would be if I were in her shoes.

Janie Daniels has yet to visit Mark. I would probably be more like Janie.

Sally decided she no longer wants to obtain her P.I. license. My time in the bunker made her realize that the job may not be as exciting as she first thought. Shooting at people and being locked up underground, are two different things. Turns out, Sally is claustrophobic, so the bunker was a deal breaker. Teeny was relieved by her change of heart. He doesn't want a similar situation befalling her. And no matter how much he loves her, he is happy that they will not be working together. If she is at the office every day, he will not be able to cheat on his diet, and that is a deal breaker for him.

After years of working at the convenience store, Thomas resigned. Scotto's meal kits and online fitness platform have become very lucrative. He offered Thomas a job and T accepted without a second thought. He loves showing off his skills in Scotto's videos. I still plan on kicking his ass occasionally after my foot completely heals— just to keep him humble.

Jared quit working at the motel and took Thomas's place at the convenience store. Now, rather than dealing with a jerk-clerk, I will be dealing with a perv-clerk.

Leonard Shipley still shoots me the middle finger every time that he sees me, unless my mother is there. He is still employed at the convenience store. He is biding his time until the heat dies down from his last workers' comp fraud, before he attempts faking an injury again.

Mama is still dealing with menopause, but thankfully, she has learned to manage the symptoms better. I have become more aware of what will set her off, although sometimes it is still dicey.

Gertie Rose still suspects that I am secretly into kinky stuff. But she did stop offering to put in a good word for me with Devin Harlow, when she saw the black diamond that Jack gifted me. The necklace isn't the same as *putting a ring on it*, but I guess it made her think he is serious about our relationship.

When Gertie learned that I had been kidnapped while working a case for Tara, she asked if she would receive a finder's fee. Of course, I was confused until she said the reason Tara sought me out, was because Gertie had recently touted my skills as a P.I. in front of Tara. I'm still not certain if she thought she deserved a finder's fee for referring a client to me, or for Tara's intruder being found. Either way, I let her take my new Bronco for a short spin. She was happy about that, so we called it even.

I have not spent time with Colton during the past three months. We have not spoken other than the occasional text, including the one I sent him on Christmas Day, telling him that I was happy that I did not have to gift him with soap on a rope. He thought it was hilarious. He seems to sense me pulling away from him, but he has not questioned the issue.

Jack lifts me slightly and spins me around on the dance floor. I spot Colt across the crowded bar now. Our eyes meet. He raises his bottle of Blue Moon in my direction and smiles. I return the smile, knowing if I ever need someone to help me get rid of a body, he is my man. Time or distance will never change that.

He is sitting across the booth from Morgan Vanover. She is three years younger than us, and she recently moved back to

Justice to open a veterinary clinic after her divorce. The light hanging above the booth they occupy, glints off her shiny blonde hair. She is laughing at something he said and appears to be infatuated with him. He smiles. A genuine smile. I hope that she ends up being his one and only.

Jack pulls me in close as we dance cheek to cheek to a slow song. I feel like the luckiest girl in the world. I have cheated death twice now, and I hope that I do not learn from experience how many times you are allowed to do that.

The song ends. Sally is suddenly standing on top of the bar with her bullhorn.

"Ladies, gents and drunken sots, can I have your attention, please? It has been brought to my attention on more than one occasion that I should fix the hole in the wall over there," she says, pointing to the destruction that was caused by her shotgun blast, when she shot at Clayton Butcher. "I have finally decided to give in to the pressure and tonight that spot will be getting a facelift."

She jumps down from the bar and grabs a big rectangular box. She strides across the room with Teeny in tow. The couple occupying the booth quickly scrambles when Teeny approaches with a hammer, resembling Thor. He proceeds to tap a nail into the wall above the hole. Sally hefts the box up onto the table. "Can I get a drum roll," she asks of the band. A ping, ping, ping, thump sound erupts from the stage as she pulls the contents from the box. Teeny is standing behind her, blocking everyone's view with his massive girth. When they step away, the painting Celeste Daniels did of me has taken up residence over the shotgun hole.

"Feast your eyes on this most exquisite piece of artwork!" She exclaims.

Everyone, including myself, erupts into laughter. After she announces a round for everybody on the house, I ask her, "How did you manage that? Celeste said the painting wasn't for sale."

"Turns out everything can be bought for a price. We passed the hat around and the amount we came up with was the price Celeste was willing to accept. Well, that and a little negotiating on my part. I volunteered Teeny to be her next muse. He agreed but he drew the line at posing nude. Your fella here put the most money in the pot," she says, tipping her head toward Jack.

"Oh, you did, did you?" I ask.

"You're totally going to make me pay for that later, aren't you?"

"I have a bad feeling, I just might," I say, giggling. I look across the room at the painting once more, and my left eye starts twitching.

acknowledgments

To my readers and fans of Elle Riley, Thank You. I was in awe of the support that I was given with my debut novel. Because of you, I have found the courage to continue writing. Your reviews and feedback mean so much to me. Every time that I find myself discouraged, or in a writing slump, someone asks me, "when will the next book be published?"— because they are anxiously awaiting the release. You probably do not realize it, but you are helping me achieve my dream. I love all of you!

My husband, James is my biggest supporter. He often reminds me that I am my own worst critic. Without his encouragement, I would not have published my first book, let alone a second. He listened to me change the plot of this book, no less than five times, while hanging in there with patience. He's a keeper.

My son, Tristan helped with editing and answered all my questions. He never complains. He's a trooper.

My son, Ethan acts as my sounding board. I often read scenes to him. I can gauge by his reactions if they are good or bad. Although, he will never tell me if they are bad. He has a great sense of humor, so if I get a chuckle from him while reading a scene, I know I've hit the mark.

Thank you, Sensei Kenny Kidd for helping me work out Elle's sparring scene. When in doubt, ask an expert, which he is. Also, thanks for your support and friendship.

A special thanks to Angie, George, Jamie, Jess and Shari. You guys are awesome!

Last, but not least, Thank You to all my family and friends. You have championed me from day one. I am humbled by your love. Please know that it is returned to each of you a thousand-fold.

Made in United States
Orlando, FL
07 June 2024

47621823R00172